Have you ever dreamed about starting a new life? Running away from your school, your town, your home, even your family and friends, and starting over somewhere else. Changing how you look, what you like, who you *are*. In a new place, you'd have no baggage. Your past and future would be a blank canvas. Of course, you'd also no longer be *you*, and that might mess with your head. And it would suck to have the people back home *worry* about you, going so far as to, say, put your face on a milk carton. Which is why it's just a fantasy.

But for one manipulative girl from Rosewood, it isn't a fantasy. It's survival.

And to her four enemies, it might mean the end of their pretty little lives–*forever*.

BOOKS BY SARA SHEPARD

Pretty Little Liars
Flawless
Perfect
Unbelievable
Wicked
Killer
Heartless
Wanted
Twisted
Ruthless
Stunning
Burned
Crushed
Deadly
Toxic
Vicious
Pretty Little Secrets
Ali's Pretty Little Lies

The Perfectionists
The Good Girls

The Lying Game
Never Have I Ever
Two Truths and a Lie
Hide and Seek
Cross My Heart, Hope to Die
Seven Minutes in Heaven
The First Lie (a digital original novella)
True Lies (a digital original novella)

For Adults

The Heiresses
Everything We Ever Wanted
The Visibles

Vicious

A PRETTY LITTLE LIARS NOVEL

SARA SHEPARD

HARPER TEEN

An Imprint of HarperCollinsPublishers

Produced by Alloy Entertainment
1700 Broadway, New York, NY 10019

Library of Congress Control Number: 2014946654
ISBN 978-0-06-228705-2

Typography by Liz Dresner

16 17 18 19 20   CG/RRDH   10 9 8 7 6 5 4 3 2 1
❖
First paperback edition, 2016

To Henry

If you want a happy ending,
that depends, of course,
on where you stop your story.

—ORSON WELLES

IDENTITY CRISIS

Have you ever dreamed about starting a new life? Running away from your school, your town, your home, even your family and friends, and starting over somewhere else. Changing how you look, what you like, who you *are*. In a new place, you'd have no baggage. Your past and future would be a blank canvas. Of course, you'd also no longer be *you*, and that might mess with your head. And it would suck to have the people back home *worry* about you, going so far as to, say, put your face on a milk carton. Which is why it's just a fantasy.

But for one manipulative girl from Rosewood, it isn't a fantasy. It's survival.

And to her four enemies, it might mean the end of their pretty little lives—*forever.*

The first thing Alison DiLaurentis noticed when she woke up was how buttery-soft her sheets were. Her down pillow was fluffy, and her blanket smelled like fresh fabric softener. A band of sun streaming in from the window warmed her legs, and a bird chirped euphorically in the trees. It was like she was sleeping in paradise.

She sat up and stretched, then broke into a grin as it hit her again. She was *free*.

Score another win for Ali D.

She picked up the remote and turned on the small television at the foot of the bed, which was already set to CNN. The same story she'd been following last night was on the news again: *Pretty Little Murderers Go to Trial.* Last year's school pictures of Spencer Hastings, Aria Montgomery, Emily Fields, and Hanna Marin were splashed across the screen. The reporters recounted the tantalizing tale of how the four girls had brutally murdered Alison DiLaurentis and were now on trial, facing life in prison.

Ali's smile broadened. This was playing out exactly as she'd planned.

"Traces of Alison's blood were found in an abandoned pool house in Ashland, Pennsylvania. The police are working hard to find her body," a reporter was saying. "Investigators also found a journal of Alison's, in the woods outside the pool house. It details how the girls methodically captured and tortured her."

A short man with curly gray hair and wire-framed glasses popped onto the screen. *Seth Rubens*, read the caption under his name. *Defense Attorney.* He was the lawyer representing the girls. "Not only did my clients not torture Alison," he said, "they also had nothing to do with her murder. The trial will prove—"

The newscast cut him off mid-sentence. "Opening statements for their trial will start next Tuesday. Stay here for full coverage."

Ali flopped back on the bed and wiggled her toes. So far, so good. Everyone bought that she was really dead, and everyone thought those bitches had killed her. It had been a bold move, but she'd pulled it off. She'd even done it mostly alone.

It had been risky returning to Rosewood, Pennsylvania, after her last scheme to bring her sister's old friends down had failed. But it had pissed her off that things had gone so wrong . . . *again*. After all, she'd plotted everything so meticulously: her boyfriend and accomplice, Nicholas, had painstakingly infiltrated the girls' lives the previous summer. First he'd used his massive trust fund to fly to Jamaica and set up an elaborate hoax for all the girls. Then he'd bounced to Philly to target Spencer, to Iceland to ensnare Aria in an international incident, and back to Philly again to gather secrets about the other two. When shit started to go down and the Liars spiraled out of control, Ali and Nick started rumors that the bitches had a suicide pact—and spread it to the press, to kids at school via Facebook, even to random people around Rosewood. Knowing the girls were looking for Ali, Ali and Nick laid out clues to her whereabouts, luring them to the basement of a ramshackle building in Rosewood. The girls were supposed to die down there. The cops were supposed to come after it was all over, when Ali and Nick had safely escaped, and think it was a group suicide.

But that wasn't how it had happened. Somehow, the girls had been saved, and the cops had hauled Nick off to prison. Ali had gotten away, but worry plagued her. How long would Nick stick to the lie they'd agreed upon: that Ali had died in the fire in the Poconos a year ago and that he'd gone after Spencer, Aria, Emily, and Hanna alone? Prison probably sucked, especially for a rich kid who was used to sleeping on zillion-thread-count sheets and who'd had to shoplift a sound machine from Target because he needed white noise even when on the lam.

After all that, drums still beat in Ali's head, overpowering all thoughts of lying low. *You have to get them*, she thought. *You have to finish this.*

And so she had. First she penned a journal, a story so brilliantly crafted it probably would have received an A+ in AP English. She twisted her relationship with Nick into something sordid and abusive, poor little sick Ali dragged into a murderous rampage with no way of escape. *Nick killed my sister. Nick killed Ian. Nick set fire to Spencer's woods. Nick killed Jenna Cavanaugh.* It was all Nick's idea, and he'd pulled Ali along for the ride.

She wrote that Nick had barely cared for her after the Poconos fire and forced her to take part in *more* nefarious activities, threatening to kill her if she told anyone or tried to leave. She wrote about clawing her way out of that basement to get away from him. Several entries talked about how wonderful it felt to be free—but how scary, too. She wrote that she'd been hiding in a barn in Limerick, Pennsylvania, though actually she'd been in the pool house at Nick's parents' vacation home in Ashland . . . which would play into the second part of her plan.

She'd also written whole chapters about the Liars, creating a different picture of them than what the public assumed. *My sister's dear old friends*, she called them, splattering salt water on the diary to look like tears. *I hope they forgive me and understand that I wasn't the one behind all this. I've wanted to tell them so many times.* Ali wrote that she wanted to go to the cops with her story, but she was afraid they wouldn't believe her. She wrote about wanting to anonymously turn in the journal, but she didn't know who to trust.

As her coup de grâce, she detailed how the Liars had tracked her down, finding her in the barn and tying her up. She begged them to listen to her side of the story, but the Liars threw her in Spencer's trunk and dragged her away—although, really, she hadn't been dragged anywhere, and was still at the pool house, waiting for them to find her. *Writing this with my hands tied up*, Ali had penned, actually tying her hands together so her handwriting was properly sloppy. And: *This journal is my only friend.* And: *I've tried to tell them the truth again and again, but they just won't listen. They're crazy. All of them. I know they're going to kill me. I'm never getting out of here alive.* Her last entry was two choppy sentences: *I think today is going to be the day. I'm so scared.*

It was kismet: The date of the last entry jibed almost perfectly with when the Liars really *did* find the pool house. Ali knew they'd come—she'd planted that receipt in the pocket of the hoodie she let Emily tear off her for that very reason. To sufficiently hook them, she made sure the place smelled overpoweringly of the vanilla soap she used. She knew they'd come inside the pool house and touch everything, leaving their fingerprints everywhere. They fell for every one of Ali's tricks as though she had them under a spell. Sure, there were a few surprises—like the cameras they set up in the trees—but even those she made work to her advantage, especially when Emily had her colossal freak-out on-screen. The prosecution team would log that into evidence.

Now, Ali sat down at the laptop propped up on a small desk in the corner and opened a website. A huge banner saying *Hang the Liars!* splashed across the top of the page. *We Are Your Ali Cats, Ali!* Letting out a little coo of happiness, she leaned forward and kissed the screen. The Ali Cats, a special fan club that had started last year, were completely devoted to *her.* They had been the sweetest surprise in all of this. Ali loved them, her special helpers, her extra credit. Some of them were dedicated enough to risk *everything* for her. She wished she could write to them and thank each one of them.

After reading a few posts from Ali Cats all over the

country, clamoring for the Liars to go to prison for the rest of their lives, Ali shut the laptop and moved to the closet. All her new clothes—mostly white or pale-colored shirts, shorts, and skirts in several sizes larger than she was used to—hung in a neat row. The stuff *totally* wasn't her . . . but that was the price she had to pay. As she slid the hangers from one side of the rod to the next, she felt a small, nagging twinge inside her. This latest escape *had* come at a bit of a price. She'd had to get rid of a few of the Ali Cats—but that was necessary. And then there was Nick. She'd had a few dreams of him escaping from prison, finding her, and demanding to know how she could have blamed him for everything. But betraying him was necessary, too.

A knock sounded at the door. Ali whipped around, her heart pounding hard. "It's just me," came a voice. "Are you up?"

Ali's heart slowed down. "Uh, yeah," she said.

"I was just about to go out and get some breakfast. You want anything? Pancakes, maybe, like yesterday? An omelet?"

Ali thought a moment. "Both," she decided. "*And* some bacon," she added. "And grapefruit juice, if you can find some."

A shadow flickered under the door. "Okay," came the voice. "Be back soon."

Ali listened as the footsteps grew softer. She turned back to her closet and pulled on a white T-shirt and a long, white, gauzy skirt, which was beyond hideous but fit her expanding hips. She glanced at herself in the mirror and almost didn't recognize the girl looking back, a larger, unwieldy creature with mousy-brown hair and blotchy, messed-up skin. It was only a temporary situation, though—soon enough, she would go back to being beautiful. This was who she needed to be right now: someone *other* than herself. A nobody. A nothing. A ghost, which made it even more appropriate that most of her new clothes were white.

Outside, a car swished past. A boat horn honked. As Ali thought of her imminent breakfast, all the wary twinges faded away. How unbelievably luxurious that deciding what she would eat was her one and only concern! All that other stuff? She didn't feel shitty about it at all. Only the strong survive, after all. And soon enough, she'd have a new life. A *better* one than what she'd had in a long, long time.

And those four bitches would have no life at all.

1

BAD NEWS, AND MORE BAD NEWS

On a balmy Thursday morning in mid-June, Emily Fields sat next to her best friends Hanna Marin, Spencer Hastings, and Aria Montgomery in a large, airy conference room that overlooked the Philadelphia waterfront. The room smelled like coffee and Danishes, and the office bustled with the sounds of ringing phones, whirring printers, and *click-clacking* high heels on female attorneys rushing off to court. When Seth Rubens, their new lawyer, cleared his throat, Emily looked up. By his pained expression, she suspected she wasn't going to like what he had to say.

"Your case doesn't look good." Rubens stirred his coffee with a thin wooden stick. He had bags under his eyes, and he wore the same cologne as Emily's dad, a summery scent called Royall Bay Rhum. The smell used to cheer Emily up, but not anymore.

"The district attorney has gathered a lot of evidence against you for Alison's murder," he went on. "You being on the scene when the crime happened. The shoddy cleanup job. Your prints all over the house. The tooth they found at the scene. Emily's, er, *episode*"—here he glanced nervously at Emily—"prior to the event. I'm happy to represent you, and I'll do all I can, but I don't want to give you false hope."

Emily slumped down. Ever since their arrest for the murder of Alison DiLaurentis—also known as A, their longtime enemy, almost-killer, and diabolical text-messager—Emily had lost ten pounds, couldn't stop crying, and thought she was going crazy. They were all out on bail after only a few hours in jail, but their trial would begin in five days. Emily had been through six lawyers, and her friends had done the same. *None* of the lawyers had given them hope—including Rubens, who'd allegedly gotten mafia bosses out of mass-killing charges.

Aria leaned forward and looked the lawyer square in the eye. "How many times can we explain this? Ali set us up. She knew we were staking out that pool house. She knew we were getting desperate. That blood was on the floor when we got there. And we were upstairs when whoever it was cleaned it up."

Rubens looked at them tiredly. "But you didn't see who that was, did you?"

Emily picked at her thumbnail. And then, suddenly, she heard a giddy, taunting, crystal-clear voice: *You didn't. You know I've got you right where I want you.*

It was Ali's voice, but no one else seemed to hear it. Emily felt another barb of worry. She'd started to hear Ali a few days ago, and her voice was growing louder.

She thought about the lawyer's question. In their hunt for Ali, they'd targeted a house in Ashland, Pennsylvania, the property of Ali's boyfriend Nick Maxwell's parents. At the very back of the property was a dilapidated pool house, the perfect place for Ali to hide out and plot her next move against them. They'd started to monitor the place, but then Spencer unwittingly told her friend Greg that they'd set up surveillance cameras. In a horrible turn of events, Greg ended up being an Ali Cat, one of Ali's online minions. Their camera feed of the cabin was disconnected almost the second Spencer broke the news.

As soon as that happened, Emily and the others drove up to Ashland to see if Ali was at the pool house, dismantling the cameras. But all they found was blood on the floor. They'd gone inside to look around, then heard a *slam* and run upstairs. The smell of bleach had wafted through the air, and someone—surely Ali, though they hadn't seen for certain—stomped around in the kitchen, messily cleaning it up. When they came back downstairs, the house was empty. Then they'd called 911. Little did they know the police would blame *them*.

But that's just what happened: The cops came, swabbed for evidence, and deemed that the blood type matched Ali's. They'd also found a tooth that matched Ali's dental records. Then they accused the *girls* of trying to clean up the crime scene—their prints were all over the place, after all, and they'd been *in* the house. The surveillance cameras had recorded the girls sneaking in the door moments before.

You're totally mine.

There was Ali's voice again. Emily blinked hard. She looked around at her friends, wondering if they heard their own versions of Ali's taunts in *their* heads.

"And the dress?" Aria asked, referring to the dress they'd found in the pool house's upstairs loft. It had also been covered in blood.

The lawyer checked his notes. "Forensics says it only has A-positive blood on it—Ali's blood type. I wouldn't bring it up. It doesn't really help your case."

Emily sat up straighter. "Couldn't Ali have cut herself, spread her blood around the pool house, and then cleaned it up? She could have pulled and planted that tooth, too. She was in The Preserve for *years*. She's crazy."

Not as crazy as you! the Ali in Emily's head tittered. Emily made a face, wanting Ali's voice out. Then she noticed Hanna looking at her curiously.

The lawyer sighed. "If we had evidence of Alison in that pool house—*alive*—at the same time you were there, we might be able to make that case. But all we have is a video of you girls sneaking in through the front door. Ali isn't there."

"Ali probably snuck in through a window," Spencer piped up. "In the back, maybe. There were no cameras there."

The lawyer stared at his palms. "There's no evidence supporting that. I had the police dust for prints on the windowsills around the property, and they found nothing."

"She could have used gloves," Hanna tried.

Rubens clicked his pen. "This is all circumstantial evidence, and we have to consider that it's coming from you four girls and that you are somewhat notorious, er, characters." He cleared his throat. "I mean, your nickname is the *Pretty Little Liars*. You've been caught in lies before—very public lies. You were on trial for killing a girl in Jamaica, and you confessed to at least pushing her off a balcony. And everyone knows what Alison did to you and how much motive you'd have to get rid of her. And like I said, there was Emily's episode . . ."

Everyone turned to look at Emily. She stared down at the table. Okay, so she'd lost it in the hunt for Ali. But that was because Ali had almost drowned Emily in the Rosewood Day Prep pool . . . and then one of her Ali Cats had killed Jordan Richards, the love of Emily's life. She hadn't meant to go to the pool house and freak out. She hadn't *meant* to trash the place and vow loudly that she was going kill Ali, which the surveillance camera had recorded. It had just . . . happened.

"And then there's that journal."

Rubens reached for a large binder on his right. Inside was a photocopy of the journal Ali had purportedly written and stashed in the woods, in an easy enough hiding place for the cops to find. Emily hadn't wanted to read it, but she'd heard plenty about it. Ali had painted herself as the innocent victim and Spencer, Aria, Emily, and Hanna as her vengeful captors. Entries talked of the girls verbally and physically abusing her. As Rubens opened the binder, Emily caught sight of the words *tied me up*. Then she saw the phrase *they don't understand*.

Poor, poor me, Ali sang in Emily's head. Emily must have groaned, because Spencer looked up at her, eyes wide. Emily's cheeks blazed. She had to be careful. Her friends already thought she was troubled—and that was when she *wasn't* hearing voices.

Aria glanced at the binder, too. "Surely that won't count as evidence, will it?"

"Especially because of what Nick said this morning." Emily fumbled for her phone and showed the lawyer an article she'd found before the meeting. She pointed to the headline. *Maxwell Says Journal Is All Lies*, it read. *His Love and Loyalty Only Go So Far*. "If Nick says Ali lied about the stuff about him in the journal, it throws the validity of the rest of the thing into question, right?" she asked hopefully.

Rubens shrugged. "We're talking about a confessed murderer's word here. Sometimes judges take journals very seriously. And when someone writes, *I'm scared*, or *I think they're going to kill me*, and then she winds up dead . . ."

"But she's *not* dead," Emily blurted. "The police found *one tooth* and blood. That's *it*. Won't it be hard for them to convict us of murder without a *body*?"

The lawyer shut the binder with a slap. "That's true. And you have that going for you." A strange look came over his face. "So let's hope detectives don't find the rest of her."

Everyone stared at the lawyer, startled. "Are you saying you don't believe us?" Spencer finally sputtered.

The lawyer raised his palms, but didn't confirm or deny it.

Hanna put her head in her hands. Spencer tore her Styrofoam coffee cup into small pieces. Aria laid her palms flat on the table. "Can we give our side of the story in court?"

Rubens tapped his pen against the table. "I'd rather not put you girls on the stand. Then the DA will get to cross-examine you, and he's going to be ruthless—he'll find all sorts of ways to trap you in your story. Let me paint a pic-ture of you girls. I'll bring the right facts to light. But even with all that, I don't know what chance we have. I can try and offer some theories of other people who might have killed Alison. Someone in Jenna Cavanaugh's family, for example. Someone in Ian Thomas's family. Someone else who hated her. But you are still the most compelling and logical suspects."

Emily glanced at the others. "But she's not *dead*," Spencer repeated.

"Is there anything that can truly save us?" Aria asked weakly. "Anything that will guarantee we go free?"

Rubens sighed. "The only thing that I can think of is if

Alison DiLaurentis herself strolls into that courtroom and turns herself in."

Like that *will ever happen*, Ali said loudly in Emily's head.

The lawyer blew air through his cheeks. "Get some sleep, girls. You look exhausted." He gestured to the plate of Danishes. "And have one, for God's sake. You don't know when you'll get the pleasure of a Danish from Rizolli's again."

Emily flinched. It was pretty easy to interpret what *that* meant: Prisons didn't serve pastries.

Hanna snatched a bear claw and shoved it into her mouth, but everyone else filed out the door without even looking at the breakfast spread. At the elevator bank, Spencer stabbed the DOWN button. Suddenly, she looked at Emily with alarm. "Em," she hissed, her eyes on Emily's hand.

Emily looked down. A long line of blood dripped from her cuticle down her wrist. She'd picked her skin until it bled and hadn't even felt it. She fumbled for a tissue in her bag, feeling her friends' eyes on her. "I'm fine," she said preemptively.

But they weren't the only ones concerned about her; Emily's family was acting even stranger. Unlike the other myriad of incidents when Emily had gotten in major trouble and her parents had disowned her, this time, her family continued to let her eat meals with them. They even bought her favorite foods, did her laundry, and checked in on her incessantly, as though she were a newborn. Her mom made stilted, polite conversation with her about TV shows and books and paid rapt attention whenever Emily said *anything*. Last night, Emily's father had leapt up from the chair, saying the TV was all hers and she could watch whatever she wanted and could he get her something? Emily had longed for this sort of attention from her family for so long—basically since the beginning of A. But it felt strange now. They were only doing it because they thought she was crazy.

The elevator dinged, and the doors slid open. The girls shuffled in silently, heads down. Emily could feel the other people in the elevator staring. One girl not much older than them pulled out her iPhone and started typing something on the screen. After a moment, Emily heard the *snap* of the device's camera and noticed that the phone was aimed at her face.

She wheeled around and stared at the girl. "What are you doing?"

The girl's cheeks reddened. She covered the phone's lens with her hand and lowered her eyes.

"Did you take a *picture* of us?" Emily screeched.

She tried to grab the phone, but Spencer caught her arm, pulling her back. The elevator dinged, and the girl darted into the lobby. Spencer stared at Emily. "You have to get a grip."

"But she was really rude!" Emily protested.

"You can't freak out about it," Spencer urged.

"Everything we do, Em, everything we say—we have to think about how the jury is going to interpret it."

Emily shut her eyes. "I can't believe we have to appear in front of a jury at *all*."

"Me, neither," Hanna whispered. "What a nightmare."

They walked across the lobby, past a guard's desk. Emily glanced out the revolving doors. Sunlight sparkled on the sidewalk. A group of girls in colorful sundresses and sandals passed, laughing giddily. But then, beyond them, she thought she saw a shadow slip into an alley across the street. The hair rose on the back of her neck. Ali—the *real* Ali—could be anywhere. Watching them. Waiting to strike.

She turned back to her friends. "You know, we could take action," she said in a low voice. "We can look for her again."

Spencer's eyes widened. "No way. Absolutely not."

Aria's throat bobbed. "It's impossible."

But Hanna nodded. "I *have* wondered where Ali went. And Rubens did say that was the only way we could go free."

"Hanna, *no*." Spencer gave her a sharp look. "We have no leads."

That's right, Ali tittered in Emily's mind. *You'll never find me.*

Emily pulled out her phone again. The Nick article was still on the screen. "Nick's so angry. Maybe he'll help us out. Give us something."

Spencer snorted. "Unlikely."

"Yeah, and I hate the idea of facing him in prison," Aria said nervously. "Don't you?"

"If we go together, I think we can handle it," Emily said, trying to sound firm.

"Maybe," Aria murmured unhappily.

Hanna tucked a lock of auburn hair behind her ear. "What are the chances the cops will even let us visit someone in prison? We're out on bail. We can't exactly move freely and do whatever we want."

Emily looked at Spencer. "Could your dad pull some strings?" Spencer's father, a powerful lawyer, knew everyone from the DA to the mayor to the chief of police. He could make all sorts of things happen.

Spencer crossed her arms over her chest. "I don't think it's a good idea."

"*Please?*" Emily cried.

Spencer shook her head. "I'm sorry. I don't want to."

Emily's mouth hung open. "So you're going to give up? That's not like you, Spence."

Spencer's chin wobbled. "What I don't want to do anymore is play Scooby-Doo. It only leads to more problems."

"Spence," Emily protested, reaching for Spencer's arm. But Spencer shook her off, letting out a pained note that echoed through the lobby. She spun around and walked through the revolving doors.

A long silence followed. Emily felt that same weight pressing on her chest once more. She didn't dare look at

Hanna or Aria because she knew she'd burst into tears if she did. Maybe Spencer was right. Maybe it *was* a terrible idea to go looking for Ali again.

That's right, Ali shrieked in Emily's head, louder than ever. *This time, I've got you for good.*

2

SPENCER'S NEW TUTOR

Spencer Hastings walked quickly to the end of the Center City block. She glanced over her shoulder, half-sure that her friends were running after her, trying to convince her to embark on another crazy, frustrating, and fruitless Ali search. But the street was empty. *Good.*

She was done trying to search for Ali. After the past two weeks, after coming so close to finding Ali and then losing her so dramatically, she was giving up. She'd gotten everything she wanted only to have it all taken away—she no longer had any college future, she no longer had a book deal, and her bullying blog, which had so recently been a huge success, hadn't had any hits in days except for people writing posts about what a horrible person she was. *Fine, Ali, you win*, she'd finally conceded. As far as Spencer was concerned, it was time to face her fate: prison.

Maybe it wasn't the worst thing in the world, though. She was Spencer Hastings, and if she was going to have to go to prison, then she was damn sure going to do everything she could to make it as tolerable as possible. It was the same approach she'd taken before attending Camp Rutabaga in fifth grade: She'd interviewed previous summers' campers and counselors, read message boards, even tramped over the campgrounds during the winter to get the lay of the land. She'd learned never to swim before 11 AM, when they added new chlorine to the pool; to avoid the peas in the mess hall; and that the surest way to win Color War was by mastering the rope bridge—and she had done so by practicing on a course she'd built beforehand in her backyard. And so she'd started her prison prep by reading the bestselling memoir *Behind Bars: My Time in Prison*. When she realized Angela Beadling, the author, lived in Philly, Spencer had gone on her website, and found that she consulted for individual clients as a Prison Life and Acclimation Specialist. She'd immediately called and made an appointment.

Her phone bleated, startling her. She looked at the screen. *Dad*. Emily hadn't called him behind her back, had she? Spencer bit her lip and answered.

"Hey, Spence," Mr. Hastings said soberly. "How are you holding up?"

Spencer swallowed hard, all thoughts of Emily fading away. She appreciated her father's efforts to stay in touch—it was more than her ice-queen mother was doing at the moment. "Okay," she said, trying to sound positive. "I just came from a meeting with Rubens, actually."

"Really?" Mr. Hastings sounded enthusiastic. "And how did that go?"

Spencer skirted a green recycling can. She didn't have the heart to tell her dad that Rubens had told them exactly the same thing as every other lawyer. Mr. Hastings had pulled all kinds of strings to get them a meeting, after all. And though they hadn't talked about it—and would probably never discuss it in a zillion years—a huge, dark secret lingered between them. Not long ago, Spencer had found out that her father was Ali and Courtney's dad, too. She knew he must have conflicted feelings about how messed up both of those girls had turned out, but Real Ali was *still* his flesh and blood. Spencer couldn't help thinking that his careful, deliberate supportiveness was a clear message that he didn't believe for a second that he was letting any paternal feelings get in the way.

"Um, great," she said. "He seems really professional, and he's going to represent all of us." She took a breath, considering asking him about visiting Nick—her dad would definitely help. But she decided it wasn't worth pursuing.

"Well, glad to hear it," Mr. Hastings said. "Hey, if you're still in the city, want to grab some lunch? I can meet you at Smith and Wollensky."

Spencer stopped and looked around. She'd forgotten that she was close to her dad's place on Rittenhouse Square. "Um, I can't," she blurted. "I'm already on SEPTA. Sorry!"

Then she hung up as fast as she could. With just her luck, she'd run into her dad on the street right now and be forced to answer questions. And she had no idea how she would explain where she was *really* going.

She reached into her pocket, looked at the address she'd written on a crumpled Post-it, and then entered it into Google Maps on her phone. It didn't take her long to get to the building, a pretty white house with molding that looked like birthday-cake frosting. The car parked in front was a British racing green Porsche 911. An American flag hung from the eaves and there was a huge pot of flowers on the porch. Spencer walked up the steps and looked at the name on the mailbox. ANGELA BEADLING. This was it. Spencer was a little surprised—the book had been a bestseller, sure, but she hadn't expected Angela to live somewhere quite so cushy.

She rang the bell and waited. Behind her, there was a loud slam, and she whirled around, her heart jumping in her throat. The street appeared deserted, so she wasn't sure who could have made that slam. Someone in the house next door? The wind?

Ali?

No way. Ali wasn't here. She couldn't be.

A steely-eyed woman with blond hair, a sharply pointed nose, and thin lips appeared in the doorway. She was wearing a menswear-cut pair of trousers and an oxford shirt. Spencer stared at her. The woman stared back. It was the woman from the book jacket, all right. Except she wasn't pleasantly smiling like she was in her author photo.

"Are you Spencer?" the woman asked gruffly. She stuck out her hand before Spencer answered. "I'm Angela. It's three hundred just to come through the door."

"O-oh." Spencer fumbled for her purse and handed over a bunch of crumpled bills. Seemingly satisfied, Angela stepped through the doorway and waved Spencer into a huge space decorated with eighteenth-century French furniture. A tapestry depicting a sour-faced king and queen sitting on thrones in a royal court decorated the back wall. The chandelier over their heads held real candles, though none were lit at the moment. Three ceramic Buddhas stared at Spencer from the mantel. They weren't calming in the least.

Angela plopped down on the largest leather couch Spencer had ever seen and spread her legs across it so that Spencer couldn't share the space. Spencer drifted toward an upright chair in the corner. "So," Spencer began, sitting down. "Thanks for agreeing to meet with me. I really enjoyed your book."

Angela smirked. "Thanks."

Spencer leaned down and pulled her laptop from her bag, opening it on her lap. She took a moment to create a new document in Word and titled it *Prison*. "So I guess we'll just start from the beginning, right? Like in 'Chapter One—Getting There.' Am I really going to be strip-searched?"

Then she heard Angela snickering and looked up. "Honey, this isn't SAT prep."

Spencer felt her cheeks blaze but didn't close the laptop.

Angela lit a Newport Light on a long, gold cigarette holder. "I know who you are and what you did. You'll probably get medium security, is my guess. I don't think they'll do minimum for you, but maybe not maximum, either."

Spencer's heart pounded. *Medium*, she typed. Just hearing the designations made things seem much more real. "Actually, I *didn't* do anything," she corrected Angela. "I'm wrongfully accused."

"Uh huh. Everyone says that." Angela tapped the cigarette into a brown ashtray. "All right, we *will* start at the beginning. This is how it's going to go down. First, they're going to strip-search you. Then, you'll be assigned a bunk, where more than likely your bunk-mates will be murderers like yourself—they like to keep similar criminals together. You won't see your friends, if you're all convicted. And don't even try to make other friends, because they're all backstabbing bitches. Now, with this consultation, I can specialize in either tricks to deal with the guards, how to handle the gangs, or how to manage a relationship while behind bars—you got a boyfriend?"

"N-no," Spencer stammered. Angela was talking too fast. She hadn't even had a chance to type.

"Well, then, I suggest we talk about dealing with the girl gangs—just like in chapter ten." Angela rolled her eyes and took another drag. "If you want to hear about the guards, too, that'll be an extra one-twenty-five."

Spencer's mouth felt dry. "Maybe we could talk about the, um, useful parts of prison? Like the college programs? Work-study initiatives?"

Angela stared at Spencer for a beat, then burst out laughing. "Honey, if anything, they'll do a GED program. And of course they have a lot of law books in case you want to appeal your case, which *everyone* does, not that you really get anywhere with that."

Spencer's heart beat faster. "What about exercise? Your book didn't mention it, but I've read that correctional facilities value physical fitness and health, so . . ."

Angela snorted. "They let you walk around the yard. Don't think you're getting a spin studio or a Pilates class."

"But . . ."

Angela leaned forward, her cigarette blazing. "Listen, honey. I highly suggest we use the rest of this time to talk about girl gangs. A girl like you needs street skills. You go in there spouting Shakespeare, taking notes? You're going to get your ass kicked."

Spencer blinked hard. "I thought that if you just minded your business and did what you were told, people would leave you alone."

One corner of Angela's mouth quirked into a smile.

"It depends. Sometimes, you slip through the cracks. But sometimes, trying to lay low makes you a target."

Suddenly, all of Spencer's tough resolve crumbled. She shut her laptop, realizing why Angela had laughed at her for wanting to take notes. What was the point?

"There's *no way* to make it better?" she heard herself squeak.

Angela snorted. "You can survive, sure. But better? That's why they call it *prison*. The best approach, honey, is to figure out a way *not* to go. Prison will ruin your life, mark my words."

A shiver ran up Spencer's spine. "Why were you in prison, anyway?" It was another thing Angela didn't mention in her book.

Angela shook another Newport out of the pack. "That doesn't matter."

"Did you kill someone?"

"*God*, no." Angela looked at her sideways. "If I did, do you really think I'd be out already?"

"Then what? Assault? Robbery? Drugs?"

Angela's lip curled. "Those aren't nice things to assume."

Spencer suddenly *really* wanted to know. So she employed an old trick she had used in debate club when she wanted to intimidate an opponent. She folded her arms across her chest and stared at Angela, sphinxlike.

Angela's expression soured. She blew out another plume of smoke. Five seconds passed, and finally she threw up her hands. "Jesus. Stop looking at me like that. It was fraud, okay? I created fake identities for people to keep them *out* of prison. Set up new lives for them. Figured out ways for them to start over."

Spencer blinked hard. "Wait, you're serious?"

Angela rolled her eyes. "Why would I lie?"

"Did the cops find these people you helped?"

Angela shook her head. "All except for this one stupid bitch who didn't follow the rules—she got in touch with someone from home, and the cops were monitoring the phones. They traced her fake ID back to me. I had to plead guilty to some of the other people I helped, but those people were long gone. As far as I know, the law never caught up to them."

Spencer ran her hands over the top of her computer, her heart beginning to thrum a little faster. "So it's like the witness protection program . . . except not through the police."

Angela nodded. "You could say that, sure. It's a new life."

"Do you . . . *still* do it?"

Angela's eyes narrowed. "Only for very special cases." She stared right into Spencer's eyes. "It's not for everyone, you know. You can't leave any traces behind. You can't be in touch with anyone you know from your previous life. You have to start over as if you were . . . I don't know. Dropped down here from an alien craft. Some people can't deal."

Spencer couldn't believe it. For the past two weeks, lying on her bed, she'd *fantasized* about someone who, like a travel agent, could get you a passport and travel documents that would extract you from your current predicament and plop you into a world where you were no longer in trouble. And here was someone who actually *did* it, sitting across from her.

She considered what it would be like, leaving Rosewood and never looking back. Becoming someone else entirely, and never, *ever* telling anyone the truth. Never seeing her family again. She'd miss them. Well, maybe not her mom, who really didn't seem to care that Spencer was on trial for murder, but she'd miss her dad. And she'd miss Melissa, who she'd become closer to lately—Melissa had been very vocal about how Spencer was wrongfully accused, though she'd stayed away from explicitly talking about Ali to the press. She'd miss her friends, of course—it would be so strange not to *talk* to them ever again. But what did she have to live for here? She had no boy in the picture. No college future. And *anything* was better than prison.

She looked up and stared into Angela's eyes. "Would you do it for me?"

Angela stubbed out her second smoke. "Starting price is a hundred."

"Dollars?"

Angela tittered. "Try a hundred *thousand* dollars, honey."

Spencer's jaw dropped. "I-I don't have that kind of money."

"Well, then, this conversation never happened," Angela said, her voice suddenly going scary-cold. "And if you tell anyone that it did, *I'll hunt you down and destroy you.*" She recrossed her legs and continued, her voice normal again. "So. Do you want to talk about girl gangs or what?"

Maybe it was the menthol smoke, maybe it was the pissed-off-looking king and queen staring at her from the tapestry, or maybe it was the threat of that giant chandelier breaking off and crushing her head, but suddenly Spencer felt dizzy. She stood from the chair. "Actually, I-I'm sorry. I think I should go."

"Your loss." Angela waggled her fingers. "I get to keep the three hundred, though."

In seconds, Spencer was on the porch again. Angela didn't follow her out.

A car honked noisily a few streets away. Spencer slumped against the wall, her breath fast. In those ten seconds when she had thought disappearing was actually plausible, she'd started to envision a new life. Living quietly. Making a few acquaintances, friends. Then going to college as another person. Still living a purposeful life. Still *succeeding.* Still being Spencer Hastings, just with a different name.

Prison will ruin your life, mark my words.

She pulled out her phone and looked at it, suddenly humbled. Angela was right: Prison would eat her alive.

She dialed Emily's number. It rang twice before Emily answered.

"I changed my mind," Spencer said before Emily even had the chance to say hello. "I can talk to my dad. Let's go see Nick."

3

THE INTERROGATION

Hanna Marin steered her Prius down a winding road that led out of Rosewood. The late-spring air smelled like Flowerbomb perfume, the bright sun was hopefully giving her face a bit of color, her three best friends were crammed into the car with her, and the radio was turned up loud. To most passersby, they probably looked like a bunch of girls on a summer road trip. Not accused murderers on their way to talk to their own almost-murderer, in prison. Her cell phone pinged, and as she slowed to a stoplight she glanced at the screen. *What time should I come over?* her boyfriend, Mike, had texted.

Hanna ran her tongue over her teeth. Thank God she hadn't lost Mike after the paparazzi released those photos of her canoodling with Jared Diaz, her costar in *Burn It Down*, a movie chronicling her and her friends' struggles with Ali. Now she and Mike were closer than ever. Since she was let out on bail he'd come over every day, bringing takeout and girly movies that he actually watched with her and tried his hardest not to make fun of.

She looked around, taking in the wide fields and red barns. For a brief second, she considered telling Mike what they were up to. Bad idea, though: Mike fancied himself as Hanna's knight in shining armor. He'd probably try and rescue them.

Didn't sleep well last night, thinking of taking a nap, Hanna typed back quickly. *Maybe this afternoon?*

There was a pause before Mike texted back, *Sure.* When another text pinged in, Hanna figured it was from Mike again, not buying it. But then she saw Hailey Blake's name.

Hanna raised her eyebrows. Hailey was a tempestuous, badass, mega–movie star who'd become Hanna's friend during her brief stint in *Burn It Down*. Hanna had thought Hailey would drop her after Hanna was unceremoniously let go from her role as herself—and, oh yeah, after she was arrested for murder—but Hailey had been texting her even *more* lately. This one said: *I just saw another report about you on CNN. Your hair looked REALLY GOOD.*

Hanna dropped her phone to her lap. Leave it to Hailey to be unfazed by Hanna's predicament. It was nice that *someone* in Hollywood still thought she was the bomb. Hank Ross, *Burn It Down*'s director, who'd said Hanna was "a natural" and "had a bright future," wouldn't even return her calls. Neither would Marcella, Hanna's brand-new agent.

Whenever Hanna thought about her almost-shot at

stardom, she burst into tears and couldn't breathe. It hurt more than when she had realized Mona, her old bestie, was the first A and had tried to kill her. It hurt more than when she had found out Ali had a twin and had never told her. It even hurt more than when her father, whom she'd once loved more than anyone in the world, had dropped Hanna cold, saying she "wasn't good for his political campaign." Acting had been all hers . . . and she was actually good at it. She'd thought it could be her future.

But now . . . well. Her only chance at stardom was on *America's Most Wanted.*

"Green light," Emily croaked impatiently from the back.

Hanna pressed the gas, glancing at Emily in the rearview mirror. Her old friend looked thinner, and her eyes bugged out from her head. Hanna was still really worried about Emily—because she'd almost jumped off a bridge in Rosewood, and then because she'd had that freak-out at the pool house where they'd tracked Ali, and didn't tell them. And lately, Em had seemed sort of . . . *twitchy.* Like an invisible person was giving her electric shocks. She was also incredibly wired this morning, like she'd drunk a zillion Red Bulls. Hanna wondered if she'd slept last night.

Then again, the rest of them didn't look so hot, either— Hanna included. Spencer sucked on the straw of her water bottle so forcefully that lines formed around her mouth. Aria wouldn't stop clanging her bracelets together. Hanna had probably redone her lipstick six times, something she always did when she was upset. Were *any* of them ready to talk to Nick?

Hanna turned onto a road marked ALLERTON PRISON, NEXT LEFT. The squat, drab, boxy prison buildings appeared in the distance, surrounded by a menacing mess of barbed wire. Hanna pulled through the entrance and parked. Everyone was silent as they walked into the visitor's gate and handed over their IDs to a woman behind a desk. As the woman took their names and contacted a guard inside, Hanna glanced surreptitiously around, her heart pounding hard. The air smelled of rotting meat. From somewhere inside the walls came a deep, manly bellow that sounded like a cross between a roar and a moan.

A guard poked his head into the waiting room. "Visitors for Maxwell?"

Everyone shot to their feet. The guard motioned for them to follow, and soon enough they were in a long, narrow room. The guard directed them to a private vestibule at the very end, and they shuffled forward. There were no other visitors in the room. A fluorescent light flickered overhead.

A door on the far wall opened. A guard pushed a guy in a prison jumpsuit and handcuffs into the room. Hanna's stomach twisted. There he was. *Nick.*

He'd lost a significant amount of weight since she'd last seen him in the basement, and he looked entirely different from when she'd *first* seen him, when he'd fed her and a new friend, Madison, drink after drink at a dive bar in Philly. Without even peeking around, Hanna could tell that her friends were each having their own struggles with the Nick *they'd* known—the shape-shifter who'd tricked them into trusting him—and the Nick who loved Ali. It was a thrill to see him in prison garb, though. If only Ali were by his side, behind bars, too.

Nick raised his head and saw them. His eyes narrowed. His mouth set in a straight, angry line. He glanced at the guard and shook his head, murmuring something that looked like *no*.

Spencer jumped to her feet. "We're not here to curse you out. We're on your side."

Nick peeked at them again. There was a shadow of a bruise by his eye. His chest heaved up and down, as if he'd been running hard. Finally, he lowered his shoulders and slumped toward the seat across the table from the girls. He was so close Hanna could reach out and touch him if she wanted. She stared at his hands. The skin under his fingernails was filthy.

"Look, you know as well as we do that Ali's not dead," Spencer started, when no one else spoke. "She's too smart for that. We heard what she wrote about you in that journal. She lied about us, too. She screwed *all* of us. We should be on the same side here."

Nick's eyes danced. "I don't know, girls. Maybe you *did* kill her." He cocked his head teasingly. "I distinctly recall the rage in your eyes in that basement when we trapped you. I distinctly remember how badly you wanted her gone."

Hanna curled her fist. "Yeah, and *I* distinctly recall how easy it was for you to torture people, judging by what you did to *us* that night." She didn't blink. "Who's to say you didn't do that to Ali?"

The playful look on Nick's face vanished. "*I* loved her."

"Do you still love her now?" Hanna challenged.

Nick muttered something Hanna couldn't hear.

Aria shifted her weight. "Look, we're trying to find Ali. Bringing her back, making her explain—it will help you, too. You'll serve much less time. We know you didn't orchestrate those murders. We know you weren't the ringleader."

Nick's jaw was so tense that ropy cords stood out on his neck. "I hate you bitches," he whispered raspily. "You were supposed to die in that room. Ali and I were supposed to escape together."

"But instead, she left you for the police to find," Emily pressed. "She *framed* you."

Nick's bottom lip twitched. "She was trying to save herself. It was part of our plan."

Aria snorted. "It was part of your plan for you to take the blame for all her crimes?"

"Of course it was. We were in love. I love her. She *loved* me."

Emily leaned forward. "No, she didn't," she said in a strong voice. "Know how I know? She told me so when she tried to drown me. She said I was the one she always loved. She told me she was just using you. She *laughed* about it."

Hanna turned and gaped at Emily, but Emily didn't meet her eye. Emily hadn't talked much about Ali trying to drown her at the Rosewood pool, but Hanna suspected it had shaken her to her core.

Nick glanced at Emily suspiciously. "She didn't say that."

"Yeah, she did," Emily stated. "She said you were pathetic. A *nothing*."

A conflicted expression crossed Nick's face. Hanna's heart started to pound. He was going to crack. She could feel it.

Spencer shifted her weight. "Tell us where she is. *Please*."

Nick snorted. "Like I'd know."

"She was last at your parents' property in Ashland," Hanna pressed, her words coming out in a jumble. "Had you told her about that place?"

He averted his gaze. "We'd been there a few times. It wasn't surprising that she hid out there."

"Does your family have other properties she might be hiding out in?" Hanna asked.

Spencer looked at Hanna. "Ali wouldn't do something so obvious. They're listed online, remember? I'm sure the cops are searching all of them."

"*I'm sure the cops are searching all of them*," Nick mocked

Spencer. He crossed his arms over his chest. "You girls think you're so freaking smart, but don't you get it? The cops *aren't* looking for her. They don't think she's out there. They think she's dead, thanks to you." He pointed at them.

"So you *don't* think she's dead, then," Spencer stated.

Nick shrugged. "I don't know," he admitted.

Hanna's heart leapt. "Where do you think she is, if you had to take a guess?"

Nick breathed in, as if he was about to speak. Then a shadow loomed over them. The guard clapped a hand on Nick's shoulder. "Time's up."

"Wait!" Emily surged to her feet. "What were you going to say?"

"Time's up," the guard repeated angrily.

"Nick, please!" Spencer called out. "Tell us!"

Nick looked at them. "Ali really liked gathering sea-shells in Cape May," he blurted. "We walked with my grandma Betty on the beach this one time. Senile old lady had no idea who Ali was, kept calling me my dad's name. It was a nice day, though."

Everyone looked at one another. "What do you mean?" Spencer shouted after him. "Is Ali in Cape May?"

"Is she with someone named Betty?" Aria tried.

But it was too late. Nick waved blithely. The guard shoved him through the door. It slammed hard, the metal-lic sound thundering in Hanna's ears.

What seemed like moments later, they were back in the

parking lot. A skunk had just sprayed, and the air smelled rank. Hanna sighed heavily. "Well. Glad we did *that*."

Spencer touched Emily's arm. "Did Ali really tell you that stuff about not loving Nick?"

Emily shook her head. "I just thought it would get him to open up. And it worked."

Aria breathed in. "You know, maybe Nick *was* trying to tell us something."

Spencer stopped next to a pickup truck. "Meaning?"

Aria twisted her hands. "Maybe Ali *is* in Cape May. Maybe his parents have another property there, or maybe it was a hint about his grandmother having a house there," Aria said. "Senile old Grandma Betty."

"Oh my God." Hanna whipped out her phone and typed in the address for public property listings in Cape May, New Jersey. "I'll look for Betty Maxwell." Data popped up on the screen. It took Hanna several minutes to wade through a bunch of names, but then she gasped. "Guys. Someone named Barbara Maxwell owns a house on Dune Street in Cape May. Betty is a nickname for Barbara, isn't it?"

"We need to go," Emily said automatically. "*Now*."

Spencer pressed her lips together. "But that means leaving the state. Which is a no-no, remember?"

Hanna paused, remembering the police and Rubens telling them how imperative it was that they remained in Rosewood until their trial. It had been incredible that they hadn't been ordered to remain in jail without bail at their arraignment, actually—people facing murder charges usually were. Hanna wondered if they'd gotten off because they were still just teenagers. She knew they were risking everything, thinking about leaving. But she couldn't bear the thought of Ali getting away, again. "What if this is our only chance?" she squeaked.

"I agree," Aria said as they reached the Prius. "Ali could be there. Or there could be a clue that leads us to where she might have gone. We should do it."

They all turned to Spencer, who looked conflicted. "I don't know . . ."

Something snapped behind them. Hanna whirled around toward the direction of the sound and canvassed the scene. The parking lot was empty, all the cars lined up in neat rows. The wind shifted again, and her gaze drifted upward. The only thing she saw was a uniformed man standing in the guard tower. He held a huge gun in his hand.

Aria's throat bobbed, her gaze on the guard, too. Emily pressed her hand to her mouth. Hanna could tell they were thinking the same thing. Pretty soon, if they didn't act fast, a guard would be watching *them*.

Spencer made a small, choked noise. "Okay," she whispered. "We'll leave for Cape May tomorrow morning."

4

BEACH TRIP!

Aria Montgomery awoke on Saturday to two strong, warm arms wrapped tightly around her. She breathed in deeply, inhaling her boyfriend Noel Kahn's slightly sweet, slightly salty morning smell. He'd slept over the past week, sneaking through her window once her mom had gone to bed, and she had to admit it was bliss spooning him all night. *I could get used to this*, she thought headily, her eyes fluttering closed.

Except she *wasn't* going to get used to it. Because soon everything was going to change.

She sat up straight, reality whooshing back. She'd only recently reunited with Noel, and now that was all going to be taken away. Aria stared at his peaceful face on the pillow, wishing she could perfectly preserve this memory for all her future lonely, horrible nights in a prison cell. *He has serious bedhead*, she chanted silently. *He talks in his sleep about lacrosse plays. He looks so cuddly and adorable.*

Noel opened one eye. "Why are you staring at me?"

"Just trying to preserve this moment forever," Aria said breezily, then winced. The last thing she wanted to do was bring up her impending doom first thing in the morning.

But Noel sat up and looked at her with a serious expression. "Whatever happens, Aria, I'm going to wait for you. I mean it."

Aria pulled away. *Yeah, right.* It was clear she and Noel were kindred spirits, but she couldn't ask him to wait thirty years for her to *maybe* get parole. "I'll have saggy boobs by the time I get out," she blurted.

"I like saggy boobs," Noel answered sleepily. "Especially *your* saggy boobs."

Aria felt tears come to her eyes. She flopped back on the pillow and stared at the old glow-in-the-dark stars on the ceiling. "I wish I could just run away."

"Where would you go?" Noel asked.

Aria thought about the fantasy she'd turned over and over in her mind a thousand times: She had the cash now, thanks to the sale of several of her oil paintings. Couldn't she withdraw a huge chunk of change and just . . . leave? If Ali could do it, why couldn't she?

"Not an island," she said first. Her spring-break trip to Jamaica junior year—and getting into that mess with Tabitha Clark, the girl who had tried to pass herself off as Ali—had ruined her on the Caribbean. So had the senior-year Eco Cruise trip, where Aria had almost been killed by a bomb blast in the boiler room and left at sea to drown.

"What about Norway?" Noel suggested.

Aria stretched. "That would be nice. Holland is cool, too. They're very lenient there, and I love the Anne Frank museum and all the canals."

Noel laced his hands behind his head. "You could paint in your spare time. Sell a few works, set us up in style."

Aria punched him playfully. "Us? Who said *you* could come along?"

Noel looked like he was going to say something teasing back when Aria's alarm blared. Suddenly, another reality rushed to the forefront of her mind. She'd told Spencer she'd be waiting outside in a half hour.

She leapt out of bed. "I have to go."

Noel watched as Aria scuttled around, flinging her closet open, searching for her flip-flops. "You meeting with your lawyer?" he asked.

"Uh . . . no. Just hanging out with the girls." She tried to smile at him. "I'm sorry. I wanted to make breakfast for you this morning." Their on-again relationship still felt so new and tenuous. A big stack of pancakes was always the way to Noel's heart. "Rain check?"

"Can I come along?"

"No!"

Noel recoiled, then frowned. She'd said it too quickly, too harshly. All at once, Aria knew that he knew what she was up to.

"Aria." He shut his eyes. "You're not looking for Ali, are you?"

Aria turned away to her dresser and busied herself by shuffling through a stack of T-shirts. "Of course not."

"You are." Noel scuttled out from under the quilt. "It's dangerous."

It was pointless to lie. Noel was on board with everything Aria told him. He believed Ali had set them up and was still alive. But they both knew how tricky she was.

She shrugged. "It's just a dumb lead. But we're going, okay? Please don't tell anyone."

Noel looked worried. "Let me come with you, at least."

Aria dropped the shirt she was holding and grabbed his hands. "Absolutely not." Ali had hurt Noel once before, leaving him for dead in a sports shed behind the school. Aria wasn't involving him again.

"But I might be in the unique position to help," Noel said gently.

Aria felt an old, annoying twinge. *A unique position.* A few years back, he'd been Ali's only confidant, visiting her at The Preserve at Addison-Stevens. Noel had kept many secrets for Ali . . . and he hadn't shared any of them with Aria when they'd started dating. It had seemed like Noel would have done *anything* for Ali back then. They even had a secret code for when they wanted to get in touch. Aria didn't like to think about it. It was stupid, she knew, but a teeny part of her still wasn't sure if she held a candle to Ali. That Noel had briefly dated an Ali-look-alike named Scarlett while he and Aria were broken up didn't help, either.

She tried to whisk the thoughts out of her mind. "We probably won't turn up anything, anyway," she told Noel. "And I'll be back soon."

Noel still looked conflicted. "Promise me you'll stay safe, okay? Text me this afternoon." He pulled her close. "I don't want to lose you again."

Aria kissed the tip of his nose. "You won't lose me," she breathed, melting into his arms.

But that was the problem. Soon enough, he *was* going to lose her—to jail.

Unless they found what they were looking for.

An hour later, the four girls were flying across the bridge out of Philly. It was an overcast day, but the road was still busy, and a bunch of roadside farmers' stands boasting watermelon, corn, and tomatoes were crowded with families. A huge billboard that read WELCOME TO NEW JERSEY swept past, and Aria sat higher in her seat, eager to get the investigation started.

After another hour, they drove down Cape May's quaint Main Street and pulled into the first establishment they found, an old, flesh-colored motel called the Atlantic Lighthouse. A large, inground pool, complete with an old-school blue diving board and a couple of rusty-looking outdoor tables and chairs, spanned the length of the building, and there was a falling-apart, bird-poop-infested, decorative lighthouse fixed to the roof. When Aria pushed the door open into the lobby, an icy blast of AC brought goose bumps to her arms. A bleached-blond woman glanced up from the news on a small TV behind the desk and gave them a strange look.

Aria's heart lurched. Then she looked down and saw something horrifying: There, on the front page of a stack of *USA Today* newspapers, was a huge picture of Ali, a smaller picture of Ali's father, and an even smaller picture of Spencer, Emily, Hanna, and herself. *Trial Starts Tuesday*, the paper said. *DiLaurentis Father Weighs In.*

She quickly turned the paper over, her breath coming out in short bursts. Did the clerk recognize them? They were all wearing sunglasses, and Hanna had on a hat to cover up her easily recognizable auburn hair, but maybe that wasn't enough. Aria considered bolting out of the room. But that would look even more suspicious, wouldn't it?

"Um, hi," Spencer said shakily. "I'm wondering if you could give us directions to Dune Street?" That was where Betty Maxwell's house was.

The woman nodded and pointed to the left. The girls were about to leave when she cleared her throat and gestured to a plaque on the counter. CAPE MAY WEATHER REPORT, it read, listing information about the days' temperature and tides. "You hear about the storm?"

Aria relaxed a little. The woman didn't seem to know who they were.

"Supposed to be a big one, rolling in by late tomorrow morning," the woman said, then rolled her eyes. "I'm sick of this crazy weather."

Then she went back to watching her TV. The girls scuttled back onto the street and headed in the direction of Dune Street, though not before Aria snatched up a *USA Today*. She skimmed the article. Ali's father was begging for justice to be done for his murdered daughter, saying he would have a front-row seat at their murder trial. Then, she noticed something interesting. "Did you guys know that Ali's mom isn't coming to the trial?" she asked in a low voice, reading as she walked. "It says that Mrs. DiLaurentis is way too traumatized to even be in the same room as us."

Emily scoffed. "That's proof right there that Ali is still alive. A mother would absolutely be at that trial unless she knew her daughter wasn't really dead."

Spencer made a face. "Or else she's just a complete basket case and can't go through with it."

"Personally, I'm glad she's not going to be there," Aria said quietly. The last thing she wanted was to come face-to-face with Jessica DiLaurentis. Ali's mom had been icy on good days.

She folded up the paper, tossed it into the trash, and trotted to catch up with her friends. The sun was already bright and hot. A bunch of kids on their way to the beach, sand pails, boogie boards, and chairs in hand, brushed past them, calling happily to one another. The air smelled like sunscreen and homemade waffle cones.

Hanna looked around pensively. "My dad used to bring me and Our Ali—Courtney—here." She kicked a pebble on the sidewalk. "We saw Mona one of the last times. Ali was ruthless to her."

Emily sniffed bitterly. "No surprise there." Then Emily's face twisted, like she was in pain.

"You okay?" Aria asked worriedly.

"Uh huh," Emily said quickly.

Maybe *too* quickly. Aria watched her carefully. Emily had seemed so . . . *troubled* from all of this Ali stuff, and it had been so unlike her to almost jump from that bridge a few weeks ago. But every time Aria asked what was wrong, Emily brushed her off.

"I came here with Courtney once, too," Aria said. "She made fun of me for using SPF 50 sunscreen. She was like, 'That's why no guys like you, Aria. Because you look like a pasty freak.' So I used her baby oil instead. I got burned, and it sucked."

"And Courtney probably laughed, right?" Hanna muttered.

Aria stepped over a crack in the sidewalk. "She did." Sure, Courtney wasn't as diabolical as the *Real* Ali, but she had still been a manipulative bitch.

They turned onto Dune Street and looked at the numbers on the houses until they reached a two-story, green-shingled house with a front yard full of bleached-white stones. The shutters were closed, there wasn't a car in the driveway, there wasn't any porch furniture out, and it was the only house on the block that didn't have a FOR RENT sign out front.

Hanna frowned. "Did anyone check if Betty Maxwell was still alive?"

"It certainly doesn't look like anyone's here," Spencer agreed.

Emily took a few steps up the front walk. The others followed. Spencer pulled out a pair of plastic gloves from her pocket, slipped them on, and tried the bell. No answer. She turned the doorknob, but it was locked.

Emily pulled her bottom lip into her mouth, then yanked on her own pair of gloves, stepped off the porch, and began trying each of the windows around the house. She disappeared quickly around the side, and suddenly called out, "We're in!"

Everyone ran to find her. Emily had hefted open a side window enough for her to squeeze through. "I'll unlock the front door for you."

"I don't know, Em." Aria glanced back at the street. "It's broad daylight. Someone might see."

Emily scoffed and boosted herself up onto the windowsill. "Isn't this why we came?"

She slipped inside without waiting for an answer. Aria's heart pounded. She waited for an alarm to blare, someone to scream out, a dog to start rabidly barking . . . but there was nothing. A few seconds later, the front door opened, Emily on the other side. Everyone hurried through.

The house was dark and smelled like sand. Aria waited for her eyes to adjust. The room was empty, and the walls bore faded, sea-horse-printed wallpaper. The navy rug was stained and threadbare. A pile of mail sat by the door, all faded circulars from the local grocery store addressed to *Current Resident.*

Emily wandered into the kitchen. Aria watched as she opened the fridge and peered inside. It was empty, completely cleaned out. She searched cabinets and drawers, but they were all empty, too. She tried the tap, but no water came out. Spencer opened a linen closet. "Nothing," she called.

Aria tiptoed down the dark hall and poked her head into each of the bedrooms. In every one, she found a neatly made twin bed and little else. She checked under the beds, but there was nothing hiding there. There were no clothes left behind in the closets, either. She poked her head into the bathroom. There was no shower curtain, and the tub smelled of bleach. And yet, it seemed like a presence lingered there. Maybe the last person who'd stayed in the house. Or maybe a ghost.

Aria stared at a small closet at the back of the bathroom she hadn't noticed at first. Something creaked—maybe from inside. All at once, goose bumps rose on her skin. Was someone *in* that closet? *Ali?*

Her hand shook as she reached out for the knob. Her stomach swirled as she slowly turned it. There was a groan as the door opened, and Aria shielded her face with her hand, ready for an onslaught.

Silence. She opened her eyes. The closet was totally empty, the shelves wiped clean.

Sighing, she returned to the living room. Spencer and Hanna were waiting, looking equally freaked out. Then, Emily called out from the door near the garage. "Come *here*."

Everyone rushed over. Emily stuck her head into the small, empty garage. "Do you smell that?" she said excitedly.

Aria's nose twitched. She looked at the others. "Is that . . . vanilla?" It was Ali's calling card: cloying vanilla soap.

Emily's eyes were wide. "We should call the police. This is proof she's still alive."

Spencer peered back into the empty house. "Em, that's not enough to get the police here." She sighed. "Besides, she's not here *now*."

Emily stared at them. "Still. This is a *lead*."

"It's a trick," Spencer corrected her. "And it's happened before. Ali gave us a hint that she was at the pool house, but then she wiped the place clean of her prints. That's what's happening here, too."

Emily turned to Aria. "But maybe she just left. We could ask people on this street. People at the Wawa. *Someone* probably saw her. Aria, what do you think?"

Aria looked down. "Em, I think Spencer's right."

Emily smacked the doorjamb. "So we're going to do *nothing*?"

Spencer placed her hand on Emily's shoulder. "Em. Calm down."

Emily twisted away, letting out a pained keening sound. "I can't just walk away from this! I've got to get her out of my head! She's *killing me*!"

Everyone exchanged nervous glances. Aria's heart began to pound. Did Emily think that Ali was trapped inside her or something? "Em." She grabbed her shoulders. "Em, *please*. You're scaring us."

She wrapped her arms around Emily until her friend stopped flailing. When Emily turned to face them again, her face was red and she was still breathing hard, but she didn't seem as unglued. "This is the end, isn't it?" she asked in a quiet, stony tone.

Aria nodded sadly. "I think so."

Emily leaned against Aria heavily. Hanna joined the group, squeezing Emily's shoulders. Spencer piled on last, her body heaving with sobs.

"I know it's hard," Aria murmured. "We all wanted to find her."

"But it's going to be okay," Hanna said bravely. "Whatever happens, we'll have each other."

Emily looked at them and tried to smile, but then her face crumpled again.

They hugged for what seemed like ages. When they pulled apart, everyone wiped their eyes. Aria felt empty. It sucked that she wouldn't return to Noel triumphant and that they'd start the trial without proof Ali was out there. Their future was so bleak. They had little to look forward to.

They filed out the door and started down the sidewalk. In the distance, waves crashed and kids laughed. Someone was playing a radio loudly, and Aria could smell a barbecue. It seemed cruel, really, to witness such happy sights, sounds, and smells right then. And when an ice-cream truck tinkled around the corner, it was almost too much to bear. A teenage boy stuck his head out the window. "Want some?" he asked.

Hanna nudged Emily. "Get a Popsicle. It'll cheer you up."

"We'll all get something." Spencer's voice was forcedly cheerful. "In fact, we should stay here the rest of the day, guys. Eat ice cream. Hang out, get a great dinner, leave early tomorrow before the storm comes in. We could check into that motel where we asked for directions. What do you think?"

Aria thought for a moment, then nodded. A day at the beach was like their equivalent of a death-row prisoner's last meal, but they were already there. They might as well.

"Okay," Emily said. And everyone seemed to breathe a collective sigh of relief.

They took their places in line. Aria perused the ice cream choices—they hadn't changed since she was a kid. When she closed her eyes, breathing in the salty air and feeling the hot sun, she almost *felt* like a kid again—like that gangly, insecure girl who let her best friend tease her about how no boys liked her because she was so pale.

She'd go back to that day in a heartbeat—anything was better than what lay ahead. She'd even suffer through the sunburn.

5

EMILY TAKES THE PLUNGE

Emily lay perfectly still on the crinkly mattress in the hotel double bed. Hanna was by her side, sleeping on her stomach, a satin mask over her eyes and headphones in her ears. Aria and Spencer were crammed into the other double bed, breathing softly. The air conditioner rattled in the corner, and the alert light on someone's phone blinked on the desk.

The wind had begun to howl, and Emily could hear the crashing waves even from up in the room. It sounded like the storm was rolling in earlier than predicted. Last year, Emily had watched footage of a hurricane like this one. In one video, a man was stranded in his rowboat out at sea. The camera stayed on him as he tried to fight the current again and again, fruitlessly paddling. Rescue helicopters hadn't been able to reach him. No lifeguard dared to swim in, nor could a rescue boat get close. And still the news kept their cameras trained on him anyway, until the bitter end. Emily had basically watched a man die on television.

Didn't like that, did you, Em? Ali giggled in her head.

Emily glanced at the clock: 5:03 AM. She couldn't stop thinking about Ali. *It's a trick*, Spencer had said about the vanilla. But was it? Was it *really*?

Emily ran her hand along her bare stomach. They'd gotten ice cream that afternoon, then treated themselves to a fish fry that evening, even finding a place where the bartender would serve them margaritas. But Emily had barely tasted any of it. She felt like her head was clouded with fog, reacting a split second too late to what her friends said, completely missing jokes, taking too long to even blink. *Em, are you okay?* her friends kept asking. But it was like they were talking to her underwater; she could barely hear them. She'd felt herself nod, she'd felt herself try to smile. The fish-and-chips she'd ordered had been too hot, but when she'd bitten into them, she barely registered that she'd burned her tongue.

Maybe she'd never taste again. Maybe she'd never *feel* again. Then again, perhaps that was a good approach to take for prison.

Damn right, Ali agreed.

Emily thought again about the vanilla smell. Ali had been in that house—she knew it. Maybe she'd ordered a Klondike from that same ice-cream truck. Strolled down to the beach, relaxed on the sand, gone for a swim. Slept peacefully, soundly, waking every morning to read more bad news of Emily, Spencer, Hanna, and Aria. Emily could only imagine the satisfaction Ali was getting from knowing that the four of them would soon be locked up forever. She'd probably thrown her head back in laughter, thrilled she'd finally won.

But Ali would only win if Emily dutifully marched off to prison, like she was supposed to. There was another way. Another darker, scarier answer. Another path Emily could dare to walk down.

Should I? She pushed back the covers and swung her legs to the carpet, feeling a twinge of déjà vu. She pulled on her swimsuit and her shorts. Paused to listen to the wind as it howled violently, shaking the windows, creaking the walls.

Then she looked at her friends. Hanna turned over. Spencer kicked in her sleep. Emily felt a guilty twinge. She knew this would devastate them, but it was the only option. She set her jaw, pulled out a piece of motel stationery, and scribbled down the words she'd been mentally composing. Then, she slipped out the door, not bothering to take a key. With any luck, she would be gone before her friends woke up.

The hallway smelled like beer. She felt along the walls until she reached the outdoor stairs, then carefully navigated down. A gust of wind slammed her from the side, pressing her against the railing. She stood there a moment, bracing herself, thinking again of her friends and the anguish they'd soon feel, before she continued walking to the sidewalk. From there, she fought her way to the beach path, the wind pushing her back with every step. The sun was just rising, the sky a streaky mix of dark blues and pinks. A foreboding red flag indicating that swimming was strictly forbidden had been staked atop the lifeguard stand. The wind was making quick work of tearing it to shreds.

Emily struggled down the beach steps and planted her feet in the cold sand. The waves whipped to and fro with no discernible pattern. They crashed angrily, caustically, with such power that they were sure to rip apart anything that got in their way. All at once, she thought she heard something over the surf and the wind. A laugh? Someone breathing? She whipped around, eyeing the dark beach stairway, glaring and glaring until her eyes began to play tricks on her. Was that a girl crouched in the dunes, watching? Could Ali be *here*?

Emily stood up straighter, staring hard, but as much as she wanted to see something, there was nothing there. She shut her eyes and pictured what Ali would do if she saw her right now. *Would* she laugh? This wasn't part of her plan, after all. Maybe she'd respect Emily for what she was about to do. Maybe she'd even fear her.

Like the other girls, Emily had an Ali Cape May memory, too—but she and Ali hadn't come here together. Her memory was from fifth grade, before Emily and Ali were friends—so the memory was of the *Real* Ali, not of Courtney. Ali had sat a few towels away from Emily's family, looking mysterious in her large-framed sunglasses, whispering and snickering with Naomi Zeigler and Riley Wolfe. Emily had stared at her hard, feeling a spangled sensation inside her. She didn't just want to *be* Alison DiLaurentis, the girl everyone adored. She wanted to be *with* her. Touch her. Braid her hair. Smell her clothes when she stepped out of them at bedtime. Drink her up.

Ali had looked up at Emily and smirked. Then she'd nudged Naomi and Riley, and all three of them had laughed. Certain Ali had sensed her desires, Emily had jumped up and run for the water, then dived under the waves. She'd swum hard and fast, into the roaring breakers, ignoring the lifeguard's whistles that she'd gone too far. *That sort of girl would never be friends with you*, a voice in her head pounded. *And she'd certainly never be* into *you*.

A wave had caught her and pushed her under. When she'd surfaced, she was sputtering and winded. Everyone was staring at her, probably knowing her impure, ridiculous thoughts. As she'd walked back to her towel, Ali was watching her again, although this time she looked a little bit awed. "The water doesn't scare you, does it?" she pointed out.

The question had taken Emily by surprise. "No," she said calmly. It was the truth. It wasn't the waves she was afraid of.

Nor was she afraid of them now.

Emily turned to face the waves again, holding that memory of Ali–the *Real* Ali, the *crazy* Ali–tight inside her. Little did she know then that someday, that beautiful, horrible girl would be the center of her life. Little did she know that Ali would take everything from her.

"I'm not afraid," Emily whispered, pulling off her tee. She waited for the Ali in her head to answer, but surprisingly, the voice was silent.

The waves tumbled, kicking up white foam. Emily understood the power of the ocean; she knew that it might take her down fast, even faster than it had in fifth grade. In these conditions, it would pull her under, spin her like a pebble. She pictured her head hitting rock, or the nearby jetty, or simply sinking down, down, down, until she felt nothing.

I'm not afraid, she thought again, stepping out of her shorts. And with that, she walked down the beach and into the sea.

6

RESCUE EFFORTS

Crack.

Spencer sat up in bed. At first, she had no idea where she was . . . and then she saw Aria next to her and felt the scratchy motel comforter. The digital clock on the side table said it was 5:30. The room was still dark, though the wind outside was howling fiercely.

She stumbled for the bathroom, not bothering to turn on the light. After she flushed, she stood by her bed again, sensing something was wrong. It didn't take her long to realize what it was.

Emily wasn't there.

Spencer rushed to Emily's side of the bed and patted it, but the lump of pillows and blankets wasn't concealing a girl. She slid open the closet door—apparently, after Jordan died, Emily had taken to sleeping in her closet—but Emily wasn't there, either. Spencer spun around the room, breathing heavily. Something was off. Where could Emily have gone this early in the morning?

And then she saw it.

A stark white piece of paper, folded, on the desk. *Spencer, Aria, and Hanna*, it read in Emily's handwriting. Spencer snatched it up, ran to the bathroom, and turned on the light. She unfolded the paper with shaking hands. There, in messy scrawl, were four terrible sentences.

I just can't do this anymore. You guys are much stronger than me. Please don't come after me. I'm sorry.

The note fluttered from her hands. Spence rushed back into the room and grabbed her flip-flops, shoved them on her feet. "Oh my God, oh my God."

Aria shifted sleepily. "Are you okay, Spence?"

Spencer didn't answer. Staying here, explaining—it would take too long. "I'll be back," she blurted, then darted out the door and dashed down the motel stairs.

It was just getting light outside. The first place Spencer checked was Hanna's car, but it was still in the parking space; Emily wasn't inside. She ran to the pool; the surface was windswept, but no one was swimming. She gazed up the sidewalk, then in the other direction. The streets were empty. Clearly the storm was rolling in early; most people had probably left. No one would be on the beach on a day like today.

And then it hit her.

Spencer raced around the side of the motel toward the beach path. She scrambled up the steps and down them again, tripping over the dunes. When she saw Emily's clothes in a jumbled heap near the stairs, she let out a choked, muffled cry. *She couldn't. She wouldn't.*

"Spence?"

Spencer whipped around. Hanna and Aria were behind her, still in their pajamas. Both were pale. "What's going on?" Aria croaked fearfully, staring at Spencer like she'd gone crazy. "Why are you down here? Where's Emily?"

"She's . . . ," Spencer said, but then she noticed the look on Hanna's face. Hanna was looking past them at the water. She extended a shaky finger, and Spencer whirled around to follow her gaze. There, beyond the breakers, very visible, was a girl's sleek, dark head.

"No!" Spencer screamed, tearing down the beach toward the water. Emily floundered in the waves, her arms extended. A wave pounded over her, and she vanished.

Spencer turned to her friends, who'd run down, too. "She's going to die out there!"

"We should call 911," Hanna said, pulling out her phone.

"There's no time!" Spencer whipped off her shorts. "I'm going after her."

Aria caught her arm. "You'll die, too!"

But Spencer had already kicked off her flip-flops and was sprinting toward the foamy water. There was no way she could let the ocean swallow Emily up. This was *her* fault: She'd seen how out of it Emily was. She knew how hard this Ali stuff had hit her, and she'd sensed the turbulent storms that were brewing in Emily's head. Emily had attempted suicide once before—of *course* she was going to try again. Spencer should have stayed up all night to watch over her. She should have known Emily was going to do something like this. They *all* should have.

The water was cold, but she pressed forward into the depths, barely feeling the temperature on her feet and calves. The first wave knocked her sideways, almost to the sand. Spencer glanced over her shoulder at Hanna and Aria on the shore. Hanna was yelling something into her phone. Aria had her hands cupped around her mouth, probably calling for Spencer to come back in. Spencer turned back around, catching sight of Emily's head in the distance. "Em!" she screamed, wading toward her. She thought Emily heard her, because she turned and seemed to stare in Spencer's direction. But then a wave crashed over her head, and she vanished.

"*Em!*" Spencer screamed again, diving under the next wave. The current knocked her sideways, and she did one full spin before spluttering to the surface. She peered at the horizon again. There was Emily's head, bobbing above the breakers for a split second. "Emily!" Spencer roared, paddling out. Another wave dragged her under. The force of it shoved Spencer to the very bottom, tumbling her without popping her up. Suddenly, she had no air left in her lungs. She clawed and groped, but the current was too strong. *Oh my God*, she thought. *I really* could *die*.

She finally made it to the surface. Breathing hard,

she peered into the distance. Was that Emily way out there? Spots formed in Spencer's eyes. She was already exhausted. She couldn't swim that far. The others were right: This was a terrible idea. She had to go back in.

But when Spencer turned for the shore, her friends seemed so far away. A rip current had pulled her far out to sea. Spencer's mind scattered. You were supposed to do something to get out of a riptide—but what? She started to paddle for the shore, but the current shoved her back. She tried again—no luck. Her muscles burned. Her lungs ached. The waves pounded over her head, and her eyes stung from the salt.

Hanna and Aria looked more and more frantic on the shore. More people had gathered, too, their hands clapped over their mouths. Spencer paddled hard, knowing that if she kept trying, she would get in. But when the next wave crashed over her head, her body sank like a stone. Her arm twisted awkwardly behind her back, slamming into the ocean bottom. She blew out through her nose and tried to fight for shore, but her arms wouldn't work anymore. The current tossed her back and forth.

She let go, opening her eyes under the water. At first, all she saw was blackness, but then a figure emerged. It was a girl with milky-white skin and buttery-blond hair. Light emanated from behind her, creating an eerie halo. She swam up to Spencer deftly until she was so close their faces were almost touching.

It was only then that Spencer realized it was Ali. She

was *here*, somehow. Maybe she'd brought this storm.

"Go away!" Spencer screamed out, extending her hands toward the girl. But just like that, Ali dissolved into a thousand water molecules, into nothingness. And seconds later, all Spencer saw was nothingness, too.

"Spencer. *Spencer*."

Spencer swam up to consciousness. A circle of white nearly blinded her, and she covered her eyes. Then a silhouette appeared. All at once, she remembered the mermaid in the water–*Ali*.

"Leave me alone!" Spencer screamed, thrashing her arms. But the person standing over her wasn't Ali, but her father. He looked sick with worry.

And then she remembered what *really* happened: the storm, Emily's note, chasing Emily into the waves.

Spencer stared down at herself as everything rushed back. She was no longer struggling in the ocean. In fact, she was wearing a hospital gown and lying in bed with a bright light over her head. A monitor beeped steadily a few feet away.

She shakily ran her hand over her hair. It was completely dry, crusty with salt. She tried to use the other hand, but couldn't move it. She heard a clanking sound and looked over. She was handcuffed to the bed. "W-what's going on?"

"You're at a hospital in Philadelphia," Mr. Hastings said. "You were pulled out of the ocean a few hours ago."

Someone else appeared over her. It was a woman in a police uniform. "Miss Hastings?" she said sternly. "I'm Lieutenant Agossi with the Philadelphia bureau. You were not supposed to leave the state, Miss Hastings. What were you doing in New Jersey? Did you have a liaison who was helping you to escape?"

Spencer's mind felt clouded. "W-where are my friends?" she whispered. "Where's Emily? Is she okay?"

"Miss Marin and Miss Montgomery were escorted home to await the start of the trial," the officer said. "Now, are you going to answer my question?"

She glanced at her father, who was peering at her curiously. Surely he had questions about what Spencer was doing in New Jersey, too, especially after he'd gotten them clearance to visit Nick in prison. She'd told him they wanted to visit Nick to get closure, but her father was way too smart to buy that.

Then she realized what the officer had left out. "What about Emily?" she whispered, her gaze flicking from the officer to her father. "Did they rescue her? Is she here, too?"

A strange look came over Mr. Hastings's face. He was about to say something, but then his phone rang. He glanced at the screen. "It's your mom," he told Spencer. "I'll be right back." He disappeared through the door.

Spencer looked at the officer. "Is Emily okay?" she asked again.

The officer glanced at the walkie-talkie on her belt. "It was wrong of you to go to New Jersey, Miss Hastings," she said robotically. "For the duration of the trial, you'll have to wear a tracking bracelet. You'll have to forfeit all your identification. You will not be permitted to drive."

Spencer's heart pounded, and a horrible feeling seized her body. This wasn't right. Why wasn't anyone answering her? She sat up in bed as best as the handcuffs allowed. "*What. Happened. To. Emily?*"

The officer pointedly cut her gaze away. Feeling sick, Spencer grabbed her arm. "*Please*," she growled. "If you know something, you have to tell me."

The officer yanked her arm from Spencer's grasp. "Miss Hastings," she said sharply. "Do *not* touch me. You don't want to be sedated, do you?"

Spencer felt wild. "Why won't you tell me what happened to Emily?" she shrieked.

Suddenly, the door swung open. "Is she awake?" a male voice asked.

The cop turned, looking relieved. "Yes. And she's very agitated."

"Would you mind stepping out? I'll speak with her."

Spencer frowned. There was something oddly familiar about the doctor's voice. But certainly it was just her mind playing tricks—her brain was still messed up from the near drowning, right? She buzzed with anger—why the hell wouldn't anyone tell her about Emily?

The doctor stepped over to her. When he smiled, it was a smile Spencer knew all too well. Her jaw dropped open. Her eyes canvassed him up and down. And then, to be absolutely certain, she checked the ID clipped to his jacket pocket. WREN KIM, it said in bold letters. RESIDENT.

Wren as in the Wren she'd stolen from Melissa. Wren as in the first boy she'd slept with, maybe the first boy she'd ever loved.

"It's nice to see you again, Spencer," Wren said in his familiar British accent. "How are you feeling?"

A tiny squeak escaped from Spencer's mouth. This didn't feel real. None of this felt real.

She had a million questions for Wren—and was immediately barraged by a million memories. But suddenly, none of it felt pertinent. There was something she really, really needed to know that blotted out anything else. She took a breath and looked into Wren's eyes. "I'm fine," she said in a clipped voice. "But I need to know what happened to Emily," she whispered, her voice trembling. "Please tell me. Is she . . ."

Wren's gaze dropped to the bed, and just like that, Spencer knew for sure. He placed a warm, comforting hand on her arm. "Spencer, I'm so sorry. The rescue team is still searching, but they're pretty sure she's . . . *gone*."

7

FUNERAL FOR A FRIEND

"Hanna Marin! Miss Marin! Over here!"

Hanna peered out from inside her mother's car. It was Monday morning, one day after she had witnessed Emily drown in Cape May. She was at the Holy Trinity Church in Rosewood. The church was an old, venerable-but-crumbling building with a spooky cemetery out back that Hanna had once run through at midnight on a dare. But right now, she'd rather be running through that thing stark naked than facing what she was about to face. Already reporters and cameramen were descending upon them, almost looking like they were going to climb onto the hood of the car.

She glanced worriedly at her mother, who was clutching the steering wheel so hard the leather was making a squeaking sound. Ms. Marin gunned the car to the other side of the lot. The reporters lunged to either side to avoid getting run over.

"Come on," Ms. Marin said when she had parked,

turning off the car and darting out of the driver's seat. Together they scampered for the church's side entrance. The press sprinted toward them, screaming questions. *"Do you have any comment on your friend's suicide? Do you have any suicidal thoughts, yourself? Are you ready for the trial tomorrow?"*

"Vultures," Ms. Marin said inside the church lobby, once they'd slammed the door. She peered out the small stained-glass window, her eyes glimmering with tears. "On today of all days."

Hanna looked around. The lobby was packed with people and smelled like old newspapers, incense, and perfume. Her gaze drifted toward a large plaque that stood at the double doors to the church. EMILY FIELDS, read swirly letters at the bottom. And there was Emily's school picture from tenth grade—her parents had chosen it because it was one of the few photos *not* used in newscasts, magazines, promotional materials, or police files. Emily looked so much younger in it, her freckles bright, her smile wide, her eyes sparkling. It was before A. Before Ali came back. Before Emily even had an inkling about taking her own life.

Hanna felt her legs give way and grabbed onto a nearby statue of some random saint for balance. She was at Emily's *funeral.* It was unreal. Unthinkable. Impossible.

One day had passed since Emily had disappeared into the ocean. Though Hanna had rabidly watched every single Emily-related news report—first a recap of the rescue efforts, then an update that her body still hadn't been found, then a police and coast guard statement saying that considering the magnitude of the storm, it was safe to assume Emily was dead and that funeral arrangements should be made—the details had passed over her like quickly moving clouds. She kept thinking she'd wake up and it would all be a dream. Emily couldn't have *really* walked into that water. Emily couldn't have killed herself because she couldn't bear the idea of going to prison. How had Hanna not realized Emily was in *that* much pain?

The thing was, though, Hanna *had* known. How long had Em gone without a good night's rest? How much weight had she lost? Why, oh, why hadn't Hanna tried to *help* her? She should have read a book on suicide or something. Talked to Em more. Stayed up with her that last night if she couldn't sleep.

And what had it felt like to be so at the end of her rope? Sure, Hanna felt panicked about going to jail . . . but not suicidal. Why had it hit Emily so differently? Why had this affected her, someone so good, so sweet, so gentle?

How could Em be . . . *gone*?

Ms. Marin took Hanna's arm and walked her into the church. The place was packed, and everyone stared at her as she walked down the aisle. There were so many people here that Hanna knew, but how many of them were here because they missed Emily? Like Mason Byers—hadn't he laughed nastily after A had outed Emily at that swim meet? And there was Klaudia Huusko, the exchange student from Finland—had she *ever* spoken to Emily? And there was Ben, Emily's old boyfriend—he'd attacked her! Like *he* was really grieving? Even Isaac, the father of Emily's baby, was here, though he looked almost bored. The only person who looked legitimately upset was Maya St. Germain, Emily's first girlfriend and the girl whose family had bought Ali's old house. Maya's hands covered her eyes, and her shoulders shook. Mr. and Mrs. St. Germain and Maya's brother flanked her, their faces stony, their eyes glazed. Hanna wondered briefly if the family regretted ever moving to Rosewood.

Aria and Spencer were already sitting in a pew near the front. Ms. Marin guided Hanna toward them, and Hanna slid in next to Spencer. Both her old friends glanced at her emptily. Aria's hands rested limply in her lap. Spencer had a packet of tissues wadded tightly in her palm. Her eye makeup was already streaky, but Spencer didn't seem to care. Aria nodded slightly. "I think they've given up."

Hanna swallowed hard. "It's only been one day!"

"There were tons of helicopters, looking everywhere," Spencer said in a monotone. "She probably drifted farther than anyone thought. Or she's caught on something underwater, and they can't see her."

"Okay, *stop*," Aria said, her voice cracking. Her eyes were filled with tears.

Dirge-like organ music started up, and Hanna swiveled around to watch a group of clergymen process down the aisle. Emily's family followed. Each of them was dressed in black, and every single one looked zombielike.

Her gaze turned to the casket behind the altar. Even though there was no body, the Fields had decided to bury something at the cemetery anyway. It seemed almost inappropriate that the Fields had arranged a funeral so quickly—Emily *could* still be out there. But the cops had basically said that although there wasn't a body yet, there was no way Emily could have survived the hurricane conditions. Maybe the Fields just wanted to get this over with and move on.

The music stopped and the priest cleared his throat. Hanna heard him say Emily's name, but then her mind began to swim and swirl. She grabbed Aria's hand and squeezed. "Tell me this isn't happening," she murmured.

"I was about to ask you the same thing," Aria said.

The Fields family rose en masse and walked to the front. Mrs. Fields took the podium first and cleared her throat. A long silence followed before she spoke. "I'd like to think my daughter has returned to the water from which she came," she said in a hoarse voice, staring at a crumpled piece of paper. "She was a dedicated swimmer. Loved the water, loved to compete. She was going to the University of North Carolina next year, on a full swimming scholarship, and she was so excited."

Hanna caught Spencer's eye. *Was* Emily excited to go to school? And really, what were the chances she was going to go after the trial? Weird that Emily's mom would bring that up.

Mrs. Fields coughed. "She was also dedicated to her

family. Her group of swimming friends. Her community at church. In the past few years, she'd been poisoned by forces out of our control, but deep down, we all know how good Emily was. How shiny and special and sweet. And I hope that's what you will remember about her."

Hanna twisted her mouth. Swimming friends? Church friends? What about her, Spencer, and Aria—Emily's *best* friends?

Mrs. Fields left the podium, and Emily's sisters Beth and Carolyn spoke next. Oddly, both of their speeches left out Hanna, Spencer, and Aria, too. There was more talk of "poisoning" and "evil outside forces," but they didn't really elaborate on what they meant. They kept talking about how much Emily loved *swimming*. Sure, she loved to swim, but that certainly wasn't the only defining thing about her.

The whole Fields family paraded back to their pew. The church was silent as they shuffled and rustled. Hanna looked at the others. "We should say something. It's like they're talking about some other girl."

Then, wordlessly, Hanna removed a small, clothbound book from her bag and stood. Spencer caught her arm. "What are you doing?"

Hanna frowned. "I'm going to give a eulogy." She showed Spencer the book. "It's pictures of us and Em. I thought I'd talk about them here, and then we'd . . . I don't know. Bury them maybe, afterward." It was what they'd done for Their Ali—Courtney—to help put her to rest. "Em deserves a better speech than the ones we just heard, don't you think?"

Aria's eyes softened. "I brought something to bury, too." She rummaged in her bag and pulled out a tattered copy of *Your Horoscope, Explained.* "Remember that summer Em was really into doing our charts? I have notes in here that she wrote about all of us."

"Great," Hanna said, pulling Aria up. "We can talk about that, too."

Spencer looked at both of them desperately. "Guys . . . you can't, okay?"

Organ music started up again. Hanna stared at Spencer crazily. "What do you mean?"

"Don't you get it?" Spencer whispered. "*We're* the poisoners. We're the evil outside forces."

Hanna shifted. She realized, suddenly, that people were staring at them.

Abruptly, Spencer stood from her seat and motioned for the others to follow. They walked into a drafty little hallway. A door stood open to a small room filled with toddler toys. Down the hall was a bulletin board boasting Bible verses.

Aria looked at Spencer. "Why would you say that?" she whispered.

Spencer glanced into the church again. "I called Mrs. Fields this morning and asked if I could give a eulogy. She admitted that she didn't even want us here. Said it was inappropriate. But I said we'd be quiet. We just wanted to honor her death."

"*What?*" Hanna gasped. She peeked through the doorway and peered at Emily's mother, who was sitting straight-backed in the pew. Her hair was molded into a stiff shape. Her shoulders were perfectly squared. Come to think of it, Mrs. Fields hadn't even looked at any of them once since the funeral began.

"But Mrs. Fields *knows* us," Aria squeaked.

"Yeah, well, not anymore," Spencer murmured bitterly.

Hanna couldn't believe it. "Didn't you argue with her?" she asked. "Didn't you try to make her understand what Em meant to us?"

Spencer scoffed. "Um, no, Hanna. I pretty much got off the phone as quickly as I could."

Hanna began to feel the hot, bubbling sensation of anger inside her. "So you just took the abuse? You let her call us inappropriate? You just let her believe something totally false?"

"*You* can take it up with her if you want," Spencer whispered, her eyes flashing. "But the impression I got is that Mrs. Fields basically thinks we caused Em's death."

"Only because you let her believe that!" Hanna argued. And then, frustrated, she shoved the book of pictures back into her purse, crossed her arms over her chest, and said the thing that had been prodding the back of her mind all morning. "Okay, fine. You know what? Maybe Mrs. Fields is right. Maybe we *did* cause Emily's death."

Spencer recoiled. "Excuse me?"

Hanna stared at her evenly. She was so angry she could

barely see straight, though she wasn't sure *who*, exactly, she was angry with. Maybe just the situation as a whole. Maybe everyone. "Well, you must believe it, too, Spence— or else you wouldn't have gotten off the phone with your tail between your legs. And maybe she's right. Maybe we shouldn't have stayed in Jersey after Betty Maxwell's house was a bust," she declared. "We should have come home, where Emily would have been safe."

Two bright spots appeared on Spencer's cheeks, even more apparent under the hallway's harsh fluorescent lights. "Huh. It was my suggestion to stay in Jersey. So it's *my* fault she's dead. Is that what you're saying?"

Hanna rolled her jaw, at first not answering. But then she swallowed a lump in her throat. "It did seem kind of clueless. 'Let's get ice cream! Let's have a good time!' And then Emily sits there, all night, like a freaking zombie! That big ocean, that storm, it was so tempting—we should have seen this coming."

Spencer's eyes narrowed. "You could have said, 'Hey, I think Emily's going to drown herself, so maybe we should leave.'"

Hanna's shoulders tensed. Spencer didn't have to use quite such a dopey tone when impersonating Hanna's voice.

"And *you* were sleeping next to her, Hanna," Spencer went on. "Why didn't you wake up when Emily got out of bed?"

Hanna clenched her fists. "You can't blame me for *sleeping*. I was tired."

"Oh, right, you need your beauty sleep," Spencer said mockingly. "God forbid Hanna Marin doesn't go one night without an eye mask and headphones."

Hanna stomped her foot. "That's not *fair!*"

"Guys," Aria said softly, grabbing their arms. "It's clear both of you are just mad at Mrs. Fields, not each other. So you missed Emily's cues. You can't beat yourselves up."

Spencer yanked away and sneered at her. "Uh, excuse me? *You* missed Emily's cues, too, Aria. We were *all* there."

Aria's mouth made an O. "*I* didn't want to stay in Cape May."

"Then why didn't *you* say something?" Spencer growled, looking more and more affronted. "Why am I the only one who makes the decisions? And have you forgotten that I was the one who got up and found that note? Have you forgotten that I went into the water after her and nearly *died?*"

"No one told you to go in the water," Hanna said under her breath. "Don't be such a martyr."

It was too much, and Hanna knew it. Spencer gasped and raised her hand toward Hanna. Hanna ducked away, nearly cracking her head on a coat rack in the hall. "Were you just going to *hit* me?" she squeaked.

"You deserve it," Spencer growled through her teeth. "Someone needs to knock some freaking sense into you."

Hanna's mouth dropped open. "What about *you*, Spence? Someone needs to knock you off your high horse." She lunged for Spencer.

Aria caught her arms and pulled her back. "Guys. *Stop.*"

"Yes, Spencer, stop being such a bitch!" Hanna wailed.

"*I'm* being a bitch?" Spencer hissed. And then, before anyone could say anything else, Spencer spun around and marched toward the back door.

"Where are you going?" Aria cried out, taking a few steps after her.

Spencer pushed on the heavy door to open it. "Away from you people."

"I'll come with you," Aria offered.

Spencer's eyes flashed. "*No.*" The door slammed as she marched out.

Silence followed. Hanna ran her hands down the length of her face, her heart drumming fast. She turned back to Aria, whose face was pale. "What the hell was that?"

Aria riffled the pages of the horoscope book. She shifted uncomfortably. "That was too far, Han," she said sternly. "We're all hurting." Then she hurried out the door behind Spencer.

"Hey!" Hanna shrieked, but Aria was already gone. What the hell had just happened?

Then she looked around, her skin prickling. To her horror, quite a few people from the church were peering out the doorway, right at her, as if they'd heard every word.

Hanna spun around and walked the opposite way down the hall, away from the door Spencer and Aria had gone through. She came to a hallway full of conference rooms and sank down on the wall until her butt hit the cold linoleum floor. She wanted to cry, but she couldn't. It was strange to feel both angry and numb at the same time, but that was the only way to describe it.

After a while, she heard footsteps. Mike stood over her. "Han," he said, crouching down.

Hanna stared up at him. She'd been in such a fog she hadn't even realized he'd come today.

"Hey," Mike said gently, taking her hands. "Are you okay? Why did you guys leave the church? What happened?"

Hanna swallowed hard, then gazed in the direction in which her friends had run. "Oh, just two of the few remaining good things in my life crumbling away," she said in a choked voice, realizing as she said it that it was utterly true.

8

ESCAPE ARTIST

Aria barely noticed that she'd crushed a few flowers in the beds as she stamped out of the church. Nor did she pause to appreciate the crisp, blue sky, the meandering bumblebees, or how her stiff suede heels were rubbing against her ankles. All she wanted was to catch Spencer and try to talk some sense into her.

That argument . . . why *today*, of all days? Emotions were way too raw to fight. They needed to stick together—the trial started tomorrow.

Aria peered into the parking lot and saw Spencer storming toward a row of cars. "Spence!" she called out. "Hey!"

Spencer glanced at Aria over her shoulder, then picked up her pace. "I don't want to talk."

Aria ran to her and caught her arm. "We're *all* upset. This is . . . horrible, Spence. It's totally not fair that Mrs. Fields feels that way about us." She waved her hand toward the parking lot. "I'm half in the mood to smash all the windows of her car! And you almost died, too, and I respect how traumatic that was. But we have to–"

"You know, maybe Emily's mom is right," Spencer interrupted. "Maybe we *are* poisoning influences on each other. Maybe we need some space."

Aria felt like the wind had been knocked out of her. "Don't push us away," she begged. "It's not us you're mad at. All of this is just messing with your head."

"With good reason!" Spencer's eyes were wide. "Emily's dead, Aria. She couldn't take it, so she *killed herself.* Maybe we *all* should take our lives—it's probably the best choice."

Aria gasped. "How could you say that? You don't know for sure that we're going to prison!"

Spencer chuckled sarcastically. "Haven't you listened to the sixty lawyers we've already talked to? They *all* think we're going down. And I'm sorry, but if it wasn't for Emily pushing us to look for Ali, if it wasn't for us being so scared to cross Emily because she seemed so fragile, she might still be here! And we might not be in the amount of trouble we're in!"

"So, what, now this is all Emily's fault? But Spence–"

Spencer cut her off. "Leave me alone, okay?" She turned and ran between the cars.

Aria knew better than to follow, but she felt hurt and confused. She looked at the church again. She should go back inside—her family was still in there. But what she really wanted, she realized, was to drive somewhere. Get away from this place, this loss. And even though she wasn't sure why, this place reminded her of Ali. *All* of Rosewood reminded her of Ali, really—she was everywhere. And this fight, their issues with one another—that seemed like another one of Ali's master plans. Instead of banding together against Ali, they'd turned on one another, growing weak, growing angry, losing everything. That was what Ali wanted, right? For them to lose everything? As Ali would say, *Score another win for Ali D.*

She trudged to the auxiliary parking lot, where she'd left the Subaru. As she turned the corner, a red flashing light caught her eye. The familiar black-and-white pattern of a Rosewood police car stopped her cold. The police were waiting for her.

The ankle bracelet. She'd totally forgotten. The cops were meeting her here to place it on her ankle as well as collect her passport, driver's license, and anything else that served as an ID. The police had wanted to do it yesterday, but Rosewood PD didn't have bracelets on-hand and they needed some sort of court order in place. Aria had even heard they were going to put a GPS chip and a recording device on her cell phone. They would know where she was at all times, and hear every conversation she had.

Aria placed her hand on her bag, where her IDs were tucked into the leather side pocket. The idea of forfeiting her passport, with its extra pages for stamps, made her stomach suddenly swirl. Traveling defined her. And not having a passport made everything more, well, *real.*

Without a license, without an ID, she was no longer Aria Montgomery. She was just a girl waiting to go to jail.

She thought about what she'd said to Noel in bed the other day. *I wish I could just run away.*

A tiny seedling of an idea took hold in her mind. *No,* Aria told herself. But it pressed on her again and again. It was so tempting—and it was one thing Ali probably would never count on. Emily had escaped Ali with death, but that wasn't the only answer.

Could she?

"You okay?"

Aria whirled around. Noel, dressed in a dark suit, was shifting from foot to foot a few yards away. In the craziness of the past twenty-four hours, she'd only been able to talk to him on the phone. She hadn't even known for sure he was coming. Now, she stepped back into the shadows and fell into him, her eyes filling with tears.

"I heard you fighting with Hanna and Spencer," Noel murmured in her ear. "It seemed kind of . . . brutal."

Aria lowered her shoulders. "It's because the Fieldses didn't want us here. They hate us. *Everyone* hates us."

Noel patted her back. "*I* don't hate you."

Aria knew Noel meant that. She wanted more than anything just to stay here and hug him. But she also knew what she had to do this instant . . . and not a moment later.

She wiped away a tear. "I'm going to miss you."

Noel cocked his head. "Aria. *You're* not dead. And you're

not in jail yet." His smile wobbled. "We still have to think positive."

Aria stared at the ground. If only she could tell Noel she meant something else, but there was just no way.

He squeezed her hands. "We need to talk about what happened in New Jersey, too. *Did* you find Ali there? Are you afraid of something?"

"No. We didn't find a thing." She couldn't look at him. "I have to go."

Noel's brow furrowed. "Go . . . where?"

But she was already walking away. "I love you," she blurted before darting around the corner. "Tell my parents not to worry about me. Tell them I'll be fine."

"Aria!" Noel called out. But Aria kept running as fast as she could. And when she glanced over her shoulder after climbing the hill that led to the next street over, Noel wasn't following.

She pushed through a thicket of trees and exploded into someone's backyard, darting around a swing set and a sandbox. The SEPTA station was at the end of the road, and she reached it quickly, stumbling down the hill. The neon sign above the train tracks said the next train into Philly was due in two minutes. Aria looked nervously toward the street, terrified that the police would roar up any second. Surely all the funeral-goers had emptied out by now. Surely they'd figure out soon enough that she'd given them the slip.

But no cars had arrived when the train roared into the

station. Aria glanced over her shoulder once more, then clambered up the metal stairs. The train pulled away noisily, the car rocking on the rails.

"*Ahem.*"

She let out a little yelp. The conductor had appeared from out of nowhere, looming over her. "Where to?" he asked in a bored voice.

Aria swallowed hard. "The airport," she said, handing over a ten. "K-keep the change."

The conductor took it, then passed on, keys jingling at his waist. Aria let out a long, freaked-out breath. *You're going to be fine*, she told herself, instinctively reaching into her bag and making sure her passport was still there. *You're going to be just fine.*

If only she could believe it was true.

9

SPENCER FOLLOWS UP

A few hours after the funeral, Spencer sat silently in the passenger seat as her mother steered her Mercedes up 76 to the city. Mrs. Hastings made a sour face, and then gestured violently at the car in front of her. "Don't you *dare* cut me off, Ford Fiesta," she warned.

Spencer squeezed her palms together. Her mom only snarled at other drivers when she was really, really pissed off, and right now it was pretty clear what was making her angry. Yesterday, at the hospital, a cop had explained to Mrs. Hastings that since Spencer no longer had a driver's license, someone would now have to drive Spencer to her appointments, lawyer's meetings, and the trial. Mrs. Hastings had made a pinched face. "But I have things to do," she'd whined. "This is an extreme inconvenience."

Needless to say, her mom hadn't had a heart-to-heart with Spencer about what had happened in Cape May. No questions about what they were doing at the beach to start with. No inquiries about how she felt about Emily's death or how scared Spencer must have been when she tried to rescue her. Her mom probably found it easier not to get emotionally involved.

Thank goodness for Melissa, who'd been calling Spencer nonstop since she was released from the hospital, bringing her takeout in bed, and staying up late to watch *Arsenic and Old Lace,* their favorite old movie, with her. Melissa had apologized profusely for not being there at the hospital when Spencer woke up—she'd been working all weekend, and no one had even called her until Spencer was released. Spencer had said it was okay—after all, it would have been *très* awkward with her, Melissa, and Wren all in the same room.

Spencer had considered telling Melissa about the Wren coincidence, but there had never been a perfect moment for it. Whatever. She just had this one return checkup with Wren at the hospital, and then she'd never see him again.

Within minutes they were speeding down Market Street, and Mrs. Hastings pulled into Jefferson Hospital. "I'll wait there." She gestured to a café on the corner of 10th and Walnut.

Spencer mumbled thanks and climbed out of the car. As she walked into the antiseptic-smelling lobby, she felt light-headed. She glanced in a large mirror just past the information desk, taking in her streaky makeup and the strained look in her eyes. She'd been crying a lot lately.

Her hands balled into fists at the memory of the fight they'd had after the funeral. How dare Hanna say those things! How dare she and Aria just sit there and say they hadn't even wanted to *stay* in Cape May, and imply this was all her fault? Didn't they realize how guilty she already felt? Didn't they understand she was already worrying about the same thing? She hated herself for the snarky things she'd said to Hanna . . . and then that she'd almost hit her. Who had she turned into? Who had *all* of them turned into? She pictured Ali lurking somewhere close, laughing her ass off. Stupid bitch.

Spencer took a deep breath. She needed to move on, take a step, go to this appointment. She wiped her eyes and stepped into the elevator.

Wren's office was on the third floor, across from a patient wing. The waiting room was generic, with lots of magazines strewn around the tables and a *Live! with Kelly and Michael* broadcast on a flatscreen in the corner. Spencer gave her name at the front desk and sat primly in the chair. When she tried to cross her ankles, her foot banged against the monitor the police had clamped around her leg after the funeral. She glowered at its blocky, imposing shape, hating that it was attached to her at all times.

The door opened, and there was Wren. "Ah. Spencer," he said. "Come on back."

Spencer held her chin high and didn't make eye contact with him. Wren led her straight to an examining room and had her sit in a chair opposite him. She stared at his Adidas sneakers, irritated that they were the same shoes he'd worn last year while he was in med school. He still smelled the same, too—like cigarettes. She wondered if he still smoked; they'd shared a cigarette together the first time they'd met at the Moshulu restaurant.

"So," he finally said in a grave voice, tapping the top of a manila folder. "How was Emily's funeral? That was today, wasn't it?"

Spencer bristled. "How did you know that?"

Wren stared at his hands, looking ashamed. "I'm sorry. It was on the news. Look, I know it's got to be hard. You guys were close, right? You used to talk about her a lot."

Spencer stared at a chart of the human body and made a noncommittal groan.

"Is it all right if I check you out now?" Wren asked tentatively, placing the folder on the table.

Spencer shrugged. "Do what you gotta do."

Wren rose and pressed a stethoscope to her back, then her chest. Spencer felt her cheeks burn—his hands were so close to her boobs—but she continued to sit straight and think impersonal, unsexual thoughts.

"I've read a little about the trial," Wren said softly. "It starts tomorrow, right? You must be under a lot of stress. Are you sleeping?"

She shrugged. "Not really."

"Would you like me to prescribe a sleeping pill?"

"I didn't do it," Spencer blurted, then gasped. She

hadn't meant to tell him anything remotely personal.

Wren looked at her. "Of course you didn't. I never believed that for a second."

A lump formed in Spencer's throat. He was the first person, it seemed, who believed she was innocent simply based on her character.

"But they can't just convict you with what they've got, can they?" Wren pressed. "It sounds like there isn't even enough evidence."

Spencer picked at her cuticles. "There's Alison's blood, and they found a tooth. According to the many lawyers I've talked to, that's enough."

"You don't even think she's dead, do you?"

Spencer looked down. The cops had wrangled out of her why they'd gone to New Jersey. She'd told them they were looking for Ali on a tip, though she certainly hadn't said anything about breaking into an old woman's rental. Naturally, it had made the news. *Liars Desperately Trying to Raise Ali's Ghost*, the headlines said. They looked even crazier than before.

Wren fiddled with his prescription pad. "So you think there's no way you'll get off?"

Only if I come up with $100,000, Spencer thought, remembering Angela. The conversation felt like a million years ago.

When she looked up again, Wren was staring at her so sympathetically, almost like he wanted to hug her. She inched closer to him, desperate for human contact.

But then she flinched. What was she going to do, make out with the first guy who was nice to her?

Spencer tightened her jaw. "The bandage on my arm needs to be changed." She rolled up her sleeve and revealed the old bandage.

Wren glanced at it for a long beat, then sighed. "Look, I hate what I did to you," he said quietly. "And I hate that you still hate me."

Every muscle in Spencer's body tensed. Okay, so Wren had cheated on Melissa with her. And then she'd fallen in love with him, and *then* he'd cheated on her with Melissa. But it was ancient history. She didn't want to give him the satisfaction of thinking it ever crossed her mind.

"It would mean so much to me if I knew you forgave me." Wren stared at her imploringly. "I've felt awful about hurting you, Spencer. I've never let myself forget it."

Spencer knew that if she spoke she'd give something away, so she just shrugged.

"So *do* you forgive me, then?" Wren's voice rose.

She bit down hard on the inside of her cheek. Her resolve was crumbling. "God. *Fine.* I forgive you."

Wren looked circumspect. "Are you sure?"

"*Yes*," Spencer said, then took a breath. "Yes," she repeated. And she realized—she did. Mostly. There was so much other bullshit to deal with right now, Wren fooling around with both sisters at the same time hardly registered on her Crazy Life Meter.

Spencer thrust out her arm. "Can you bandage this now?"

"Of course, of course," Wren said quickly.

He rolled the stool back to Spencer and carefully wound a new bandage around her arm. She tried not to stare at his long, graceful fingers, and she was glad he was no longer listening to her galloping heart. Every so often, Wren paused what he was doing to give her a tiny smile.

"All done." Wren pressed the bandage to stick. "I think that should hold you for a while."

"Great." Spencer jumped up and grabbed her bag. "So I can go now?"

"Yes." Wren's cheek twitched. "Although . . ."

"I'll see you," Spencer said at the same time. Then she looked at him. "Sorry. Go ahead."

Two pink splotches appeared on Wren's cheeks. "I-I was just going to say that I have your phone number, and I'll stay in touch." He fiddled with his stethoscope. "Maybe you'd like to get coffee sometime?"

Spencer stared at him. On one hand, it was a teensy bit flattering that he was asking her out. On the other, it sort of enraged her. Did he really think she had time for him right now on top of everything else? "I don't think that's a good idea," she said bluntly.

He blinked. "Oh?"

She shrugged. "Melissa and I are in a good place. Better than we've ever been. And no offense, but you coming back into our lives—well, I don't want to mess that up."

Wren nodded slowly, his expression turning sad. "Ah. I see. Well, okay then."

Spencer paused a moment, then gave him a firm nod good-bye. She felt satisfied with her decision—adult, even. Melissa was far more important than any boy.

Even if it was bedroom-eyes, sexy-voiced, gentle-doctor-hands Wren.

10

TOUCHDOWN

"Miss? Miss?"

Aria jolted awake. A pretty blonde in a tight blue uniform stood over her with a strange expression on her face. "You're in trouble," she said smoothly.

Aria's heart leapt to her throat, and she looked around. Rows and rows of airline seats stretched in front of her, and there was that familiar droning sound of an engine in midflight. The cabin smelled like feet. A sleeping passenger across the aisle had a guidebook that said *Go Paris* folded across his lap, and two people in front of her were speaking softly in French. It was only then that Aria realized that her buying a ticket for and boarding a flight to Paris had not been part of her dreams. It had really and truly happened.

She looked at the stewardess again. *You're in trouble.* How stupid was she to think she could get away with this? It had been inconceivable that the police hadn't been waiting at the airport when she got there, or that no one had shown up when she'd withdrawn that huge sum of cash from the ATM for the ticket to France, or that the clerk at the US Airways desk didn't pale and reach for a phone when she saw Aria's name on the passport. And that she'd actually boarded the plane without incident, and that it had actually taken off? It almost seemed criminal.

Of *course* she was in trouble. She'd escaped the country, like a terrorist.

But then the stewardess pointed to Aria's legs, which were in the middle of the aisle. "You'll be in trouble when we bring the cart through," the woman explained. "Can you move?"

"Oh." Aria pulled her legs back under her seat. The stewardess gave her a tight smile and sauntered on.

Aria ran her hands down the length of her face. *That* was close. Then she peeked out the small porthole in her row. It was almost light outside, but her watch read 2:45 AM. Everyone in Rosewood was probably sleeping. She pictured Noel in his bed. Had he tried her window last night? Was he worried? Had he told the police about what she'd said to him before she left? And what about her family? They must be sick with worry by this point. She pictured her mom pacing. Mike rolling over in his bed, sleepless. And Hanna and Spencer. She swallowed hard, pausing on them. Would they be angry that she hadn't included them in her plan? Only, that was crazy—she'd had no choice. One girl could escape much easier than three. Besides, there hadn't been time to involve all of them. And anyway, after the fight, she felt kind of stung. It wasn't like she'd deliberately left them out of her plan, but, well . . . it was probably better if she had a little space.

But as soon as she thought that, she felt kind of bad. They would be going to trial without her. Facing an onslaught she'd run from. It was selfish, she knew. Maybe *too* selfish.

"Good morning, everyone, this is your captain," said a man's voice. "We will be landing at Charles de Gaulle airport shortly. The local time will be 8:45 AM."

People started to stir. Aria's seatmate, a businessman who'd thankfully said nothing to Aria the whole flight except for "excuse me," wiped some drool off his cheek and stuffed some documents into his briefcase. Aria slowly put her iPod and the magazines she'd bought at the airport into her bag and watched as the Paris skyline materialized in the distance. In what felt like just seconds later, the plane thudded to a landing. Overhead lights snapped on. Elevator music blared through the cabin. People stood up and reached for their bags. Not a single person looked at her suspiciously.

Aria's heart pounded as she unbuckled her seat belt and waited for the line in the aisle to clear. The stewardess said a clipped "bye-bye" to the man in front of her, but skipped over Aria entirely. The terminal was fairly quiet, their flight the only one getting in at that time. Everyone streamed toward customs; Aria didn't know what else to do but follow. If only there was a way to avoid yet another set of eyes staring at her, but short of diving out a window and running for a fence, she couldn't think of a way around it.

Everyone crammed through the customs door and took their places in a winding line. Aria glanced at the officials at the front, her stomach churning. She touched her phone, which was tucked in her bag, switched off—even turning it on might tip off the cops to her location. Still, she wished she could check the voicemail and the texts. How many people had called her? Noel for sure. Mike? Her parents? Hanna? The cops?

Suddenly, looking at the passengers in front of her, something stopped the breath in Aria's lungs. A girl with a reddish-blond ponytail bounced in place, headphones over her ears. She had a gym bag on one shoulder, and she wore a blue sweatshirt that had the words DELAWARE VALLEY SWIMMING CHAMPIONSHIPS on the back. Emily had had that same sweatshirt.

Aria's heart lifted. Maybe it *was* Emily. Maybe, somehow, she'd survived the ocean. Maybe she'd had the same idea Aria had to get the hell out of the country. How wonderful! Aria wouldn't be so alone! They could figure out what to do together!

Aria pushed through the crowd, never feeling so happy in her life. "Am I glad to see *you*!" she crowed, tugging Emily's arm.

The girl turned. The corners of her lips turned down, and she had no freckles. Her eyes weren't as keen as

Emily's had been, her expression not as insightful. The girl cocked her head tiredly, taking in Aria's disheveled black dress from Emily's funeral, streaky makeup, and messy hair. "Sorry?" she asked in a Southern accent.

Aria stepped back, her mouth wobbling. "O-oh," she stammered. "Never mind."

The girl slipped her headphones over her ears. Aria returned to her spot in line, all at once not able to breathe. She'd hoped that escaping overseas would lessen the Emily blow a little—at least, over here, not everything would remind her of Emily. But after only a few minutes in the Paris airport, she felt more bereaved than ever.

The customs process moved quickly, and before long, a customs officer motioned for Aria to step forward. Her legs felt wobbly and weak as she stepped forward. A police dog waiting by the door stared straight at her, ears perked.

"Passport?" the officer said in a bored voice.

Aria's fingers trembled as she removed the little book from her bag. The officer stared at it, then Aria's face. There was a long pause as he looked at something on his computer screen. A whooshing sound rushed in Aria's ears. Was he checking a list? Silently sounding an alarm that the criminal had been located?

"Are you here on business or pleasure?" the officer asked.

His thin, high voice disarmed her. She stared at him, almost wanting to laugh—did she *look* like someone here on business? "P-pleasure," she stammered.

"For how long?"

"A week." It was an arbitrary length of time, but the officer nodded, seemingly placated. Aria could feel a thin bead of sweat trickling down her back. She felt the sudden urge to pee. She glanced toward the doors, horrified that the police dog was *still* staring at her.

Stamp.

To her amazement, the officer was handing back her passport. "There you go, Miss Montgomery. Have a nice stay."

Aria took it from him slowly, not quite believing it was happening. But as soon as she got the passport back, she scurried toward the huge door marked EXIT. And then, finally, blissfully, she was in the regular terminal, on official French soil, people streaming around her and noises blaring from every direction. She was instantly lost in the crowd. Aria headed toward an escalator, locating a taxi-stand sign overhead. She wasn't staying in the city, though. Or even this country. The police would track this flight in no time. Her plan was to get out of France on a train, or in a hired cab that wouldn't ask for ID.

Her heart began to pound again—but this time, from excitement. Where would she end up? She wasn't even sure—anywhere within the EU that didn't ask for passports at the borders. Milan, maybe. Or perhaps a sleepy Spanish town. Or maybe Denmark, or Switzerland. It thrilled her to be in Europe again. The whole world had opened up once more.

Screw you, Ali, she thought giddily. And she wondered, too; even though that girl in the terminal hadn't been Emily in the flesh, perhaps Emily was watching over her from beyond the grave. Maybe she'd supernaturally guided Aria here, making sure no one caught her, paving the way for Aria to get into the country without incident. After all, what Emily wanted more than anything in the world was for all of them to beat Ali and walk free.

And by some crazy twist of fate, at least for Aria, that was exactly what was happening. If only she could have brought her friends with her.

11

YOU SHOULDA PUT A
LACROSSE BRACELET ON IT

"So what are you going to go with, the gray suit with the pinstripes, or the basic black?"

Hanna looked up from her vanity. It was Tuesday, and Mike was standing in front of the full-length mirror in her bedroom, holding two of her outfits up to his body and pivoting back and forth like a beauty queen. "Personally, I'd like you to show off your legs," he said. He hung the demure suits back in the closet and pulled out a tight, sparkly, ultra-short dress Hanna had worn out with Hailey Blake. "*This* would wow the jury, don't you think?"

"Yeah, especially with this." Hanna held up her leg, showing off her ankle monitor. The thing was *so* annoying: She had to wrap a plastic bag around it to take a shower, she couldn't turn over in bed without it clunking around, and she couldn't pull a single pair of skinny jeans over it. Still, she couldn't help but crack the tiniest smile.

Mike was just trying to make her feel better, but it was tough on today of all days.

On cue, the morning news on the TV in her room resumed after a commercial break. Hanna's own face from the *last* time they were in the courtroom, for Tabitha Clark's murder, appeared on the screen. "The murder trial of the Pretty Little Liars begins this morning," the reporter said.

The image switched from Hanna's face to Aria's and Spencer's, and then a picture of Emily. "After Emily Fields's tragic suicide on Saturday, there was talk of delaying the proceedings, but the prosecution team wants to push forward."

The pointy-nosed district attorney named Brice Reginald popped up. Hanna already hated his slicked hair and penchant for bow ties. "I feel for Ms. Fields's family, but there's another family who needs answers— the DiLaurentis family," he said in a smooth, nasal tone. "We expect Mr. DiLaurentis at the trial this morning, and I've assured him that it will be a quick procedure with favorable results. Justice will be done for his murdered daughter."

Hanna scoffed. If she were Ali's dad, she wouldn't show her face in that courtroom. He had to know Ali was a coldhearted killer and liar. Then again, he actually *wasn't* Ali's dad—that was Mr. Hastings. And *he* was attending . . . supporting Spencer. Her head started to hurt with how messed up it all was.

She wondered, too, where Jason was in all this. It was clear Mrs. D was wallowing at home, too overwrought to attend, but what was Ali's brother's excuse? Maybe he was smart and didn't believe the hype.

"What about the defense's position that Alison DiLaurentis is still alive?" a reporter asked the lawyer.

The DA sniffed. "It's very clear Ms. DiLaurentis was murdered."

Hanna made a small *eep*. Mike muted the TV. "There's no use watching this." He walked over and wrapped his arms around her shoulders. "It's going to be okay. I promise. I'll be there the whole time."

Hanna was about to answer him when his phone beeped. He glanced at the screen, and his face clouded.

"Is it a reporter?" Hanna asked, feeling jumpy. She'd gotten so many calls from nosy people in the past twenty-four hours that she'd had to clear out her voicemail twice. Mike had mentioned they'd gotten his number, too.

"No," Mike murmured, his eyes still on the screen. "My mom still can't get ahold of Aria."

Hanna cocked her head. "Since when?"

Mike's fingers tapped the keyboard. "Since last night. And I didn't see her this morning, but I thought she was at Noel's or something—it was early. But the cops came to the house just now. Aria never met them after the funeral to hand over her IDs and get her ankle monitor. And apparently she made a big ATM withdrawal at the airport."

Hanna wrinkled her brow. "You're kidding." She could hardly believe Aria would do such a thing. "Do you think she took a flight somewhere?"

"I don't know. But that would be really, *really* stupid." Mike glanced at Hanna, his expression frantic. "I can't believe she didn't call anyone. You haven't heard from her?"

Hanna pulled her bottom lip into her mouth. "No," she said in a small voice. She'd called Aria a million times since their fight, but it had gone straight to voicemail.

Mike's mouth twitched. "What did you guys fight about, anyway?"

Hanna slapped her arms to her sides. "Emily, Ali . . . I don't even know."

She'd tried to understand the fight, but it was no use. *Did* she blame Spencer for Emily's plunge into the ocean? Spencer had been the one who suggested they stay the night, after all, and in hindsight, they all should have gone home—Emily would have been the safest, not to mention they might not have gotten caught for violating the terms of their bail.

But it wasn't like they knew that was going to happen. It reminded Hanna of the accident she'd gotten into last summer: She'd driven Madison home because Madison was too drunk to drive, but she hadn't made A's car come out of nowhere. She hadn't planned to crash.

Hanna had tried Spencer's phone yesterday, too, but she'd hung up before the call went to voicemail. She hadn't known what to say. *I'm sorry?* Was she? It was annoying, too, that Spencer hadn't called *her*. She should have, at least to apologize for freaking out on Hanna at the funeral. Why did Hanna have to be the one to crack first?

Mike sat down on the bed and turned his phone over in his hands. "Where do you think she went?"

Hanna raised her shoulders. "Maybe nowhere? Maybe it was just to fool the police?"

"My money's on Europe," Mike said softly. He rubbed his hands through his hair. "I just hope she's safe." Then a strange expression crossed his face. "Or you don't think she did something horrible, do you? Like Emily?"

"We don't know that Emily's dead," Hanna said automatically.

Mike cocked his head. "Han. We kind of . . . *do*."

Hanna shut her eyes. She wasn't so sure. Last night, she'd looked up all kinds of articles about people who'd miraculously survived tempestuous waters and tsunamis. The human drive to persevere was astonishing. Maybe Emily had decided, once she was out there, that she didn't want to die after all!

Then her gaze drifted to the plushy chair in the corner of the room. The dress she'd worn to Emily's funeral was lying there, as were her clutch and shoes and the program she'd grabbed on the way out. EMILY FIELDS, it read on the front, accompanied by several pictures of Emily through the years. There was one of Emily as a young girl, long before Hanna knew her, standing in a field of dandelions. There was another from when they'd just become friends in sixth grade—Emily at a swim competition, pulling on her goggles. Several others from junior high and high school, Emily always looking fresh and sweet and happy.

When Hanna shut her eyes, wrenching scenarios flashed in her mind. She thought of Emily's bed, unslept in, its covers probably pulled tight, its pillows fluffed. She thought of all the things Emily would no longer touch, no longer use, no longer be part of. She picked up her phone and began to compose a text explaining how low she felt . . . until she realized. She'd addressed the text to Emily. Of course she had: Emily was always the one she could go to with raw, vulnerable feelings.

Her jaw wobbled. She sank to the bed and put her head between her legs. Mike's hand pressed on her back. "Hey," he said soothingly. "It's okay. We'll get through this."

"We will?" Hanna sobbed, feeling the tears spill down her cheeks. "I just can't believe this is my life. *All* of it." She shook her head. "Emily's gone, Spencer's not speaking to me, and soon enough, I'm going to *jail*, Mike. *Prison*. I have nothing. No future, no friends, no life . . ."

"Hey." Mike frowned and placed his hands on his hips. "You haven't lost everything, Hanna. You still have me."

Hanna wiped her eyes. "But how long are you honestly

going to wait for me? I might be in prison for thirty years or more. I mean, you can't go *that* long without sex." She was trying to make a joke, but when she tried to smile, she just started crying harder.

"You're worth the wait." Mike's fingers made slow circles on Hanna's back.

"You say that now, but . . ."

Mike drew back. "You don't believe me?"

"It's not that. I just . . ." Hanna stared blankly at the TV on the other side of the room. A beautiful Brazilian supermodel was sensuously drinking Diet Coke through a straw. "The world is full of girls, Mike," she said softly. "And I wouldn't want you to stop living because of me."

He looked annoyed. "Don't even say stuff like that. You want me to prove that I'll wait for you?"

He shifted in front of her. When Hanna opened her eyes again, she realized he was down on one knee, staring into her eyes. "Marry me, Hanna Marin," he said urgently. "Marry me today."

"Ha," Hanna said, reaching for a Kleenex and blotting her eyes.

Mike removed the yellow rubber lacrosse bracelet from his wrist and held it out to her. "I don't have a ring, but take this," he said. "I mean it. Let's get married. Like, tomorrow."

Hanna blinked. "You're serious?"

"Of course I am."

She wiped her nose. "Like, with a ceremony and

everything? And with a document, to make it legal? *Can it be legal? Are we old enough?*"

Mike frowned. "I think so. And yes, I want it to be totally legal. I want *you*, Hanna. And I want you to know that I'm always going to want you, no matter what."

Hanna stared at the rubber bracelet in her hands. It had been awarded to him when he made varsity lacrosse. Once, in Jamaica, before their run-in with Tabitha, she and Mike got a couples' massage. Hanna had commented on how he'd left the bracelet on even though the masseuses instructed them to remove all jewelry. *Removing this would be like removing a part of myself,* Mike had said, a totally serious look on his face.

She considered being with Mike for the rest of her life, and it didn't take long for her to realize she liked the idea. She was touched, too, by the gesture. Mike knew full well what their fate might be. He knew the pitfalls of being with someone in prison—or at least she hoped he'd absorbed those parts in *Orange Is the New Black* and not just the lesbian scenes.

She looked up at him. "Can we have a real wedding?"

He shrugged. "Whatever you want."

"So I'd get to wear a dress? And throw a party?"

Mike smiled. "Is that a yes?"

Hanna licked her lips, suddenly feeling shy. "I think it is," she whispered, and then threw her arms around him. "Yes, Mike Montgomery, even though it's crazy, I'll marry you."

"That's just what I wanted to hear," Mike whispered back, and slid his lacrosse bracelet on her tiny wrist. Hanna shut her eyes and laughed. Wearing the bracelet felt better than any diamond ring on her finger. It was, literally, priceless.

12

COURTROOM DRAMA

Never in her life did Spencer think she would visit the Rosewood Courthouse as many times as she had in the past several years. She knew the place like the back of her hand by now, including which side entrance to use to avoid the press, which vending machine actually spit out the correct snacks, and which bench in the courtroom had an irritating squeak when you sat on it.

But walking up the stone steps on the first day of her murder trial, the place looked entirely different. There were so many more cameras than usual, even at the side entrances, and everyone was screaming her name as she rushed inside—including a bunch of people gathered together in a tight knot, all of them wearing T-shirts that said *Ali Cats Unite*. Spencer stopped cold, surprised at the sight of the Ali Cats up close—they all looked so *ordinary*. The woman in the front, who was overweight and had shiny red hair and bore a startling resemblance to Spencer's old piano teacher, lunged forward, leering at

Spencer. "Are you ready for prison, bitch?" The rest of the group cackled. Spencer shot away quickly, her heart thudding hard.

Inside, security had set up extra metal detectors, but even so there were long lines. The lights in the courtroom seemed to be harsher and brighter, almost like interrogation fluorescents. And this time, the jury box was full of people who were all staring at Spencer judgingly.

She tried not to look at them as she filed into the room, but it was tough. Every movement she made, every tuck of her hair behind her ear or wipe of her nose, she feared the jury would see as arrogant, or icy, or immature. *I didn't do it*, she tried to convey, peeking over and noticing that one of them looked like her uncle Daniel. Which wasn't entirely a good thing—Uncle Daniel categorically hated children.

Then her gaze settled on a youngish girl at the very end of the jury box who was staring at her with even more disdain than the others. *Ali Cat*, a voice in her brain whispered, the image of the group outside still so fresh. Was it possible?

Her phone beeped. Spencer reddened and silenced it, but she checked the screen before slipping it into her bag. Two messages had come in. The first was a text from a 215 number she recognized but didn't have in her contacts: *Hope you're feeling okay. Are those sleeping pills working? Please reach out if you need to talk. I'm here. Wren.*

Her first feeling was annoyance. Hadn't she told Wren

she wasn't interested?

The second note was an email from George Kerrick, who worked for the bank who held Spencer's trust fund. *Dear Spencer, I have inquired about your wish to withdraw funds, and your account is on strict lockdown. I'm sorry; there's nothing more I can do at this time.*

She glowered at the screen. Reaching out to Kerrick had been her one attempt to come up with $100,000 for Angela. But who had ordered a lockdown? Spencer's mom? The police?

There were some shuffling sounds, and Hanna filed in and took her place on the other side of their lawyer. Spencer glanced at her, then looked away. There had been a few missed calls from Hanna on Spencer's phone, but Hanna hadn't left her a voicemail. Spencer suspected Hanna wanted her to apologize—it was the way she got, Spencer remembered, when they used to have fights in seventh grade. Hanna had even once frozen Ali out until *Ali* crumbled and said she was sorry. But what about what *Hanna* had said? Spencer was unbelievably hurt that Hanna could accuse her of being responsible for what had happened to Emily. Dealing with Emily's death was already hard enough.

After a moment, Hanna thrust her chin in the air and turned away. *Fine*, Spencer thought.

More people filed into the courtroom until the place was almost filled. Spencer noticed Ali's father—who wasn't *really* her father, ironically—standing at the back of the courtroom alone. Then she saw her own dad on the other side of the courtroom, glancing surreptitiously in Mr. DiLaurentis's direction. She felt a lump in her throat and turned away. It was so weird to consider what was going through both their minds.

She scanned the aisles some more, expecting Aria, but she still hadn't arrived. Finally, Aria's father materialized in the back of the courtroom and motioned Rubens over to talk. As Byron Montgomery whispered in his ear, Rubens's expression shifted. Then Rubens strode to the judge's bench and spoke softly. Hanna whispered something to Mike. Finally, Rubens returned to their aisle.

Spencer stared at him. "What's going on?"

"Aria Montgomery is missing," he said in a low voice. "The police have reason to believe she was at the airport yesterday, and that she boarded a plane to Paris. Her name was on the flight manifest. The French authorities are on it, but everyone's hunch is that she's out of Paris by now."

Spencer gasped. "How did Aria get to Europe? Weren't the cops tracking her?"

Rubens shook his head. "She left before they could attach her monitor."

Spencer ran her hand over her hair. Aria had had the same idea she did—except she'd followed through on it. It was a brilliant plan, maybe one that Spencer should have thought of. Brilliant, but reckless. Escaping to Europe without taking the proper steps to disappear seemed really foolhardy. Aria was going to get in major trouble. She wondered, too, if *this* was why her account was frozen. The authorities thought—with good reason—that she was going to do the same thing.

She glanced at Hanna, and Hanna met her eyes for a second. Spencer considered saying something to break the ice. This was way bigger than their stupid fight, after all. She wondered, too, if Hanna had seen the Ali Cats outside.

But then she had a thought and turned to Rubens. "Will the jury judge *us* because of this?"

Rubens made a face. "Well, it doesn't exactly look good for the two of you. One of you commits suicide, the other flees to Europe? That's not exactly innocent-person behavior."

Spencer closed her eyes. That was what she'd feared he'd say.

Rubens leaned in. "We're going to continue with the hearing anyway. Aria will be tried in absentia. The police are going to want to question you girls about it after court adjourns today, though."

Spencer wrinkled her nose. "*I* didn't have anything to do with Aria's escape."

"Me neither," Hanna piped up.

"You all took off to New Jersey together. You're her number-one accomplices. Just tell them the truth, and there won't be any trouble."

The judge banged his gavel and called the lawyers to his bench. After some talk, Seth and the DA introduced themselves to the jury, and then it was time for opening statements. Spencer's heart pounded. It was happening. Their trial for murder was about to start.

The prosecution went first. Dressed in a pinstriped suit and expensive-looking loafers, his hair slicked back from his face and his skin oddly tanned, Brice Reginald, the District Attorney, sidled up to the jury box and gave each of the jurors a smile Spencer could only describe as *icky*. "We all know about Alison DiLaurentis," he began. "It's hard not to, isn't it? Pretty girl goes missing, on the cover of *People* magazine, captivates the country's attention . . . and then we find out her mentally unstable twin–the *real* Alison–killed her. Or . . . *did* she?" He looked at the jurors, his eyes dramatically wide. "Was Alison Courtney's killer? Was she really the monster people think she is? Or was she an innocent victim, first played by her manipulative and unstable boyfriend, Nicholas, and then tormented by the four young women who were her sister's best friends?"

At this point, his attention turned to Spencer and Hanna. Naturally, the jury stared at them, too. Spencer put her head down, feeling even her scalp burn. Never had she felt quite so shamed.

"What is real in this case, and what is made up?" the lawyer went on. "Who is playing for sympathy, and who is the true victim? Over the next few days, I am going to tell you who Alison *really* was. A girl who was sent to a mental hospital by concerned parents . . . but who was browbeaten there. A girl who escaped from a hellish situation only to fall in with a young man who forced her to abet in murder after murder, and who escaped from *him* only to fall prey to four girls who wanted revenge at any cost. And I'm going to tell you about four girls from Rosewood who had a vendetta they wanted to settle. On the surface, they seem like sweet teenagers who were at the wrong place at the wrong time. But if we dig deeper, *this* is who they really are."

He turned to a TV screen by the judge's bench and pressed PLAY on the DVD player. A surveillance tape appeared. It was the feed they'd set up to watch the pool house—Spencer recognized the rickety front porch and spidery tree branch. There, on the screen, was Emily, whirling around the room, smashing various things to pieces.

Her stomach clenched. It was heartbreaking to see Emily alive again, whole and real and also . . . *crazy.* Emily's eyes were wild as she wheeled about the space. Her nostrils flared, and she actually *growled.* And at the end of her rampage, she looked straight into the surveillance camera, teeth bared. *"I will never love you! Never, ever! And I will kill you! You will pay for this!"*

Spencer's heart dropped like a stone.

The DA turned off the TV. "I will describe to you exactly what these girls did to Alison, which includes beating her to the point of knocking out her teeth and slicing her up so that she bled profusely. These were girls whose lives were on the rise. And yet, that wasn't enough.

What they wanted, what they *craved*, was getting Alison out of their lives once and for all." He looked around at the courtroom with a triumphant and righteous smile. "Yes, we should be sympathetic that these girls had some near misses with Nicholas Maxwell. But we should blame the person who deserves it—Maxwell, not Alison. The girls should have listened to her pleas that she was innocent. But they are here because they didn't, and it is up to you to make the right decision to convict them for their heinous, violent crime."

He ended with a flourish of his hands. Spencer almost thought he was going to take a bow. She turned to her lawyer, horrified. "None of that is even *true!*" she whispered. "Can't you, like, object or something?"

"Not during opening statements," Rubens said through his teeth.

Then it was Rubens's turn. He strode to the front of the courtroom, and then made his way to the jury box, smiling at them sheepishly. "Mr. Reginald paints a pretty picture," he began. "And maybe it's true. *Some* of it, anyway. Maybe Nicholas Maxwell coerced Alison. Maybe she isn't guilty of as much as we think. But that's not what the case is about. This case is about whether or not four girls murdered Miss DiLaurentis. And I'm here to tell you that they did not."

There was a long pause. The jury shifted.

Rubens took a breath. "It's not even clear, in fact, that Alison is dead." The DA let out a guffaw. "Yes, some of her blood was found. And there is certain evidence that puts my clients in the same place where a murder may have occurred, though I certainly have theories about others who might have wanted Alison DiLaurentis gone and could have pulled off such a thing. However, we don't even know if a murder *did* occur, and that her body is missing leaves a huge gap in this case. Mr. Reginald has told us one way to look at this story, and I will tell you another: These girls were set up by the very girl who we think is dead. She spilled her own blood. She pulled her own tooth. She cleaned up the mess with bleach, making it look like the girls were responsible. She faked her death and framed the girls because it was her perfect escape—for all we know, she is out there somewhere, enjoying her life, while my clients are on trial for *their* lives."

Spencer's heart thudded. So he was using their theory. She checked out the jury's expressions. Most of them looked perplexed. The young woman Spencer had focused on earlier looked downright disgusted.

Rubens came to a stop by the judge. "I'm here to describe to you how that might have happened. And like Mr. Reginald said, it's up to you to make the right call on what went on that night."

There was a lot of shuffling and whispering. Spencer was dying to see Mr. DiLaurentis's expression, but she was far too scared to turn around. Finally, the judge cleared his throat. "We'll adjourn for an hour and then call the first witnesses," the judge ordered. Then he stood and marched into his chambers.

Everyone else in the courtroom rose and filed out. Only Spencer remained seated, staring at her feet. She felt even more doomed than before. After a moment, she looked up and saw Hanna staring at her. "And so it begins," her friend said softly.

"Yeah," Spencer answered.

She wanted to reach out and touch Hanna. But she also felt so awkward . . . and drained . . . and totally not in the right headspace to make amends. So she stood abruptly from the seat and pivoted toward the center aisle. And just like that, even though she knew deep down she really *needed* Hanna, she walked off to seek a private refuge where she could process everything alone.

13

HOW TO PLAN A
WEDDING IN FIVE DAYS

Hanna and Mike sat on the couch in Hanna's living room, Hanna's miniature pinscher, Dot, snuggling in Hanna's lap. A woman named Ramona, who had angularly cut, ice-blond hair, harsh gray eyes, and high cheekbones, and was wearing a Chanel suit and very expensive-looking five-inch snakeskin heels, sat opposite them, a large binder on her lap. "Are you telling me," she said in an intimidating voice, "that you want me to pull together an unforgettable wedding by the end of the *week*?"

Hanna swallowed hard. Maybe calling Ramona, who was supposed to be the best wedding planner in the business—she'd apparently arranged a ton of starlets' nuptials all over the country—was a crazy idea. So, probably, was asking that she have it at Chanticleer, her favorite mansion on the Main Line. "I realize weddings normally take a while to plan," she said meekly. "Is there *anything* you can do for us?"

"Oh, I can do anything you want," Ramona said haughtily. "I've planned weddings with far *less* time. It just means we have to start *now*."

Then she looked at Fidel, her gaunt, ponytailed, effeminate assistant who'd trailed in timidly behind her. He was twitching in the shadows, taking notes on an iPad. "Bring in the samples!" she boomed. Fidel skittered out the front door.

Hanna squeezed Mike's hand. They were doing it. *Really* getting married. Sure, the wedding plans were a bit overshadowed by everything else going on, but Hanna was happy to have something good in her life to take her mind off all that, at least for a little while.

There was a swift knock on the door. Dot sprang up and started barking. "*Entrée*, you fool!" Ramona bellowed, and Fidel burst into the foyer pushing a wheeled clothes rack with one arm and balancing several white bakery boxes in another.

Hanna's mother, who had been in the kitchen, hurried down the hall to grab the boxes before they fell. "My goodness!" she cried. She opened the lid of one of them and swooned. "Wedding cake samples, Han!" she cried. "From Bliss Bakery, and Angela's—these are the *best*!"

Hanna smiled gratefully. It wasn't any mom who would take her daughter's announcement that she was hastily getting married before she was probably going off to prison in stride. Ms. Marin had basically said that if Hanna was happy, then she was happy. She'd even agreed to sign off on the marriage certificate—which a parent had to do, as Hanna and Mike were both under eighteen. And she'd even left a few copies of *Brides* and *Vogue Weddings* on Hanna's bed this evening and said she would handle securing a DJ for the night—her advertising company had some connections.

Mike's parents had accepted it, too: Hanna had received a congratulatory hug from both Ella Montgomery and Byron's new wife, Meredith, that morning. Of course, in that family the wedding was overshadowed by Aria's disappearance, for good reason.

Hanna glanced at Mike, who was sitting next to her. He hadn't said anything in a while. In fact, he seemed out of it. "Are you okay?" she whispered.

Mike flinched and returned to earth. "Yeah," he answered. "Of course. Just, you know . . . thinking about Aria."

Hanna swallowed hard. Of course he was. She'd been thinking about Aria a lot, too. It astonished Hanna that she'd actually escaped. The cops had interrogated her this afternoon with questions about Hanna helping to escort Aria out of the country. It was even on CNN this evening. Apparently, authorities all over the EU were searching for her. Her picture was up everywhere, and already people in Spain, France, Luxembourg, and Wales claimed to have seen her, though Hanna hadn't been able to tell if any of the leads were valid.

"Are you sure you don't want to postpone this until

she's found?" Hanna whispered.

Mike shook his head. "No. Let's do it." He leaned in closer. "And we don't *want* her to be found, right?"

Hanna bit her lip, frowning. Mike was right—in a way. Hanna wanted Aria to be free of this. On the other hand, her absence made it *way* worse for her and Spencer. Another story on CNN was how guilty they looked now that Emily was dead and Aria was AWOL. Several legal experts had said they might as well enter a plea bargain and be done with it.

She turned back to the clothes rack Fidel had pushed into the center of the living room. At least fifteen wedding dresses wrapped in plastic hung from the bar. There were shoe bags bearing names like Vera Wang and Manolo Blahnik. A final hanger held a small velvet bag containing jewelry. An assortment of veils and tiaras were draped over the top bar, and a sudden smell of floral perfume had filled the room.

She looked at Ramona. "Is that stuff for *me*?" She leapt up and looked at the tags. The dresses were in her size. She peeked in one of the shoe bags. The gorgeous pair of off-white pumps also looked like it would fit her. "How did you know what to choose?" She'd only contacted Ramona a few hours ago, and the woman had asked her the briefest of questions.

Ramona rolled her eyes. "That's why I'm the best. Now, go try some things on. Your groom and I will talk about the menu, things like that."

Mike suddenly looked intrigued. "Can we have Hooters cater chicken wings?"

Hanna shrugged. "If you want, I guess."

Mike's eyes lit up. "What about Hooters girls *serving* the wings?"

Ramona looked horrified, and Hanna was about to shoot him a look. But then she realized—this was Mike's wedding, too. And she'd do anything to take his mind off Aria. "If you promise not to touch the Hooters girls, then yes," she said primly.

"*Sweet!*" Mike crowed. He pulled out his phone. "I'm calling them right now."

"I'll handle it," Ramona grumbled, gesturing to Fidel. He typed something on the iPad. Then Ramona turned to Hanna. "And are you thinking about bridesmaids? We should get them in for a fitting, too."

"Yes," Hanna said automatically. "I want Aria, Spencer, and Emily."

Everyone gasped. It took Hanna a moment to realize her gaffe, and she hiccupped. "Or, um, *not* Emily, obviously." She suddenly felt disoriented. "And maybe not those others, either." It wasn't like Spencer would want to do it. And Aria . . . well, that was out of the question, too. "It would probably be better if it was just me."

Ramona raised an eyebrow. "Bridesmaids are part of the fun. You choose their dresses, their jewelry, you'll have a buddy the day of the ceremony . . ."

Hanna felt her chin wobble. Mike grabbed her hand. "She said she doesn't want bridesmaids, okay?" He said it so ferociously that Hanna wanted to kiss him.

"She'll have a flower girl, though," Ms. Marin piped up. She looked at Hanna. "What about Morgan?"

"Definitely," Hanna said, mustering a smile. Morgan Greenspan was her seven-year-old cousin on her mom's side and pretty much the cutest thing ever. Every time Hanna saw her, she begged Hanna to catch fireflies with her in the backyard and told her stories about her pet Brussels griffon.

Ramona just shrugged. "Okay. We'll have to talk colors so I know what kind of flower-girl dresses to bring in. Now, why don't you go start trying on those gowns. Chop-chop!"

Hanna turned to the dresses once more, but they didn't provide her as much joy as they had only a few seconds before. *Your best friends are gone*, a voice pounded away in her head. *All of them.*

Her throat closed like it often did when she was about to cry. Hanna put her head down, gathered a bunch of dresses in her arms, and climbed the stairs to her room. Everything suddenly felt tainted. Emily was *dead*—she had to accept it. She'd read, a few hours ago, that the coast guard had given up their search for her.

She turned Mike's bracelet around her wrist. *If only you were still here, Em*, she thought. *You'd figure out a way to get us all back together. You'd fix everything.*

The light suddenly shifted, sending a golden slant through Hanna's window and skimming the top of her head. Hanna looked over, and for a moment, the space next to her on the bed felt warm, almost like there was someone sitting there. She decided to pretend it was Emily's spirit. She thought about pulling Emily close, holding her tight, and never letting her go. She could almost hear Emily's voice in her ear. *I'm glad you're getting married, Hanna. You should be happy.*

Hanna straightened up, feeling renewed. Emily was totally right. If she dwelled in her sorrow, if she fixated on everything that was wrong, Ali *was* winning. Screw that.

She turned to the dresses on her bed and unzipped the first garment bag. It was a strapless gown made in delicate silk and overlaid with lace. Tiny jewels peppered the bodice, and it had a slimming fit all the way down to the dramatic, sweeping train. Hanna gasped. Not that she'd ever tell Ramona, but she used to spend hours sketching her ideal wedding dress when she was younger—and it had looked almost exactly like this.

She slid it over her head and beheld herself in the mirror, astonished at the sudden transformation. She looked . . . *older.* Beautiful. And super thin. She twirled and grinned, unable to take her eyes off her reflection. Then, squealing with delight, she ran downstairs and peered around the corner. "Mike, hide in the bathroom. I can't have you seeing me!"

She waited until there was the obligatory slam to the

door, then flounced down the stairs. Ramona stared at her impassively. Fidel tapped notes. Hanna's mom looked like she was going to cry. "Oh, honey," she breathed, pressing her hands to her breast. "You look lovely."

The rest of the evening proceeded just like that: Hanna sent Mike out for a little while and tried on dresses, shoes, and veils. Mike returned and everyone tasted wedding cake, settling on the white buttercream from Bliss. Ramona made bullying phone calls to Chanticleer and catering companies and florists, demanding that they get their acts together by the end of this week or she'd never work with them again. With every *yes* Ramona got, Hanna felt more and more confident that Emily really *was* watching her, creating a smooth path. *You deserve to be happy*, she could hear her saying. *Even if it's only for one day.*

By the end of the evening, there was only one big thing left to decide on: the guests. Ramona had an in with a calligrapher and a stationery company, but they had to know the head count *tonight* for the invitations to go out in time.

"Well, there are the Milanos, the Reeveses, and the Parsons," Hanna said, naming her relatives and a few old family friends. She eyed her mother. "But let's *not* include the Rumsons." They had a vile daughter named Brooke who'd tried to steal Hanna's old boyfriend, Lucas Beattie, away. "Most everyone from school is a yes, though definitely not Colleen Bebris." She snuck a peek at Mike. He'd dated her for a brief time earlier that year.

"We can invite Naomi and Riley, but they should have a really crappy table assignment. And a definite no to that Klaudia Huusko girl." Klaudia had tried to steal Noel from Aria. Aria might not be coming, but Hanna still had her standards.

"Got it," Ramona said, writing everything down.

Hanna smiled nastily. If she had her way, this was going to be the party of the century, better than any Sweet Sixteen or Foxy Ball or stupid benefit at the Rosewood Country Club combined. It would be her last power play to snub those who'd pissed her off.

"Noel, Mason, all the guys on the lacrosse team," Mike listed off. "My mom, her boss at the gallery. And my dad and Meredith and Lola."

"What about your father, Hanna?"

Hanna looked up, astonished. It had been her *mother* who'd said it.

Ms. Marin jiggled her knee on the slipper chair. There was a conflicted but also principled look on her face. "I mean, he *is* your father. He would not want to miss it."

Hanna snorted. "Kate can come," she said, referring to her stepsister. Kate had found out about the engagement and sent Hanna an email, in fact, asking if she could be of any help. "But not him. We've been through too much."

She felt everyone's eyes on her, especially Ramona's. But it wasn't like Hanna was going to explain her reasoning. It was far too embarrassing to admit that your own father chose his new wife, his new stepdaughter, and even his *political* campaign over you. Again and again, Mr. Marin had given Hanna the tiniest bit of affection only to yank it away when she did something wrong. She was tired of giving him second, third, and fourth chances just because they used to be two peas in a pod. He'd changed.

And suddenly, she felt like she had to make them understand she was serious. She sprang from her chair and mumbled that she'd be right back. Once back in her room, she gazed at herself in the mirror. She'd taken off the wedding dress, but there was still a bride-esque glow about her that couldn't be undone. Her father probably would want to see her. But enough was enough. He'd hurt her for the last time.

She reached for her phone and scrolled for the number at his campaign office. An assistant answered, and when Hanna told him her name, she said, "I'll put you through" in a brisk voice. Hanna blinked hard. She'd half-expected the assistant to hang up on her.

"Hanna," her father's voice boomed through the other end mere seconds later. "It's so good to hear from you. How are you holding up?"

Hanna was both shocked and irritated by the warmth in his voice. "How do *you* think?" she heard herself snap. "I'm on trial. Haven't you heard?"

"Of course I know," Mr. Marin said softly, maybe regretfully.

Hanna rolled her eyes. She wasn't going to give in to that tone of voice. "Anyway, I just called to let you know

I'm getting married to Mike Montgomery."

"You're . . . *what*?"

She bristled. Was that judgment she sensed? "We're very happy. The wedding is next Saturday at Chanticleer."

"How long have you been planning this?"

She ignored his question. "I just called to tell you that you *aren't* invited," she said loudly, saying the words quickly before she lost her nerve. "Mom and I have got it covered. Have a nice life."

She pressed END fast, then cupped the phone between her hands. All at once, she felt even better. The gentle, Emily-like warmth in the room returned. For the next few days, Hanna would surround herself with exactly who *she* wanted—and no one else.

14

LITTLE DUTCH GIRL

Aria sat up as daybreak streamed through the long, slanting windows of her room. She pushed back the curtains and peered out. It was Wednesday morning, and bicyclists traversed the picturesque canals. The air smelled like *pannenkoeken*, the famous Dutch pancakes. A man was standing on the next street corner playing the loveliest little melody on his violin. And then, from the next room over, Aria heard one of the raucous boys let out the loudest burp ever. "I am so hungover," someone bellowed.

"Yeah, well, I think I'm still stoned."

Aria flopped back down on the bed. She *was* in a youth hostel in Amsterdam—what did she expect? At least she'd ponied up for a private room.

Even the pile of vomit in the hallway and the unpredictable hot-cold stream of water in the shower didn't dull her spirits. An hour later, she was clean, bright-eyed, and optimistic, strolling out of the Red-Light District.

The streets were mostly empty, all of the tourists who flooded this neighborhood probably sleeping off their hangovers. It was like she had the whole city to herself. She'd forgotten how much she loved Amsterdam! The slower pace, the foreign signs, the *putt-putt* of motorbikes, Amsterdam's funny trolley system, all of the quaint art and architecture . . . every detail made her realize how glad she was that she'd had the cab driver bring her here. It had been an impulse decision—Holland was lenient and tolerant—and it had been a long, boring drive through France and Belgium, Aria refusing to make eye contact or small talk with the hopefully oblivious, chain-smoking French driver and remaining slumped down so none of the other drivers could see her through the window. But it had been worth it.

The cool morning air felt good on her skin as she turned down a series of alleyways toward the Anne Frank house, which she planned on visiting that day. Might as well get some culture in, right? As Aria rounded a corner, a group of kids passed her going in the opposite direction. One of them had Emily's same copper-colored hair.

Aria flinched. She was seeing versions of Emily *everywhere*. Like the girl with the strong swimmer's shoulders she'd noticed through the windows of a touring bus yesterday, or the girl who'd thrown her head back and laughed the same way Emily did while Aria's cab driver had pulled over at a rest stop to pee, or the girl who knitted her brow, Emily-like, when someone told her something interesting—Aria had spied her at the hostel last night. It was uncanny . . . and kind of awful. Sort of like Emily's ghost was following her around, trying to tell her something.

She pressed on, passing a gift shop, a restaurant, and a little place that sold cell phones. A newsstand was next on the block, and a tabloid headline in the window caught her eye. *Pretty Little Liar trouwen*, it read. Aria blinked hard. She didn't know Dutch, but by the swirly writing and the picture of Hanna with a bridal veil superimposed on her head, she was pretty sure it meant *getting married*.

Aria ran into the shop, snatched up a copy of the paper, and flipped to the article on page eight. Not that she could understand it—the whole paper was in Dutch—but she tried to glean as much as she could from the pictures. There was one of Hanna and Mike slow-dancing at the Valentine's Dance last year. Another of Hanna on the set of *Burn It Down* before she was fired. And then images of various diamond wedding rings with a big question mark next to each.

Aria's mouth dropped open. Were they having an actual *wedding*, with guests? Did her parents approve of this? She thought of the time *she'd* gotten married—to Hallbjorn, a boy she'd known from Iceland, in a whirlwind justice-of-the-peace ceremony mainly so that Hallbjorn could stay in the country. Her parents hadn't even known about it, would have killed her if they did. She'd gotten the union annulled long before they could have found out.

But Mike and Hanna . . . they were different. Aria could actually *see* them being married. She felt a pang. She was going to miss her little brother's and her best friend's wedding. She was going to miss *everything* about Mike's life, in fact—and Lola's, and she was just a baby! Tears came to her eyes. She thought she could handle being away, but she'd focused only on the negatives—the trial, going to prison, having everything taken away from her. But here, halfway around the world, so much was *still* taken away from her. It was such a high price to pay for freedom.

Then, her gaze focused on another front page on a newspaper two rows down. This paper was in English, and Aria's face was on the cover. *Pretty Little Liar in the EU?* read the headline.

Aria's blood ran cold. She looked around the little shop. The shopkeeper behind the counter was looking at something on his phone. A teenage boy stood in front of a refrigerated case full of soda. Heart pounding, Aria picked up a Dutch sailing magazine and slid the incriminating newspaper within the pages. Terrifying phrases jumped out from the page. *Authorities report that Miss Montgomery boarded a flight to Paris . . . Interpol searching for her everywhere, with an EU-wide alert at hotels, restaurants, and transport stations . . . several tips say she is in Northern Europe, perhaps the Scandinavian countries.*

Northern Europe. That *was* where she was—sort of, anyway. Aria's hands started to tremble. She hadn't expected them to find her so soon . . . but maybe that was naive. This was *Interpol*, not the Rosewood PD.

Someone cleared his throat, and Aria looked up. The shopkeeper was suddenly staring at her, a strange expression on his face.

She slipped her sunglasses over her eyes and backed away quickly, almost stumbling over the stoop onto the street. Her chest felt tight. The shopkeeper had recognized her, hadn't he? She started walking as fast as she could down the street without breaking into a dead sprint. Any minute, the guy was going to follow her. Any minute, police cars were going to roar up and snatch her from behind.

Just keep going, she told herself. She picked up the pace and noticed other people staring at her, too. A man on a bicycle. A teenager sitting on a bench, earbuds in her ears. What if they *all* knew who she was? What if there were tons of calls to Interpol right this minute? Should she go to the American embassy? Except that was insane—they'd ship her back, and she'd go to jail.

She cut through an alley and burst onto another, busier street, blinded with panic. She ran as fast as she could, veering around bikes, cutting around open shop doors, eliciting more strange looks from passersby. Her bag thumped imposingly against her hip, but she was glad to have it—there was no way she could go back to that hostel now. Good Lord: She'd used her *own ID* to check in. When had that alert about her gone out? Had the hostel she'd stayed in received it, and did they cross-reference it with her name?

How could she have been so stupid?

The Anne Frank house loomed ahead of her, though she couldn't imagine going inside now—it was far too cramped; she'd be too exposed. She stopped at the stairs and placed her hands on her thighs, panting. She needed a second before she pressed on.

Tons of people streamed past her. Tourists. Workers. Students. All at once, this felt like the worst idea in the world. She was in a foreign country—she didn't even know the language. Nor did she know a single person here. No one would take her in and hide her, Anne Frank–style. She fumbled in her bag and pulled out her phone again. She hadn't turned it on since she'd boarded the plane—in fact, she'd even removed the battery, as she'd heard somewhere that people could track you through GPS, even if your phone was off, if the battery was still installed. But maybe she should call someone. Surrender. Maybe the police would have pity on her if she went willingly.

Her fingers closed around the battery. Just snapping it back into place might set up a signal by which people could find her. Was she ready?

She was about to do it when a hand touched her shoulder. Aria whirled around, her arms protectively in front of her face. Her phone fell from her hand and skittered across the cobblestones, but she didn't move to grab it. She stared at the person in front of her. Then she gasped.

"I knew it," he said breathlessly. "I knew you'd come here, just like you said."

Aria blinked, unsure of her senses. And she oscillated, she realized, between throwing her arms around him or running even farther away in order to protect him.

Noel.

15

SPENCER'S UPS AND DOWNS

"Miss Hastings?" the reporters screamed as Spencer hurried down the courthouse steps after the second day of the trial. "What are your thoughts on the proceedings?"

"Do you have any idea where Aria Montgomery is hiding in Europe?" another reporter bellowed.

"What do you think about Hanna Marin getting married?" someone else shouted.

"Do you still believe that Alison is alive?" A reporter shoved a microphone with a local news logo on the base in her face.

Spencer elbowed out of their way, somehow making it through the blue barricades to a "safe" area the cops had blocked off that was off-limits to the press. She scanned the parking lot for the car service her mom had arranged to take her home—apparently, Mrs. Hastings was far too busy to actually watch her daughter's murder trial today. But the car wasn't there yet. She leaned against the wall and breathed in, feeling like she might cry.

The trial had been a disaster today. The prosecution's witnesses were first, and the DA had expertly uncovered every single damning thing Spencer had done through the years. Like how she'd pushed her sister down the stairs when she thought Melissa was A. Or that she'd freaked out in therapy, certain she'd killed Their Ali, or how she'd plagiarized her Golden Orchid essay (it didn't matter that she'd confessed her crime before they gave her the prize), or that she'd framed another girl for drug possession and had aided and abetted in pushing Tabitha Clark off that balcony in Jamaica, and that she was suspected to be involved in a mass-drugging at an eating club party in Princeton. *She's a violent, psychotic liar who has a Machiavellian drive to get what she wants*, the lawyer had sneered to the jury. *We shouldn't believe anything she says.*

And as for the case the defense had on Ali? All the prosecution had to do was bring up that damn journal the cops found in the woods. *She's a different person on these pages*, the lawyer said. *Alison isn't the girl we think she is.*

The doors to the courtroom slammed again, and Spencer watched as Hanna, flanked by her mom and Mike, emerged onto the steps. She felt a pang. All day, Hanna had sat stiffly and stoically as the lawyer went through the various things *she'd* done in the past two years. But Spencer could tell by the way she spun the yellow lacrosse bracelet around and around her wrist how much the accusations got to her. A huge part of her wanted just to take Hanna's hand, but there was never an appropriate moment—whenever there was a break, Mike rushed to Hanna's side immediately, whisking her away. Spencer wondered if they were really getting married, like the reporters had said. Would Hanna actually do such a thing?

"Spencer?"

A man in a white jacket and blue scrub pants hurried toward her. Spencer's mouth dropped open. It was Wren.

"Hi," Wren said breathlessly when he approached. "How are you feeling?"

Spencer's whole body tensed. "Were you in the court-room?" she squeaked. She hated the idea of him hearing all those horrible things about her.

"No, no. I just got off work. I thought I'd pop down here and see how you're doing—I haven't heard from you. Are you sleeping better? How are your wounds?"

Wren had driven all the way here just to give her a checkup? "Um, I'm fine," Spencer said softly. "Healing nicely."

"Good." Wren's smile was twitchy. "Well, okay then. Unless . . ." He licked his lips nervously. "Unless you'd like to get coffee with me?"

"What, like now?" Spencer blurted.

Wren raised one shoulder. "I have the afternoon off. Unless you have other plans?"

Spencer lowered her shoulders. "I already told you this isn't a good idea."

"Listen, I spoke to your sister," Wren said.

"You did *what*?" Spencer shrieked. "You had no right!" Had Wren implied something happened between them? Did Melissa hate her now? Spencer glanced at her phone, wanting to call her sister that instant.

Wren held up his hand. "I just said that I'd like to take you out for coffee as a friend and I wanted to know if it was okay with her. She said it was fine. Honest."

Spencer blinked slowly. That didn't sound so extreme. All of a sudden, she felt exhausted. She didn't want to argue with Wren anymore. And honestly, it would be kind of nice if someone took her out for coffee after such a horrendous day. It would certainly beat another stiflingly silent dinner at her house, Mr. Pennythistle and Amelia staring at her like she was an alien and her own mother acting like she didn't exist.

But then she looked at the ankle bracelet. Technically, she wasn't allowed to go anywhere except for home, the courthouse, and the doctor unless she had her parents' permission. Spencer's dad would probably say yes, but he was in a work meeting all day. Spencer's mom probably wouldn't even pick up her phone.

"Would you mind coming to my house?" she asked shyly, showing him her ankle bracelet. "It would be a lot easier."

Wren didn't bat an eye. "Of course. Want me to drive you?"

Spencer shaded her eyes and watched as her car service pulled into the lot. "I'll meet you there," she said, figuring her mom would get mad if she didn't use it.

The house was empty when Spencer arrived, a good thing. Talking to Wren would be easier without her mom nosing around. Minutes later, Wren pulled up to the curb and got out. Spencer stood on the lawn, smiling at him goofily. "Want to, um, sit out back?" she asked.

"Sure," Wren answered.

She led him around the side yard to the patio, then pulled out a chair at the table for him to sit. "Um, do you want something to drink?" she fumbled. "Lemonade, maybe? Coke?"

"Whatever you have is fine." He looked at her bemusedly, like she was stressing over something unimportant.

"Oh," Spencer said. "Well, okay."

She retrieved some Cokes from the fridge and sank down in a chair opposite him. A lawn mower grumbled. The Hastings's gardener quietly pruned the bushes in the side yard. The pool glistened invitingly, and the hot tub bubbled. Spencer couldn't help but remember when she and Wren had been in that hot tub together, after hockey practice. Had that really been her life?

Wren must have been thinking the same thing, because

he said, "Things are a bit different than when I stayed here, huh?"

Spencer gazed out at the property. The grass still hadn't grown in properly where the converted barn apartment had once stood. "I should say so," she said quietly.

"I heard you were in the barn when that fire happened."

Spencer nodded, recalling that horrible night. If only someone had caught Ali *then*. "Let's not dwell on that," she said. "I do too much thinking about the past as it is."

For a while, they talked about Rosewood, and Wren's residency program, and new music that they both liked. Then Wren folded his hands. "Did I hear you'd gotten into Princeton? *And* that you'd gotten a book deal?"

Spencer sipped her soda. "Yes on both counts, not that they're happening now."

Wren made a face. "Pretend, for a moment, you aren't going to prison on a false murder charge. What's your book about?"

It still surprised Spencer that someone wanted to know this stuff—but then, Wren had always taken a genuine interest in who she was. Taking a deep breath, she began to describe the bullying blog. "I think it would have made a great book," she said wistfully. "There are so many stories that deserve to be told."

"You can still write it, you know," Wren reminded her. "After all, Cervantes wrote *Don Quixote* in prison."

Spencer looked up at him, surprised. "Really?"

"And O. Henry wrote tons of his short stories while incarcerated for embezzlement."

Spencer's eyes lit up. "I love his stories."

"Me, too." Wren placed his chin in his hands. "I was always kind of sheepish to admit it, though. O. Henry was uncool with my classmates."

Spencer snickered. "My AP English class always tried to outdo one another with obscure writers. I'm sure it would've been even worse at Princeton."

"So what would your major be, if you were to go?" Wren asked.

Spencer sat back and thought for a moment. "When I first got in, it was going to be history, or maybe economics—my dad always thought I'd be good at business school." She shrugged. "It's probably not worth talking about, though. I'm not going."

Wren laced his fingers. "I have a feeling that you will, if you want to."

"So you think I *won't* go to prison?"

He leaned forward. "I just believe that certain things have a way of working out."

Spencer's eyes widened. And then, before she knew it, Wren was leaning forward even more and kissing her lightly on the mouth. His lips tasted like sugar. His skin was warmed from the sun.

She pulled away fast, staring at him with her mouth open. As much as she tried to tear her gaze away from Wren's face, all she could focus on was a tiny droplet of

Coke on his upper lip that she suddenly felt the urge to brush away.

"Anyway," Wren said in a small voice. And then he sat back in his seat and turned toward the woods, watching the trees, as if it hadn't happened at all.

A few hours later, Spencer opened her eyes. She was lying on her bed in her bedroom, feeling groggy—she must have dozed off after Wren left, which hadn't been long after the kiss.

The kiss. It had been only a second long, but she'd thought about it quite a bit since it happened. What had it meant? Had it just been a friendly, sympathetic peck . . . or something more? And was it a good idea for her to even get into something right now?

There were clinking noises of pots banging together and silverware being pulled from drawers coming from the kitchen. Spencer rose and padded into the hall, surprised to hear Melissa's lilting voice downstairs. Her sister was laughing about something, clearly in a good mood. Apparently she hadn't seen the trial recap on CNN.

She walked downstairs and found Melissa and Darren already seated at the table. Her mother, Mr. Pennythistle, and Amelia were seated as well. "What's up?" she asked everyone.

"Spence!" Melissa's eyes lit up. "I tried calling you! I was wondering where you were!"

Spencer frowned. "I was just upstairs." She glanced at

her mother, who probably knew that, but Mrs. Hastings just shrugged.

"Sit, sit," Melissa said, gesturing at an empty seat next to her. "We have big news."

Spencer slid into a seat. Melissa's attention had turned to Darren again. It was then that Spencer noticed he was in a dark suit and a gray tie. She wasn't sure if she'd ever seen him so dressed up in her life. He was also nervously fiddling with his fork. "Did I miss something?" Spencer asked.

"Well, we were just about to tell everyone." Darren looked moonily at Melissa. "I've asked Melissa to marry me. And Melissa's said yes."

Spencer almost burst out laughing, quickly clapping her hand over her mouth before she did. Darren and Melissa were such a mismatched couple, but who was she to judge? She watched as Darren brought out a velvet ring box from his pocket and placed it in Melissa's hands. All at once, she felt a little twinge: Had Mike proposed to Hanna like this? It sucked that she wasn't speaking to Hanna and hadn't gotten the story.

"I'll do a reenactment, if you like," Darren said. "Melissa Hastings," he began in a far-too-sappy voice, "will you marry me?"

Melissa's eyes widened. "Yes!" she exclaimed. "I will!"

Mrs. Hastings whooped. Mr. Pennythistle clapped his hands. Everyone was hugging, Melissa even grabbing Spencer and pulling her into the fold. "There's more news, though," she said over the din, then took a deep breath. "I'm also pregnant!"

Spencer's jaw dropped. Darren beamed. Mr. Pennythistle clapped again. "How delightful!"

"H-how far along?" Mrs. Hastings stammered.

Melissa's gaze fell bashfully to her midsection. "Nine weeks," she said. "We just had an ultrasound, and everything looks great." She pulled out a black-and-white picture and passed it around. Amelia and Mr. Pennythistle oohed.

When the picture made its way to Spencer, she focused hard, trying to discern where the little blob's head and feet might be. She also felt a rush of love for her sister. Perhaps *this* was why Melissa didn't want to get too involved with the Ali stuff–professing she was alive to the press, et cetera. Maybe she wanted to protect her unborn child from Ali's wrath.

"Well, then, the wedding has to happen quickly," Mrs. Hastings said primly, folding her hands. It was pretty clear the baby had been a surprise to her, too. "Good thing I gave Darren one of my rings for the engagement."

On cue, Melissa pulled the ring from the box. The huge, square-cut diamond sparkled magically around the room, throwing prismatic shapes on the walls. Spencer almost burst out laughing again. "That was *your* old engagement ring from Dad, wasn't it?" she asked her mom.

"Yes," Mrs. Hastings said, a defensive edge to her

voice. "Your father is a jerk, but he has exquisite taste in jewels."

Melissa tilted her hand back and forth. "It was so nice of you to let us have this, Mom."

Mrs. Hastings sliced at her meat. "Oh, you girls are set to inherit a treasure trove of things from your father. None of it means anything to *me* anymore." Then she looked up sharply at Spencer. "Well, *you* won't get anything. You'll be in jail—it'll be no use to you there. Amelia can take your half."

Spencer's mouth fell open. It felt as though her mother had just kicked her in the stomach. She'd always known her mom could be tactless, but come *on*.

There was an awkward pause; it was clear no one knew what to say. Then Melissa touched Spencer's hand. "How does it feel, knowing you're going to be an aunt?"

Spencer tried to smile and shift gears. "Great. I'm so excited for you. And I'll try to be the best aunt ever."

"Actually, I was hoping you'd be *more* than an aunt," Melissa said cautiously, twisting her new ring around her finger. "Maybe a godmother, too?"

"*Me?*" Spencer touched her chest. "Are you *sure?*" She might very well be a godmother in *jail*, after all.

"Of course." Melissa squeezed Spencer's thigh. "I want you in our baby's life, Spence. You're the strongest person I know, especially given all you've been through." She glanced at her mother, who had jumped up from her seat and was rushing into the kitchen. "Don't pay attention to

Mom, okay?" she whispered. "I'll give you half the jewels I inherit. But only the ugly ones." She nudged her playfully.

Spencer wiped away a tear, overwhelmed by her sister's kindness. "Thanks," she mustered. "I'll take the ugliest ones you get."

Melissa dabbed at her mouth with a napkin. "I heard you're back in touch with Wren."

Even though Spencer had been forewarned, she still felt her cheeks burn. "It's just because he's my doctor," she said quickly. "We're not, like, *you* know."

"Even if you were, that would be okay."

Spencer stared at her, surprised. "Really?"

Melissa nodded. "Wren used to talk about you all the time. And what happened at the end there . . . well, I can't say I didn't sort of orchestrate it, you know?" She looked down at the ultrasound picture next to her plate. "I just want you to be as happy as I am."

"Thanks," Spencer bleated.

As she said it, she realized she kind of *was* happy. Not with the predicament she was in, obviously, but in this moment. She thought of a baby coming into their lives and how much joy that would bring. She thought of how pleasant it was to have a real, true, precious relationship with Melissa. And then she thought of Wren. Leaning toward her. Kissing her lightly. That contented look on his face afterward, as he'd stared at the trees.

She grabbed her phone, suddenly charged with

purpose. Wren's text from the other day was still in her inbox; she hit a button and composed a reply. *Thanks for coming over today*, she typed quickly. *I hope I can see you again.*

She hoped he hoped so, too.

16

DOOMED

By Thursday, Hanna had begun to notice that the judge who was presiding over their trial, the Honorable Judge Pierrot, secretly picked his nose when he thought no one was looking. And that the bailiff played Candy Crush Saga during breaks, and that Juror #4, an older woman who wore square, dark-framed glasses and seemed utterly oblivious to current events—which was probably why they had chosen her—tapped her fingers on the desk to the rhythm of "Ding, Dong! The Witch Is Dead." Hanna began to make a little superstitious game out of it: If Judge Pierrot dug around in his nose five times before lunch, she got ten points. If Juror #10 spun her engagement ring around her finger ten times in the day, she got twenty. It was easier to focus on that stuff than what was actually happening during the trial.

The testimony this morning was all about various witnesses who'd seen Hanna and the others skulking around Ashland before Ali's alleged death. Apparently they'd been much less sneaky than they all thought, because the prosecution had found *seven people* to come forward. Most of them were just random citizens who didn't have much to say, but the last woman, who wore a navy-blue suit and heels, was someone Hanna remembered. It was the lady Emily had accosted near the Maxwells' property. Emily had been so worked up, in fact, that they'd had to practically pull her off the woman to calm her down.

Which, of course, was what the woman told them. "The girl who sadly took her life seemed very troubled," she said in a dramatic voice. "I truly feared for my safety."

Hanna wrinkled her nose. It hadn't been *that* bad.

The DA called another witness, a well-dressed woman with bright-red lipstick. When she stated her name for the court, she said in a clear voice, "Sharon Ridge."

Hanna gasped. It was the woman who'd organized the Rosewood Rallies function at the Rosewood Country Club. What was *she* doing up there, testifying against them?

"Tell us about the Rosewood Rallies event," the DA said.

Sharon Ridge rolled back her shoulders, then described the event as a gala at the country club to support disadvantaged youth in the Rosewood area. "It was a very special night," she said. "A lot of people from the community came out, and we raised a lot of money."

"And you had distinguished guests, correct?" the DA asked.

Ridge gazed into the courtroom. "Yes, Ms. Marin." She pointed to Hanna. "And Ms. Hastings. As well as Ms. Fields and Ms. Montgomery, who are not here."

"And did those girls seem grateful to be there?"

She adjusted her collar. "Well, not exactly. They seemed quite distracted all night. I wanted to introduce them to people, but all of them just looked right through me. And we wanted to have a little ceremony for the girls—they'd been through so much, or so we'd thought. But when we called them to the stage, they weren't there."

"Not a single one?"

The woman shook her head. "The cameras at the main entrance show them leaving the premises around 9 PM."

"And when you say the girls were distracted, what do you mean?"

Ridge pushed a flyaway hair out of her face. "Well, I noticed Aria Montgomery flee into the ladies' lounge. Emily Fields was positively catatonic, as was Hanna Marin. And Spencer Hastings, well . . ." She trailed off, looking uncomfortable.

"What?" the DA goaded.

"I'm not sure if this has anything to do with anything, but a few people said that Ms. Hastings had a very heated fight with the boy she brought as her date. They heard the name *Alison* mentioned."

The DA put his hands on his hips. "You have this young man's name, correct?"

She nodded. "It's Greg Messner."

He looked at the jury. "I may mention that Greg Messner ended up dead later that night." Everyone gasped. "Found in a creek bed in Ashland, Pennsylvania. And you know who else was in Ashland that same evening? Spencer Hastings. And her three friends."

Rubens shot up. "This isn't a trial for Mr. Messner's death. And Ms. Hastings had nothing to do with that."

"Sustained," the judge said.

Spencer poked Rubens as he sat down. "Greg was an Ali Cat," she whispered. "He targeted me through my anti-bullying site. He'd been working *with* Ali—she'd given him instructions to get close to me and get info. Can't you tell them that?"

"You should totally tell him that," Hanna piped up, just trying to be helpful. But Spencer just shot her an *I-don't-need-your-help* look. Hanna slumped back down in her seat. So much for trying to be civil.

Rubens glanced at the girls worriedly. "Let's just drop it, okay? We'll concentrate on our own witnesses. That starts this afternoon."

Hanna drew her bottom lip into her mouth. It seemed like every avenue they pursued led to a dead end. And were *their* witnesses really going to save the day?

She ran her hands down the length of her face, her heart thudding hard. It felt like she was trapped inside a dress that was ten sizes too small for her body. She couldn't move her arms or her torso. She could barely breathe.

After that day's proceedings, she somehow made her way into the hall, where she could collect her thoughts. She looked at her phone for the first time in hours. She had forty-two new messages, and they were all RSVPs to her wedding.

Her wedding. Well, at least that was something.

She scrolled through each *yes*, astonished that so many people wanted to come. Ramona had emailed her that the hip-hop/breakdancing group Hanna wanted to perform during cocktail hour at the reception had said yes. She also mentioned that because so many celebrities were attending—not only some of the cast of *Burn It Down*, but a few local newscasters and young socialites as well—she was thinking of having something of a red carpet before the reception. Us Weekly *seems really into the idea.*

Us Weekly? Despite the courtroom circus, Hanna felt a tiny, excited flutter. She knew this wedding was a big deal—everything surrounding their lives was these days. The trial was reported on obsessively on most of the news channels every night, there were constant updates about Aria's whereabouts in Europe—the latest was that she was hiding somewhere in Sweden—and a few people had sent her Instagrams of mentions of her wedding in tabloids all over the globe. But *Us* was legit—and it didn't sound like they were covering the wedding just to be snarky.

She dialed Ramona's number and pressed her phone to her ear. "It's Hanna. Red carpet's a go. I think that sounds really fun."

"Perfect," Ramona squawked. "It's all coming together, Hanna. I think it's going to be fantastic."

"Me, too," Hanna said, her voice rising. "And you know what? Let's have fireworks at the reception, too."

"Fireworks?" Ramona paused to consider it. "I have some people I can call."

Hanna hung up and slipped her phone back in her pocket, feeling good about her latest choice. Fireworks seemed totally appropriate for her wedding reception. Most likely, it would be her last moment of happiness— and she might as well go out with a bang.

17

INTERNATIONAL INTRIGUE

"I don't think I'll ever get used to a euro as currency," Noel said on Thursday afternoon as he leafed through a stack of bills in the cheap hostel room he had rented. "I mean, look at this." He held up a ten-euro note. "It looks like Monopoly money."

Aria plucked it from his hand. "Be careful with that. Over here, Monopoly money is freedom."

"I'm just glad we're free together," Noel said, pulling Aria onto the small, stiff-mattressed hostel bed.

Aria relished it for a moment, but then she pulled away. She still felt really, really nervous about Noel being here. Especially after some of the, er, mistakes she'd made.

When she'd turned around to face him yesterday, she thought she'd inhaled stray marijuana vapors from the nearby hash bar. "What are you *doing* here?" she'd asked frantically.

Noel had shrugged. "The way you said good-bye like

that, and then when I got calls from your mom later that night wondering where you were, I started to put things together. I knew you'd left. And I knew I had to find you. You'd mentioned Amsterdam a few days ago—remember? And the Anne Frank house specifically. I just didn't know I was going to find you so quickly."

Aria had looked around him anxiously, still worried someone would spot her. "Noel, you have to go. You can't be seen with me. And aren't people looking for *you*?"

"My parents think I went to their place in Vail. I bought a plane ticket in my name for there, and I even checked into that flight but just didn't board it. I snuck back down the Jetway, bolted for the international terminal, and got on an Amsterdam flight instead."

Aria had started to feel sweaty. "Don't you understand?" she'd whispered. "I'm an international criminal! You need to stay away from me! The cops are on my tail!" People were streaming past. It felt like everyone was staring at her, hearing every word.

Noel had just taken Aria's arm and walked her down the canal. "You've only been here for one day. You haven't done anything to attract attention, right? Used any credit cards, shown your ID?"

Aria's bottom lip had trembled. She had done just those things. "Maybe," she lied. "But there are alerts about me. Interpol is looking everywhere. Anywhere I go, someone is going to recognize me." She shut her eyes.

"Maybe I should just turn myself in."

"Nonsense." Noel grabbed her hand. "I'll keep you safe."

The first thing they did was find a guy who made fake passports, who whipped up two American documents for Aria and Noel, barely looking at them and not asking if they approved of their fake names—Elizabeth Rogers for Aria and Ronald Nestor for Noel. Aria liked her fake name. Elizabeth Rogers struck her as a girl who wrote for the school paper and kept her room very neat and was too shy to have a boyfriend. A girl who would never, *ever* be on trial for murder.

Noel's steady, calming presence put her at ease—maybe she really *was* safe with him. Knowing that Amsterdam was too dangerous, they'd boarded a train with their fake passports and headed for Brussels, Belgium, checking in at a little hostel on a quiet street. Noel had taken her on a moonlit stroll along a walkway that overlooked the city. Despite Aria's protests that someone might recognize her, Noel had coaxed her to a little restaurant that served Belgian fries with mayonnaise, her favorite. They'd returned to their hostel room feeling almost shy as they fell into bed together. "Let's go to Japan," Aria had mused as she lay her head on the pillow. It sounded so foreign, so exotic, so utterly removed from anything having to do with her old life—*or* Ali. "We'll teach English. And eat sushi. And ride bicycles, and learn Japanese."

"We'll have to get a guidebook," Noel said. "See where we'll want to live."

Aria thought about this. "A beach town, maybe? Or near a mountain?"

"Ooh, I wonder if Japan has good skiing." Noel looked excited. "I've never been, but Eric has."

A wistful look crossed his face. Aria stared at her lap. Of course he'd want to call his brother and ask. But he couldn't.

Then Noel drew her into his arms. "All this sounds perfect, Liz."

"I only go by *Elizabeth*," Aria teased. "But thank you, Ronald."

"That's Ron to you." Noel laughed lightly.

And now they were packing up to leave once more. Aria had looked up flights to Tokyo and found that they were cheaper out of London, so they were planning on taking the bus through the Chunnel there. They would board a plane for Tokyo the following day.

After they were packed they walked down the rickety stairs and through the lobby. Hand in hand, they climbed onto a trolley that would take them to the suburb's train station. Most of the people on the trolley were either very old or looked like students. "See?" Noel whispered, squeezing her hand. "No one is looking at you strangely in the slightest." Noel brightened and began to unzip his backpack. "I forgot." He pulled out a plastic bag and handed it to her. "I got you something yesterday."

Aria plunged her hand into the bag. Inside was a long, blond wig. She touched a few strands. They felt like real hair. "Whoa."

"I got it while you were trying on that dress in the store last night," Noel explained, mentioning the one boutique they'd popped into during their tour of Brussels. "Just in case you feel . . . worried about someone recognizing you. I thought it would be a cute disguise."

"It's beautiful." Aria wished she could put it on right then, though she knew that might draw suspicion.

Noel's gaze fell to the bag. "There's something else in there, too."

She felt around at the bottom, then pulled out a small, vintage-looking gold bracelet etched with tiny purple stones. "Noel," she breathed. The name *Cartier* was inscribed on the inside.

"I was going to give this to you on prom night," Noel said gently. "But then everything . . . well, you know."

Aria thought about how she'd freaked out on Noel in the graveyard near prom—though she'd had good reason. She'd just found out all that stuff about his secret friendship with Ali. The next morning was when they'd found Noel in the storage shed. Nick and Ali had beat him up, presumably because he'd said too much.

"It was my grandmother's," Noel explained. "She gave it to me before she died and said that I should give it to someone really special." His voice cracked a little. "It's the last thing I grabbed before I took off to find you. My grandmother meant a lot to me, and you do, too."

Aria put the bracelet on and held up her wrist, her heart swelling with love. "Thank you."

The trolley dropped them off at the train station, and together they walked through the echoing building to find their train. They flashed their new passports, and the woman behind the glass nodded sleepily. They boarded the train quickly, swept up in the crowds and babble and movement. After ten minutes, a whistle blew, and the train chugged out of the station. Aria stared out the windows, her stomach jumping with excitement, her new bracelet encircling her wrist.

Noel laid his head back on the seat. Aria gazed blankly around the cabin, then plucked a magazine from the mesh pocket in front of her. She had a sudden, prickly premonition, and sure enough, when she turned to one of the first pages, her own face stared back at her. It was a blurry picture of her at the Philadelphia airport, still dressed in her black sheath from Emily's funeral. *Aria Montgomery on the Lam*, it said.

This article didn't say much more than the one Aria had read in Amsterdam, though this one had interviewed several people who claimed to be "Aria's closest friends." One of them, laughably, was Klaudia Huusko, the exchange student who lived with the Kahns. "Aria push me off ski lift," they quoted Klaudia as saying—it was just like a trashy paper to play up her fakey pidgin English.

"She also spy on me. She very sneaky girl. I hope she not in Finland, she might hurt my family."

Another was Ezra Fitz. Aria almost dropped the paper when she read his name. It included a picture, too—Ezra looked kind of bloated, and he was wearing an unflattering pair of black-framed glasses. "Aria always spoke of her love of Europe, so I have no doubt she went there," he said. Then there was a line about how Ezra's book, *See Me After Class*, was coming out next October. *Publicity whore.*

Aria looked up. Someone was staring—she could just feel it. She glanced around, then spotted a man standing at the back of the car. He wore a trench coat and had his hands shoved deep into his pockets. Even when she met his gaze, he didn't look down.

Aria pretended to busy herself with the buttons on her coat. When she peeked at him again, he was *still* looking. Her breathing quickened. The man looked older, professional. He took out his phone and started saying something inaudibly into the receiver. Every so often, he glanced at her again, his expression more and more punishing.

Sweat pricked her forehead. Slowly, casually, she tapped Noel's shoulder. "Um, I think we need to get off this train."

Noel looked confused. "Huh? Why?"

Aria put her finger to her lips. "Just follow me into the next car in a few minutes, okay?"

She stood up, slinging her purse over her shoulder. She could feel the man's eyes on her as she pushed through the door into the next car. The door slammed, and she wobbled up the aisle. Swallowing hard, she ducked into the bathroom and locked the door.

She stared at herself in the mirror, then smashed the blond wig on her head. Instantly, she was transformed into someone else—but was it enough? She fumbled for her sunglasses in her bag, then put on a hat, too.

Noel was waiting for her when she came out of the bathroom door. Aria could tell he wanted to ask questions, but she didn't say a word, instead looking around him for the guy. He was in the next car, still on the phone. Would he soon realize she wasn't coming back?

Blessedly, the train screeched into a station. A clipped voice called out the station name in Dutch, French, and German, and Aria grabbed Noel's hand and yanked him to the platform. She ran all the way to the stairs, then glanced over her shoulder. The man wasn't following.

"*Now* can you tell me what's going on?" Noel cried as they clambered down the steps.

"I felt like someone was watching me," Aria said under her breath. "Did you see him? That guy at the end of the car?"

Noel's mouth twitched. "That guy came up to me and asked if I had a light for his cigarette. H-he heard my accent, asked where I was from."

Aria gawked. "And what did you say?"

Noel's throat bobbed. He glanced at the train again. "I said the U.S. That's it. Then I got away from him. Excused myself." He shook his head. "Aria. It was probably nothing. You're being paranoid."

Aria felt an uneasy pull in her stomach. "I kind of have a reason to be."

Noel nodded. Then, a curiously excited smile danced across his lips, and he touched a strand of her wig. "You're sexy when you're an international criminal."

"*Stop.*" Aria smacked him playfully. But she appreciated Noel's attempt at making light of the moment. Maybe the man *wasn't* after her. And now, in the swirl of people, she felt anonymous once more. It sort of *was* sexy—she felt like a character in *Murder on the Orient Express*. And suddenly, she felt so overcome that she took Noel's hand and pulled him under the stairwell. She kissed him like it was their last day on earth.

Or like it was their last day of freedom.

18

THE JEWEL IN THE CROWN

Later on Thursday, after Spencer had suffered through yet another long, horrific court day, Rubens motioned for her and Hanna to speak to him in the hall. Spencer kept her head down, avoiding the reporters who were clamoring just past the courtroom doors. A bunch of their witnesses were there, too. Like Andrew Campbell, who Spencer hadn't seen in months, but who'd given a sweet testimonial on the stand that she was a good person. Kirsten Cullen was there, too, as were a few of Spencer's teachers, and there was even a representative from the Golden Orchid essay committee. Spencer had plagiarized her sister's paper, but it had taken a great deal of fortitude and character to come forward to say that she'd lied. It was not, the representative said, the behavior of a murderer.

Spencer could sense them all there, and she wanted to take the time to thank each one of them. But Rubens was motioning her and Hanna forward. She shot them cursory smiles, then hurried after him.

Rubens led them into a conference room with a long wooden table and a huge oil painting of a snub-nosed man in an old-timey George Washington wig. He sat down and folded his hands, then let out a long sigh.

"I'm going to level with you." Rubens looked back and forth between the two of them. Spencer and Hanna were sitting as far apart as they possibly could, not looking at each other. "I've heard rumors that the DA is bringing in a surprise witness. It's unusual, since they've already presented all their witnesses, but it can be done if someone doesn't agree to testify until late in the game. It's someone whom they claim will put the nail in the coffin."

Hanna wrinkled her nose. "Who would that be?"

"Yeah, aside from Ali's ghost coming in and saying we killed her," Spencer added drily, fiddling with a button on her blazer.

Rubens tapped his pen on the table. "I'm not really sure who it might be, but it seems like the DA has something up his sleeve—something not good. I'm wondering if it makes the most sense for you girls to enter a plea bargain."

Spencer flinched. "*What?*"

The lawyer didn't look like he was joking. "We make a deal. It'll mean a very high fine. And it'll still mean prison time. But it might mean *less* prison time."

Spencer stared at him. "But we didn't *do* it."

"We shouldn't have to go to prison at all," Hanna added.

Rubens rubbed his temples. "I understand that. But what you girls are looking for—absolute exoneration—it might not happen. I just want to manage your expectations."

Spencer sat back. "You're supposed to prove to the jury that this crime can't be proven beyond a shadow of a doubt. All the cops have are a tooth and some blood and us at the scene when we weren't supposed to be there. Emily freaking out, all this stuff about our pasts—it doesn't make us killers. Why are we giving up?"

Rubens shrugged. "It's true that the lack of Alison's body should be important, and I'm going to emphasize that in my closing statements. I'm not giving up, okay? I'm just throwing this out there as an option." Then he stood. "Think about it, okay? We're in recess for another few hours. We could end this today."

And go to prison immediately? Spencer thought, her stomach pulling. *No, thanks.*

Rubens exited into the hall, leaving Spencer and Hanna alone. Spencer glanced at her old friend, feeling awkward. "This *sucks*," Hanna finally mumbled.

Spencer nodded. She stared at the lacrosse bracelet on Hanna's wrist, wanting to say something. Anything. If only she could reach over and give Hanna a big hug and all would be forgiven.

Then she noticed something tucked into Hanna's bag.

It looked like an invitation. Spencer squinted harder, noticing Hanna's own name, along with Mike's. *Hanna Marin and Michelangelo Montgomery invite you to their wedding at the Chanticleer mansion this Saturday at eight o'clock in the evening.*

It stung, especially because she hadn't been invited.

Hanna noticed Spencer looking at the invites. Her face paled. "Oh, Spence. Actually—here." She plunged her hand into the bag and handed her an invite.

Spencer stared at it. Her head shot up. "You don't have to invite me just because I happened to see this."

Hanna's eyes were wide. "No, I *want* to invite you!" She laughed nervously. "Spence, I want to be friends again. That argument was stupid. We need to get past it, don't you think?"

Spencer rolled her jaw. She wanted to believe Hanna, but something about what she'd just said didn't sit right. She couldn't get their argument out of her mind. *Don't be such a martyr.* No one had ever been that mean to her, not even Melissa.

Then she realized what it was. Hanna hadn't said she was sorry for blaming Spencer for Emily's death. What she really, really wanted was an apology. Not a wedding invitation.

Hanna stared at her with big doe eyes. Spencer straightened her spine and handed the invite back. "I'm busy that night," she said in a clipped voice, then swung around and marched out the door.

"Spencer!" Hanna said, chasing her. Spencer kept going, outpacing Hanna.

Spencer pushed through the back entrance, her emotions scrambled both from Hanna's invitation and Rubens's suggestion for a plea bargain. *Should* they do that? It would put an end to the trial and the persecution. But making a deal meant they were guilty of something—and they *weren't*. Spencer didn't want to go to prison for less time; she didn't want to go at *all*.

She shut her eyes and thought again of Angela naming that outlandish price to help Spencer to disappear. She'd racked her brain but had come up with no other way to find the money. The prospect was as good as dead.

"Spencer."

She whirled around. Melissa was hustling behind her down the ramp from the courthouse. Spencer's jaw dropped. "You were in there?"

Melissa nodded. "I had to see how things were going." She cast her eyes downward, looking about as defeated as Spencer felt. "I didn't realize it was so bad, honey. Need a hug?"

Tears filled Spencer's eyes. She melted into her sister, squeezing her tightly. Then Melissa patted her arm. "C'mon. I'll drive you home. I canceled your car service."

Spencer climbed into her sister's Mercedes and sat back against the warm leather seats. As they wound through Rosewood, Melissa tried to take Spencer's mind off things by chattering about the baby items she was planning to register for. "It's crazy, all the things you need for such a little person," she said. "So many blankets and bibs, bottles and toys, and we don't know whether to co-sleep or use a bassinet . . ."

Her ring flashed as she gesticulated with her hands. It was incongruous to see Melissa wearing their mother's old ring; Spencer wondered what her dad thought about it. Her mother's nasty words floated back to her, too. *You girls are set to inherit a treasure trove of things from your father. Well, you won't get anything. You'll be in jail—it'll be no use to you there.*

Suddenly, an idea struck her. She let out a gasp.

Melissa looked up. "You okay?"

Spencer tucked a lock of hair behind her ear and tried to smile. "Sure."

But the rest of the way home, she jiggled her leg repeatedly. When she was little, she used to sneak into her mom's closet and look at the jewels inside her red-and-black enamel jewelry box. Sometimes, she'd even try them on. Was it still there? When had her mother last taken stock?

Could Spencer actually consider *taking* some of that jewelry . . . to pay Angela?

As soon as her sister pulled into the driveway, Spencer gave her another grateful hug, ran into the house, and slammed the door. She waited until Melissa pulled out again, then shot upstairs. As usual, her mom's bedroom suite smelled like her mother's signature Chanel No. 5, and it was five-star-hotel-room spotless, the pillows fluffed, the bedspread smoothed, all clothes put away. Their cleaning lady even ironed Spencer's mom's sheets every morning before placing them on the bed.

She stepped toward her mother's walk-in closet. Mrs. Hastings's wardrobe hung on one side, Mr. Pennythistle's suits on the other, their shoes on racks upon racks at the back. And then, on a middle shelf, there it was: the same black-and-red box she remembered.

Hands shaking, Spencer tried the lid. It didn't budge. She held it up to the light, then caught sight of a little keypad by the hinge. Of course: It had a code.

She sat back, trying to remember what the old code had been. Melissa's birthday, right? She typed in 1123 for November 23, but a red LED light appeared. Spencer frowned. Why would her mother have changed it?

She tried 0408 for Amelia's birthday, and then Mr. Pennythistle's, but the red light appeared again and again. Then, feeling pretty hopeless, she typed in the code for her own birthday. The LED flashed green, and the hinge unlatched. Spencer pressed her lips together, guilt swelling over her. But maybe her mother's usage of her birthday was fairly arbitrary, just another semi-significant number combination after lots of other semi-significant number combinations had already been used. It didn't *mean* anything, did it?

Several diamond bracelets were arranged carefully on a velvet tray. Two red Cartier boxes were nestled into a trough, along with a box from Tiffany and a Philadelphia jeweler Mr. Hastings frequented. Spencer opened the first Cartier to find the massive emerald ring her father had given her mom a few Christmases ago. The next box held a pair of diamond earrings he'd presented to her for an anniversary. There were more velvet boxes in a second tray bearing bracelets, diamond hoops and studs, a pear-shaped diamond ring that looked to be at least three carats, and a pink diamond brooch Spencer recalled her father giving to her mom for her birthday.

Spencer heard a sound and looked up. Was her mom here? Hands fluttering, she scooped up some of the velvet boxes and stuffed them into her pocket. She selected the pink diamond—her mom probably wouldn't notice it was gone—a few bracelets, and a pair of big diamond studs that looked identical to the ones already in Mrs. Hastings's ears, then rearranged everything in the box to look as though it had been untouched.

She shut the lid, darted out of the closet, and was almost to her room when someone cleared her throat behind her. Spencer wheeled around. Amelia stood in the middle of the hall, staring.

"O-oh!" Spencer sputtered. "I didn't know you were home."

Amelia looked Spencer up and down, her lips pressed tightly together. She glanced at Mrs. Hastings's open bedroom door and said nothing.

Spencer's heart jumped. "I, um, wanted to borrow my

mom's curling iron," she blathered. "It's much nicer than mine." It was the first thing she could think of.

But then her stepsister's gaze fell to Spencer's hands. Not only were they curling iron free, but she was wearing the pear-shaped diamond ring she'd snuck out of the jewelry box. Spencer's heart jumped. *Just get out of here*, a voice in her head screamed. *Go before you dig an even deeper hole.*

She pushed past Amelia into her own bedroom, slamming the door loudly. After a moment, she heard Amelia close her own door and the classical SiriusXM station snap on. The guilt started to snake around her like a noose. Amelia was going to say something. Should Spencer just put everything back?

But the only thing she could picture in her mind was the four block walls of a prison cell. And the lawyer's words: *It makes the most sense for you girls to enter a plea bargain.* They felt like the only two valid thoughts in her brain, crowding out everything else.

She fled out of her room and slipped into Mr. Pennythistle's office. He had a separate landline from the home phone, which she knew was being monitored. She hated using this phone in case the cops were monitoring it, too, though she doubted they were quite that thorough. And anyway, she'd only be on with Angela for a few moments—not long enough to trace.

Angela answered on the first ring with, "Who's this?"

For a moment, Spencer couldn't find her voice. "I-it's Spencer Hastings," she finally got out. "I just wanted to let you know I have the money you're looking for so that I can . . . you know. So that you can help me with what I need."

"I'm listening," Angela said gruffly. "When can you get this money to me?"

"Well, it's in jewelry, not cash," Spencer explained. "I can't get to you because I have a tracking bracelet on, but I'm good for it, I swear. I want to go as soon as possible," she added. "Whenever you can make it happen."

There was a pause. Spencer checked the clock, remembering from an old episode of *24* that she had only another twenty seconds or so until the call could be tracked. "All right," the woman on the other end finally said. "Send me a photo of the jewels so I know they're up to snuff. And then I want you outside your house on Saturday night at 10 PM. *Sharp*. We'll make the transaction *and* get you gone all in the same day. You're a minute late, or the jewels are shit, and all bets are off. Got it?"

"Of course." Spencer's hands were shaking. "But you'll be able to remove my ankle bracelet when you pick me up?"

Angela snorted. "I have ways of getting that thing off and duping the system for a little bit. But you'll be on borrowed time. We'll have to get you out of range, and *fast*."

"Thank you," Spencer said, feeling a prickle by her eyes. "I'll see you then."

There was a sharp *click*, and Angela was gone. Spencer

stared at her reflection in the vanity across the room. Her pockets bulged with jewels. She closed her eyes. *Saturday night.* That was two days from now. She could make it until then.

She had to.

19

CEASE AND DESIST

Aria picked up the bag of Scrabble tiles and gave it a swift shake. "If I pick one more vowel, I'm going to lose my mind."

She plunged her hand into the bag, selected a tile, and turned it over in her hand. An *E*. "Oh my *God*," she said dramatically, falling back on the mattress. "I'm doomed. Can E-I-E-I-O count as an Old MacDonald word?"

Noel mustered a weak smile. As he rearranged the tiles on his Scrabble shelf, his gaze slid toward the window. The sun was high in the sky. "Can't we go out for just a little bit?" It came out as a whine.

Aria's mouth twitched. "I'd rather not."

Noel stood up from their hotel bed and wandered to the chaise in the corner. The room in the little Belgian suburb was much plushier and more expensive than Aria would have preferred to stay in, but they'd gotten off the train in the middle of nowhere, and this was all they could find. At first, they'd tried to make the best of it:

Aria marveled over the hotel's library, claiming it would keep them busy for days. When she found the Scrabble game tucked onto one of the shelves in the lounge, she made a huge deal out of challenging Noel to a tournament. She'd talked up the hotel gym and said they could watch movies. Staying there was going to be so much fun!

But none of the machines in the gym worked. The movies for purchase were all in Dutch or German without subtitles. It seemed like everything on the hotel restaurant menu featured pickled herring, and Aria was pretty sure the Scrabble game was missing most of the consonant tiles.

She wanted to believe what Noel kept insisting: The guy on the train didn't know who she was. Look at all the articles, after all—they said she was in Sweden, or Spain, and one even mentioned Morocco!

But all last night, paranoid thoughts had spiraled in her mind. The safest thing to do was to lie low in the room until everything blew over. She'd tried to make it fun and sexy, giving Noel a massage, dancing for him to Miley Cyrus's "Wrecking Ball" on VH1, fantasizing about the many places they'd visit in Japan. She'd even let him win at Scrabble. But you could only make a 300-square-foot hotel room fun for so long. It was Friday now. She was running out of things to do.

She picked up the remote and turned on the TV, clicking it to CNN International, searching for news about the trial. Aria was pretty sure closing statements were today. And what was going on with Hanna and Mike's wedding? Noel had said he'd seen a newscast about that in the Amsterdam airport. If only she could just look online, but she feared someone tracking her search. Even tuning in on TV felt criminal.

Noel grabbed the remote from her and switched to another station that looked like the Dutch version of the Food Network. "You're worrying too much," he said. "You have to calm down. We have the fake passports. We've been careful. And besides, I came all the way to Europe to find you." He fluttered his eyelashes. "At the very least you could show me some of the sights, you know?"

Aria swallowed hard and looked out the window. Maybe Noel was right. And it was true—he *had* come all this way. This couldn't exactly be fun for him. Maybe if she put on the blond wig and some sunglasses, she'd be fine.

"Okay," she conceded. "Let's go out for a bit. Just nowhere too public, okay?"

"Thank God." Noel's face flooded with relief. "I was starting to lose it in here."

It was chilly outside, so they put on hoodies and scarves. The blond wig made Aria's scalp itch, but she didn't dare go out without it. The walk down to the elevator was okay, mostly because there was no one in the hallway. So was the stroll through the lobby—the clerk was looking at something on her computer screen, paying no attention to them. But as soon as they hit the street, Aria's throat began to close. It seemed like everyone on the sidewalk had frozen and was looking at her. Was the doorman peering at them strangely? What was that guy doing across the street, just staring into his cell phone?

"I saw a cool-looking café a few blocks away," Noel said. "Want to go there?"

"Uh . . ." Aria touched the blond strands of her wig. She couldn't imagine going somewhere so public. But maybe the café was dark inside. Maybe they could be escorted to a private room. Maybe no one in the place would have seen the APB with her face on it. *Act normal*, she told herself.

She started down the street, her hand tightly gripping Noel's. Halfway down the block, she noticed a black sedan parked across the street. Its windows were tinted, but she could just make out that someone was inside. As they turned left, the sedan's lights flipped on, and the car began to slowly creep after them.

She dug her nails into Noel's arm. "I think that car is following us."

"What?" Noel swiveled around.

Aria dug her nails harder. "Don't *look*."

Noel sighed loudly. "No one's after us."

"I can just tell." She walked fast but not *too* fast, pretending to be just another pedestrian out for dinner. "Why aren't they driving faster?"

Noel twisted his mouth. "Because this is, like, a fifteen-mile-per-hour zone?"

But Aria had a horrible sense, one much more pressing than the one she'd felt even in the newsagent's in Amsterdam. This was the end of the road. Someone had recognized her—maybe it *had* been that man on the train. He'd tipped off the authorities, they'd put out an alert, and someone at the hotel had made the call. Aria and Noel had basically just delivered themselves straight to the waiting Feds. She might as well knock on the window and offer up her wrists for handcuffs.

"What do you want to do?" Noel asked.

"I don't *know*," Aria said through her teeth, wishing there was an alley to duck into. The car slunk behind them, though it was quite far away, as if the driver was trying to figure out if it was really them. Or maybe he was calling for backup. "We can't go back to the hotel. They'll follow us."

"Aria, they're not following us," Noel said. "We should keep walking."

Aria stared at Noel fearfully as they clomped past a bakery. "We shouldn't have left the room. I shouldn't have given in to you."

He set his jaw. "So now it's all my fault?"

Aria said nothing.

"What were we supposed to do, hide forever?" Noel asked.

"*Yes!*" Aria shrieked, slapping her arms to her sides. "We were supposed to hide however long it took!"

Noel let out a strange laugh. Aria turned and looked at him. "What?"

He flinched. "Because this isn't *you*, Aria. And honestly, I thought this was sort of going to be . . . fun. Not like . . . *this*."

Aria set her jaw. "Well, I'm sorry this isn't more of a vacation for you. But I didn't *ask* you to come, Noel. I would have been fine on my own."

Noel squinted at her. "You didn't seem very fine when I found you. You were a total mess."

"I'm sorry I've caused you so much stress," Aria said bitterly, ignoring his comment. Then she looked up. "You know, if it were someone *else* here, someone *else* you were protecting, I bet you wouldn't complain about this not being fun."

Noel looked at her sharply. "Someone else meaning *who*?"

The words had come out of Aria's mouth so quickly she hadn't exactly had time to process them. "Forget it," she said. "I'm just upset."

Noel put his hands on his hips, stopping next to a dry-cleaner's. "You're talking about Ali, aren't you?"

Aria turned away. She hated how well Noel knew her. "Maybe," she said, feeling something inside her break. "You would have done anything for her, Noel."

"No, I wouldn't." Noel's nostrils flared. "The only person I'll do anything for is *you*." He glared. "Why can't you believe that?"

Aria stared at a shimmering puddle of oil on the street.

Would she ever forgive Noel for Ali? Ali clouded everything in Aria's mind. Two nights ago, when he'd given her that bracelet, she'd had a fleeting thought: *Had he thought about giving this to Ali once, too?* Even the blond wig: It looked, she realized now, like *Ali's hair.*

"It's still so hard," she said in a raspy voice. "And I can't help but think that if you hadn't trusted her so much, maybe we wouldn't be here at all."

Noel recoiled. "Meaning?"

"Meaning . . ." Aria gulped. *Meaning you could have warned someone. Meaning you could have stopped her. Meaning Ali wouldn't have been let out of the hospital, and she wouldn't have killed all those people, and she wouldn't have come after us and I wouldn't be in this situation.*

But that felt too much to say aloud. It was too much blame to put on him. And she knew it wasn't right—it was as wrong, in fact, as Hanna blaming Spencer for Emily's death simply for suggesting they stay at the beach overnight. There were a lot of factors at play. Noel didn't pull all the strings. No one did.

Noel was staring at her now like he understood exactly what was happening in her brain. He took one big step back, his mouth opened wide. "My God, Aria," he whispered. "Your perception is so, *so* warped."

She held up her hand. "I don't—"

"Deep down, you still blame me. You still hate me. I risk my life to come to Europe for you, and even *that* isn't enough."

"Noel," she said, stepping toward him. "That's not . . ."

But Noel held up a forbidding arm and whipped around, back toward the hotel. "Just leave me alone for a little while, okay? I need to think."

"Noel!" Aria shouted after him. But Noel started to jog, heading back toward the car that was following them.

"Noel!" Aria called again. He picked up the pace. His hair flopped up and down. He darted into the street, nearly getting run down by a man on a motorbike. "Noel!" Aria screamed. "Just *stop*!"

Just then, all four doors of the sedan opened. Four figures in black shot out, descending on Noel all at once. Aria heard a scream, and then realized it was coming from her own throat. In seconds, the officers had Noel on the ground. The sun caught something silver, glinted, and then Aria heard the sharp *snap* of handcuffs closing around his wrists. She clapped her hand over her mouth.

There were footsteps behind her, and she turned. Two more officers ran at her from the opposite direction, yelling what was probably *stop* in Dutch or German or some language Aria wasn't familiar with. The word *interpol* was emblazoned on their jackets. In the blink of an eye, they had Aria in a headlock. She squirmed, trying to breathe. They clapped handcuffs on her, too. It was like that old adage Aria had read in *Catch-22* for English class: *Just because you're paranoid doesn't mean they aren't after you.*

It was all over in a matter of seconds, and the Feds

were loading both of them into two separate cars. Aria wanted to catch Noel's eye—she'd been right all along. But suddenly, it felt like not much of a victory. She would have *rather* he was right.

Because now, they were totally and completely ruined.

20

FINAL STATEMENTS

On Friday afternoon, dressed in her most expensive black dress and highest heels, Hanna sat in her mother's car on the way to the courthouse. From the outside, no one would know she was on her way to the end of a trial that would probably put her in prison forever. She looked like a girl who was chattering on her cell phone, planning something big. Which she was.

On her list was to make sure the caterers were coming sharply at 1 PM, that the rabbi her mom had insisted they use was still confirmed, and that *Us Weekly* was on board to cover the red carpet at the reception. But at that moment, she was talking to her stepsister, Kate.

"So the seating is done?" she said into the phone.

"Yep," Kate answered. "You and Mike are at a private table. Your mom and paternal grandma aren't sitting together, as you requested. And I organized the rest of the tables by people's party preferences—you know, the vegans all together, the people we think will be heavy drinkers in a corner, and I mixed up a bunch of guys and girls so there will be fun dance-floor possibilities. Oh, and I put myself with the lacrosse boys, if that's cool."

"Of course it's cool," Hanna said, feeling grateful. She and Kate had had their moments, but Hanna was thrilled that Kate was taking part in the wedding prep. Kate had also handled the wedding favors—iPhone covers in their wedding colors, mint green and coral—as well as put together a video montage of Mike-and-Hanna pictures to show at the cocktail hour. "This is a huge help," she added. "Wanna be my bridesmaid?"

Kate laughed uncomfortably. "Oh, Hanna, no. You should give that honor to Spencer." She coughed. "Although, um, I didn't see her on the guest list. Was that a mistake?"

Hanna fiddled with Mike's lacrosse bracelet on her wrist. *No, it's because she refused to come.* She knew how hurt Spencer had been when she saw the wedding invite in Hanna's bag, and, okay, it *had* kind of been a last-minute decision to invite her. But Hanna really did want her to come—why couldn't Spencer understand that? What did she want from her? It was like there was a wall up between them that was growing taller by the day.

In a parallel universe, Aria, Emily, and Spencer would be her bridesmaids—and they'd do an awesome job. Spencer would be fantastic at organizing the table seating and keeping the caterers in line. Aria would make such adorable homemade favors for the guests. Emily would give a tearful, heartfelt speech that would bring down the house. Even though Hanna knew it wasn't possible, she'd gone ahead and ordered three sequined headbands for the girls anyway, as if they really were her bridesmaids. They'd be the perfect accessory for the Vera Wang bridesmaids dresses Hanna had picked out—though not bought, she wasn't *that* crazy. And when the headbands had arrived that morning, Hanna had gotten such an overwhelming wave of sadness she'd had to splash her face with cold water. The worst was seeing the headband she'd picked out for Emily among the others. It had a sequined butterfly on it, and was a shiny blue that would have matched Emily's coloring perfectly.

Hanna realized she'd never answered Kate's question, but they were now pulling up to the courthouse, so she just said that she had to go and hung up. After they parked, Hanna and her mother had to fight through an onslaught of reporters, microphones, and cameras to the main entrance. A man caught her eye as she pushed through the doors to the courtroom. Hanna looked away fast. It was Ali's father. He'd attended the proceedings religiously, sitting quietly in the back. She wondered if he reported on the proceedings to his wife every evening. Told her how the state was totally going to win this case. Assured her that justice would be done. She remembered, suddenly, something Emily had said in Cape May, when she'd found out

Mrs. D wasn't attending the trial—that a mother would definitely be there unless she had at least a hunch her daughter *wasn't* dead. Then again, maybe Mrs. D just hated them as much as everybody else in America did—in the world, really.

Soon Hanna was sitting at her regular post next to Rubens, inhaling his sickly sweet cologne. He grunted a hello to her, and she grunted back. Hanna was still pissed at him for suggesting the plea bargain idea the other day. Then again, maybe Rubens was pissed at her and Spencer for not taking him up on it.

Rubens turned to Hanna, and then Spencer, who'd taken her seat on his other side. "I have some news. First of all, I just got word that Aria Montgomery has been found."

Hanna's heart went still. "I-is she okay?"

"Where was she?" Spencer asked.

"Outside Brussels. The police are bringing them back now. She won't make it to the rest of the trial except for the jury sentencing."

"Wait, you said *them*," Hanna said. "Was someone *with* Aria?"

"Her boyfriend, I believe." Rubens glanced at his phone. "They're bringing him back, too."

Hanna clapped a hand over her mouth. *Noel* had followed Aria to Europe? She swore Mike had told her he'd gone to his parents' house in Colorado. She wondered what Mike thought about this, and swiveled around to the back of the courtroom to look for him. But Mike wasn't in his normal seat.

"Second thing," Rubens said. "The prosecution is indeed calling a surprise witness."

"Ali?" Hanna blurted out before she could think.

Spencer snorted. Rubens shook his head. "No, of course not. Nick Maxwell."

All sound died away. Hanna suddenly felt numb. "W-what does that mean?"

Spencer looked excited. "This could be good. Nick hates Ali. What he said in that news article proved it. He could dispute everything in that journal."

Rubens made a sour face. "He's the prosecution's witness, though, which means he isn't going to say anything disparaging about that journal. The prosecution probably cut him a deal to change his story."

Hanna gasped. "They can *do* that?"

"That's not fair!" Spencer said at the same time.

Rubens uncapped his bottled water and took a long swig. "I never said the law was fair. But don't worry. I've got an idea."

Spencer wrinkled her nose. "*You*, an idea?" she said under her breath.

Hanna shot her a smile. She'd been thinking the same thing. Spencer glanced at her for a moment, almost like the ice was about to crack, but then looked away.

Judge Pierrot emerged from his chambers and settled down on his bench. The jury filed in as well, and the bailiff went through his usual spiel of everyone rising and blah, blah, blah. Then Nicholas Maxwell was called to the witness stand.

The back doors flew open, and two guards walked Nick, who was still in his orange prison jumpsuit and ankle and wrist chains, to the front of the room. His head was down, but Hanna still caught him shooting a conspiratorial smile in Reginald's direction. She balled up her fist. They *did* have a deal. What was Nick going to say?

"Mr. Maxwell," Reginald said, strutting up to the witness stand once Nick had been sworn in. "According to some sources, you've done some terrible things. Is that right?"

Nick shrugged. "I guess."

"Alison DiLaurentis wrote that you coerced her into murdering a lot of people. That it was *your* idea to kill her sister, Courtney. Your idea to kill Ian Thomas and Jenna Cavanaugh and set fire to the Hastings's property. That you beat her and manipulated her and basically made her your captor. Is that true?"

Nick stared at his shackled feet. A muscle in his jaw twitched. "Yeah," he finally grunted.

Hanna shut her eyes. *Unbelievable.* She nudged Rubens. "He wasn't saying that in prison the other day."

"So basically, you and Alison weren't having a love affair, as Ms. Hastings, Ms. Marin, and the other girls purported," the DA said. "You were torturing her. Keeping her alive and making her help you."

Nick nodded almost imperceptibly. Hanna clamped down on Rubens's wrist, but he shook her off. It *wasn't. Freaking. Fair.*

"And so what she wrote in that journal—that's all true?"

"The stuff about me is," Nick mumbled.

"Even though you told the press it wasn't?"

He nodded. "I was just upset. And surprised she'd expose that stuff. That's all."

"And so we can surmise, perhaps, that everything *else* in the journal is true, too?"

Nick's gaze flicked out into the courtroom, landing on Hanna. He snickered.

Reginald sauntered over to the jury. "And so if Alison had, say, begged Ms. Hastings, Ms. Marin, Ms. Montgomery, and Ms. Fields for mercy, telling them that she was innocent and that they shouldn't hurt her because she was a pawn in your game, that wouldn't have been a lie, either?"

"Nope," Nick drawled. "Alison wanted to reunite with them. She begged me again and again not to hurt them."

"Oh my *God*," Spencer hissed.

The district attorney seemed to notice this, but then he turned back to Nick. "What can you tell me about these four girls? You know them quite well, so I've heard."

Rubens shot up. "Objection!" he cried. "This man is a murderer, and he's admitted himself that he's manipulative. He can't serve as a character witness."

But the judge looked intrigued. "You can continue, Mr. Reginald."

All eyes turned to Nick again. He shrugged and glanced at Hanna and Spencer. "They want what they want," he said simply. "Whether that's to get the perfect grades at any cost. Whether it's to place the blame on someone else so they can get off scot-free. Whether it's to cover up their dirty secrets. All they care about is protecting themselves—*and* getting revenge on Alison. I got a long, hard look at their faces the day I trapped them in the basement. They weren't angry at me—not really. They were angry at *her.*"

"And what do you think they would have wanted to do to her, if they found her again?"

Nick didn't take a moment to ponder the question. "Kill her. No doubt."

Reginald turned. "No further questions."

There was a shuffling in the crowd. Hanna placed her hands over her face, too humiliated to even look around. She felt Rubens rise from his seat, but it only made her heart plummet lower. What on earth was he going to ask Nick?

Rubens walked up to the witness stand and looked at Nick. "So you're admitting that Alison was your slave and not your girlfriend."

Nick didn't make eye contact. "Uh huh."

"Are you sure about that?"

He scowled. "I just said I was."

"So what you told the police at first—that you and Alison worked together—that was a lie, huh?"

"Uh, *yeah*," Nick said, rolling his eyes.

"And what really happened was that you brainwashed Ali, right? Forced her into helping her kill her sister? And when she was let out of The Preserve again, you got to her and made her torture the girls, help to kill Ian Thomas, et cetera?"

Nick glanced into the courtroom at the DA, then shrugged yes. Hanna chewed on the inside of her cheek, wondering where Rubens was going with this. Reginald had already asked these questions.

"So you didn't love Alison at *all*?" Rubens asked. "You didn't do all you could for her? As in, hire a private nurse to take care of her burns after the fire in the Poconos, paying for it with your own personal funds?"

A tiny muscle twitched by Nick's eye.

"I know what burn victims look like, and I did see the surveillance video of Alison at that mini-mart," Rubens said. "It was clear she had scars on her face, but they looked like they'd been treated. Do you know what burns look like when they aren't properly cared for? It's not pretty."

The DA banged on the desk. "Mr. Maxwell hired that nurse to keep Alison alive so she could help him. It had nothing to do with love."

"That could be true." Rubens pressed a finger to his lip thoughtfully. "But then I got to thinking about the pictures of Alison the police found in the basement in Rosewood." He walked over to the TV monitor and flipped through the various digital evidence files, which included some shots of the Ali shrine Nick had set up. "Most of these are pictures of Alison from before the Poconos fire." He pointed at the one of Ali at the press conference her parents had held after she'd been let out of The Preserve, then at another of Ali at the Valentine's dance on the night she'd tried to kill them. "And there are even some pictures of *Courtney*, from when the girls knew her." He gestured to the right side of the screen, where there were pictures of seventh-grade Courtney with Hanna and the others. "There are also pictures of Alison before Courtney made the switch and before the girls befriended her. But then I noticed this one."

He pointed to a picture in the upper-left-hand corner. It showed only Ali's smiling eyes, the rest of her face hidden by a blanket. "The shape of her brow is a little different, and her hair is a bit darker. I asked the police to run some forensic evidence on the print, and they told me it was done on a machine at a pharmacy sometime in the last year." He stared at Nick hard. "You used a current picture of Ali, after the Poconos fire. From when she was with *you*."

Nick blinked. Again, he glanced at DA in the audience. "Maybe . . . ," he admitted.

"Look at her eyes." Rubens stretched his fingers to blow up the image. "How does she look to you?"

"She's . . . I don't know. Smiling, I guess," Nick admitted.

"Smiling." Rubens looked at the audience. "A genuine smile, I'd say. A loving smile, even. A smile that said she knew exactly what she was doing. *Not*, in other words, the grimace of a girl who was being tormented."

"Objection!" Reginald bellowed. "This is conjecture!"

But a smile began to stretch across Hanna's face. She hadn't noticed that picture of Current Ali in the shrine. But Rubens had a point—and a good one.

"And let's talk about that letter that was slipped under the door in the Poconos house," Rubens went on. "You said you wrote it, yes?"

Nick nodded. "I wrote it as Alison, to the girls."

"And this was with Alison totally objecting every step of the way, right? Just like she says in her journal?"

"Uh huh." Beads of sweat appeared on Nick's brow. Hanna's heart beat faster and faster.

"As you know, the police found that letter outside the house in the Poconos, the night of the fire," Rubens said. The letter had been a key piece of evidence in *Nick's* trial. Rubens walked over to the laptop, pressed a button, and there was the letter, suddenly, on a big projection screen. "I won't ask you to read the whole thing, ladies and gentlemen of the jury, since you're all familiar with it, but it explains what really happened the day Alison's sister switched places with her. It mentions things like the wishing well Courtney drew on the time capsule flag, and how Courtney stole Alison's 'A-for-Alison' ring. You wrote those things, yes, Mr. Maxwell?"

Nick shrugged. "They're there in print."

"I'm just wondering how you knew such specific details," Rubens said to Nick. "Did Alison tell you willingly?"

"Wait!" The DA stood up. His mouth hung open. He didn't say anything. He kind of looked bamboozled.

For the first time since the trial began, Hanna looked at Spencer and met her gaze. Spencer's eyebrows shot up. It was like a tiny glimmer of sunlight had entered the courtroom. Nick wiped his hand across his forehead. "Uh, no?" He seemed uncertain, like he no longer knew the script he was supposed to follow. "I-I forced it out of her?"

"Ah." Rubens placed his hands on his hips. "Of course. But, Mr. Maxwell, if Alison truly wasn't the one to blame in these murders, if Alison was looking for a sure way to prove to these girls that *she* wasn't the enemy, wouldn't she have fed you some incorrect details instead?"

Nick blinked. "Huh?" he said softly.

Reginald stood up again from his seat, but he didn't say anything, just stared.

"It wasn't like you'd know if the details were true or not," Rubens said. "And if Alison was smart—which she is—she would have given incorrect details, so that when the girls read the letter in that bedroom in the Poconos, they would have thought, *Huh. This isn't Ali.* They would have been scared, of course—they were locked inside the house, a match had been lit—but they might have wondered what was exactly at play."

"Maybe Alison *isn't* that smart," Nick said, but he sounded unconvinced.

Rubens shrugged. "Clearly the two of you didn't bank on the girls surviving and explaining what the letter said at all. But they did, and it seems to me that by Alison giving you specific and accurate details, she could be seen as your co-conspirator, not your captive. Now, tell the truth. Alison willingly fed you that information for the letter. But she did so because she wanted the girls to know the whole, awful truth. She asked you to write it, though, so your prints would be on it if it was found. I bet she praised you for your writing, didn't she? Made you think *you* were better suited to write such a letter, that you had a better way with words."

Nick licked his lips. "How did you know that?" he whispered.

"Objection!" Reginald said, shooting up. But then he just stared at Nick, furious.

"I'll keep you just a minute longer," Rubens said. "My last question is about Ms. Marin, Ms. Hastings, and the others' visit to you in prison last week." He smiled. "I'm assuming you had a nice talk?"

"Not really," Nick spat.

"It's funny, though, that they turned up in Cape May, New Jersey, the day after their visit. It's also funny that your grandmother, Betty Maxwell, has a vacation home there."

"Lots of people have vacation homes in Cape May," the DA called out from his seat.

"That's true." Rubens looked at Nick. "Very, very true. But I had some guys do some snooping, and do you know what they found? A witness who can put Ms. Hastings and the other girls at that beach house that day." He went to the screen and clicked on a new file. Up popped a picture of Hanna, Spencer, Emily, and Aria standing in front of the beach house they'd raided, hugging. Hanna's heart lurched—she hoped this wouldn't get them in even more trouble. But by the look on Rubens's face, maybe that wasn't where he was going.

"That doesn't seem like a coincidence, does it?" he said. "And strange—when I questioned the guard at your prison who escorted you out of the room after you spoke to the girls, he said you mentioned your grandmother Betty to them—*and* Cape May. Now, why would you do that?"

Nick's lip quivered. "I—"

"Can I offer a theory?" Rubens suggested, lacing his hands together. "I think you wanted them to go to that beach house because you can't be sure Alison's really dead. And you're furious that she pinned all of her crimes on you—*you* loved her, *you* thought you two were bound for life. You thought the girls might find her there. And you wanted them to bring her in once and for all."

"That's not true," Nick said.

"Why else would you have hinted that your grand-mother has a house there?" Rubens raised his hands in the air. "Surely you weren't offering the place so the girls could get some R & R. Will you honestly sit up here and tell me that you really and truly think Alison is dead? In front of all these people, after swearing on the Bible, with the risk of perjury on your record, you want to tell me that you really and truly believe Alison isn't alive?"

There was a deathly hush in the courtroom. Hanna peeked at Reginald. His face was pale, his mouth slack. Nick ran his hands down his face, his eyes darting back and forth. Finally, the judge shifted. "Answer the question," he demanded.

"I-I don't know." Nick's voice cracked. "She *could* be out there. I mean, probably not, but . . ."

"But she *could*." Rubens looked at the jury, his expression triumphant. "She could. And that's because Alison is the mastermind here, not Nicholas. He was a pawn in her game, not the other way around. And may I remind all of you that we are convicting Ms. Hastings and Ms. Marin—and Ms. Montgomery, when she returns—based on one hundred percent certainty that they not only *killed* Alison, but that Alison is indeed dead. And maybe, just maybe, she's not. She's been presumed dead before, after all—after the Poconos, when Nick *himself* saved her. She knows how to lie low. She knows how to evade the law. It's not unthinkable that she's doing the same thing here."

Then, dropping his hands to his sides, he looked wearily at the judge. "No further questions, your honor."

"That's the last witness," the judge said. "After closing statements, the jury will deliberate. We'll recess for one hour."

Instantly the courtroom started buzzing. The guard grabbed Nick and led him back down the aisle, but not before he shot the DA a trapped, scared glance. Rubens strode out of the courtroom, too, looking almost giddy. Hanna turned to Spencer again. Her old friend glanced at Hanna cagily, then gave her the tiniest of smiles.

Hanna smiled back just before Spencer turned away. Just like Nick's testimony, it wasn't much—just the tip of the iceberg. But at least it was something.

21

ONE LAST HURRAH

On Friday night, Spencer sat in the kitchen, helping Melissa go through bags and bags of stuff she'd purchased from Buy Buy Baby. There must have been at least fifteen tiny, neutral-colored onesies in the pile. "Now, I've heard that babies are really sensitive to dyes, so you have to wash all their clothes first," Melissa murmured, pulling out a huge bottle of Honest Company organic detergent.

"I'll be on wash duty," Spencer volunteered. Then she laughed—the baby wasn't coming for seven more months, so it seemed silly to wash all the clothes now. On the other hand, she might not be around in seven months to help. If Angela made her disappear, she wouldn't be here for the birth. She wouldn't get to meet the baby . . . *ever.*

She gathered up the onesies and began to remove their tags, trying to push the thought down deep.

"So," Melissa said as she pulled out several different

brands of bottles. "The trial was kind of encouraging today, huh?"

Spencer nodded, too afraid to speak. Everyone was abuzz about how Rubens had cross-examined Nick that day. Some reporters were saying it was a major turning point in the case, but still others continued to be focused on Reginald's version of the facts and all of the character-assassinating things Spencer and the others had done in the past few years.

The whole thing made Spencer feel jittery. She wanted to hold on to hope, but maybe that was foolish. Maybe it was better to stick with her original plan: Get the hell out of here before the final verdict was passed down.

"And I heard about Aria, too," Melissa added.

Spencer ran her fingers along a beige-and-white-striped romper. Aria's plane had landed at the Philly airport about an hour ago. A TV camera had tried to catch Aria disembarking, but a police escort had held his hand toward the screen, shielding her.

"I wish they'd never found her," Spencer said softly. It was weird: When Aria had first taken off, Spencer had been so annoyed—that Aria had accomplished what *she'd* wanted to do, but also that she'd left them to handle the trial alone. But as the week progressed, her anger had given way to acceptance. Maybe one of them deserved freedom. It was scary to imagine what Aria had been through overseas—*and* what Aria might face now that she was back. The news was that she'd receive double the sentence because she'd run off.

The side door opened, and Mrs. Hastings burst through carrying a bunch of grocery bags in her hands. Spencer rushed over to help, but her mother brushed her off. "I'm fine," she snapped, giving Spencer a strange look.

Spencer recoiled. Her mother was still staring at her. "What?" Spencer finally asked.

Mrs. Hastings dropped a bag on the kitchen table. "Perhaps you can explain why Wren Kim is in the driveway, asking for you?" Spencer's mouth dropped open. She and Wren hadn't made plans, though it was kind of exciting that he was here. Then again, her mom looked so furious. "You're not supposed to leave the house," Mrs. Hastings added. "Especially not with *him*."

"Mom," Melissa said softly from the island. "Let Spencer go. It's not going to hurt anything. Let her have some fun—hasn't she been through enough?"

Both Spencer and Mrs. Hastings whirled around and stared at Melissa. Spencer wanted to run over and give her a huge hug. After a beat, Mrs. Hastings sighed and began jerkily removing the groceries. "Fine," she spat. "If *that's* how you'd like to spend your last few days, be my guest."

Spencer bit the inside of her cheek. *Thanks for the vote of confidence, Mom.* It sounded like she was pretty sure Spencer was headed to jail.

She ran a tube of lipstick over her lips, smoothed

her button-down, and hurried out the front door. Sure enough, Wren was standing on the front porch, hands shoved into his pockets. His whole face lit up when he saw her, and Spencer felt her insides sparkle. Wren's dark hair was pushed off his face, his sharp cheekbones were especially prominent, and his trim body looked good in a vintage-style corduroy jacket and narrow-cut jeans. All of the feelings of attraction that she'd been trying to suppress suddenly let loose inside her. She wanted him. She really did. And what was amazing was that she could have him.

"Hey," he said shyly, holding out a bouquet of lilies.

"H-hi," she answered back, taking the flowers and hugging them to her chest.

Wren's throat bobbed as he swallowed. "I was hoping to take you somewhere tonight. For dinner, maybe?" He looked around. "Somewhere *off* the property? But, um, I wasn't sure if I should come inside." He made a face. "Your mom seemed kind of angry."

Spencer rolled her eyes. "She'll be fine. Let's get out of here," she agreed, grabbing her purse. But as he took her arm and led her to his car, her spirits suddenly plunged. *Saturday night, 10 PM sharp*, Angela had told her. That was . . . *tomorrow.* In twenty-four hours, she'd never see Wren again.

She decided not to think about it.

As they swung into Wren's car, she turned to him and

smiled. "You know, there are a few things I wouldn't mind doing this evening, if you're game."

He looked at her and grinned. "I'm up for anything," he answered. "As long as it's with you."

And off they went.

Two hours later, Spencer had a new pair of shoes from a shopping spree on Walnut Street, felt much more relaxed from the ten-minute neck massage she'd gotten from one of the Chinese women on the sidewalk in Rittenhouse Square, and was delightfully full after an impromptu cheese-tasting session at a small tapas bar on 19th Street. It was the most spontaneous she'd behaved in, well, maybe *ever*, and it felt good to shed that old Spencer Hastings attitude and embrace someone much more lighthearted, at least for one more day.

After a few more whirlwind stops wherever struck her fancy, she and Wren were walking hand-in-hand, her shopping bag swinging at her side, along Chestnut Street toward downtown. Suddenly, she spied something in the distance and squeezed his hand. "Let's go for a carriage ride!"

Wren looked at her, seeming startled. "*You* want to go for a carriage ride? As I recall, you told me once that you thought they were cheesy and inhumane."

Spencer frowned, vaguely remembering telling Wren that during one of their torrid make-out fests when she'd snuck into the city to be with him in the beginning of junior year. Well, that was the old Spencer. "Come on," she said, grabbing his hand and dragging him to the line of horses and buggies on the square.

After Wren handed over forty bucks to a man in a top hat, tails, and Benjamin Franklin–style wire-rimmed glasses, the two of them climbed into the backseat of the carriage and snuggled under the provided flannel blanket, which smelled a teensy bit like manure. Spencer looked at Wren and smiled. "Isn't this fun?"

"Sure," Wren said. "Then again, anything's fun with you."

He pulled her closer, and Spencer sighed happily. The whole night, they'd found excuses to touch each other—playful little hand grabs, feet brushes under the table, a knee squeeze. She leaned in to kiss him, but suddenly Wren placed his hand on her shoulder, gently pushing her back.

"Whoa, Spencer," he said, his British accent especially lilting. "We don't have to rush things. Can we be serious for a minute?"

She cocked her head. "We've been serious all night."

He raised an eyebrow. "We've been spontaneous all night. Which is, forgive me for saying this, not exactly the type-A Spencer Hastings I know. You've seemed . . . speedy. Like we're rushing from activity to activity so you don't have to think about anything."

"No, I haven't," Spencer answered automatically, though Wren was pretty much right on the mark.

His gaze fell to the leather bag he was carrying. "I have something for you."

He pushed a brown-paper–wrapped object into her hands. Spencer frowned and opened it. Inside was a copy of Nelson Mandela's memoir from prison.

"What's this for?" she asked, looking up at him.

Wren's Adam's apple wobbled. "I thought it might help if . . . you know. If you do have to go to prison. If justice isn't done. You are allowed to bring books into prison. I mean, the guard will check through it, but it's clean."

Spencer riffled the pages between her fingers. "Oh. Well, thank you."

Wren cleared his throat. "You've hardly talked about the trial with me—or what might happen. But I want you to know that you can."

Spencer was grateful that the horse-drawn carriage was passing through a particularly dark section of the square so Wren couldn't see her conflicted expression. "I'm trying not to think about the trial," she admitted.

"I know," he said gently. "But maybe you *should* think about it. And we should think about how we can see each other. I'll visit you, you know—if it comes to that. And we can have phone calls, and—"

Spencer crossed her arms over her chest. "I don't want to talk about any of that."

Wren frowned. "I'm going to be there for you, Spencer. This isn't some random little fling for me. The more I talk to you, the more I spend time with you—I know it's crazy, but well, I'm crazy about *you*, Spencer. I want to try this out, for real. See where it leads."

A lump formed in her throat. *I'm crazy about you.* The thing was, she realized, she wanted to try this out, too.

But she knew exactly where it would lead. She was disappearing the next day. Cutting off all ties. She suddenly understood what Angela had meant, when she said that some people chose prison over disappearing because they couldn't let go of their families and loved ones. If she disappeared, everyone in her life would essentially be dead.

But she couldn't think about that now. She turned to Wren and shook her finger. "You're ruining the romantic moment. Now let's sit back, look at the stars, and breathe in the horse poop, shall we?"

Wren's eyes shone under a passing street lamp. He looked so dissatisfied. "Is this because of what happened to us before? Is that why you're not letting me in?"

I'm not letting you in because I can't *let you in!* Spencer wanted to shout. She wanted to tear at her hair and punch the sky and scream until her lungs were raw. This was so unfair. She'd finally found a guy she liked, and now she had to say good-bye.

Suddenly Spencer was crying, her head in her hands, her body shaking with silent sobs.

"Hey, hey," Wren murmured, rubbing her back. "It's okay."

"I'm sorry," Spencer managed, between sobs. She almost laughed at the situation she was in. Of all the times during the entire trial that she could have broken down into a snotty mess, it had to be on her last night, while she was on a carriage ride with Wren.

Wren leaned forward and spoke to the driver, and the carriage stopped. "I live just a few blocks away," Wren said. "And you need some tea. Just tea," he added, before she could say anything else. Spencer sniffed, and nodded.

Wren turned to Spencer and offered his hand, and the two of them climbed off the carriage. Then he led her to his apartment building. They were silent as they strode through the lobby and to the elevator, but as soon as they got into Wren's apartment—a place that came back to her immediately from being there almost two years ago, with its cramped walls and beige-colored fridge and small TV wedged into the corner—Wren wrapped his arms around Spencer and pulled her into a hug. Her eyes still burned with tears, but she wasn't hysterical anymore. She glanced in the mirror and saw that her makeup was running and her face was red. Strangely, she didn't care.

"What kind of tea, chamomile or peppermint?" Wren asked, his brown eyes warm. "Or maybe hot chocolate instead?"

"Actually," Spencer heard herself ask, as she sank onto the couch. "Can you just sit here with me for a second?"

She leaned back on the cushions, and Wren wrapped an arm around her, pulling her close. As she curled into his body, her eyes teared up again. She felt so safe with him.

It scared her that she might never feel this safe again.

22

A SOBER RETURN

On Friday evening, long after the sun had set, two police officers greeted Aria at customs at the Philadelphia airport. They offered a gruff thank-you to the air marshal who'd escorted her on the plane from Brussels to Philly—who had smelled sweaty, smacked his lips when he ate the meal they'd served on the plane, and even accompanied her to the aircraft's tiny bathroom, waiting outside while she peed.

The cops took Aria by the arms and dragged her toward baggage claim. The handcuffs she had been wearing for ten hours had rubbed her wrists raw. Her head swam with fatigue, and she felt sticky, dirty, and sick. As she walked past the sparsely populated security lines, all the guards looked up and stared at her. As they passed a dead McDonald's and a few gift shops, the workers gaped. They rode down an escalator in silence, listening to Frank Sinatra on the PA system. But suddenly, at baggage claim, tons of people swam into view. Flashbulbs popped. Everyone started to shout. "Miss Montgomery!"

the reporters clamored, rushing for her.

Aria shaded her eyes, wishing she'd been better prepared. Of course reporters were going to be here. She was the biggest story on the eastern seaboard.

"Miss Montgomery!" more reporters roared. "Did you think you were going to get away with it?"

"Does this mean you're guilty?" someone screamed.

The reporters were screaming at someone else, too— and that was when Aria caught sight of Noel coming down the escalator behind her. He'd been on the same plane as Aria, though in another section, with his own air marshal. For the first half of the trip, Aria had been angry with him, but soon enough that had given way to deep regret. How was Noel supposed to know someone was *actually* watching them? And why on earth had she spouted all that ridiculous stuff about Ali? He probably hated her now.

"Mr. Kahn, why did you follow your girlfriend to Europe when you knew it was a crime?" someone shouted.

"Are you two in cahoots?" another reporter asked him. "Did you help kill Alison?"

"Out of our way," one of Aria's agents grunted, pushing aside some of the reporters and photographers.

Aria's gaze was still on Noel. He had his head down and his hoodie pulled tight. They were snapping his picture all the same. It would be everywhere. If only he'd never come to Europe. Aria had ruined his life.

"Aria!" cried a familiar voice.

Aria looked up. Her mother was elbowing through the crowd. Ella's eyes were red, and her face was blotchy, and she was wearing a pair of army shorts and Mike's Rosewood Day lacrosse sweatshirt—as if she'd had no time and these were the first things she'd found to throw on. Byron stood with her, too, looking stiff and embarrassed.

Ella grabbed Aria's shoulders. "We were so worried," she blurted, and then burst into tears.

"What were you *thinking*?" Byron called out behind her.

"Mrs. Montgomery, Mr. Montgomery." Aria's police escort held out his hand to keep them at arm's length. "We told you we'd bring Miss Montgomery home, and we'd meet you there." Aria had been granted permission to remain in her house this weekend, though under strict lockdown and constant supervision by her parents. It was a huge win, apparently orchestrated by Seth Rubens—normally, Aria would have been sent straight to prison after pulling such a stunt, but her family had paid bail. Aria asked if Noel had been given the same privilege, but the officers hadn't given anything away.

Ella gave the officer a strange look. "I wasn't just going to sit at home, *waiting*." She walked alongside Aria and out the double doors to the sidewalk. "Do you realize what you've done?"

"I'm sorry," Aria said, feeling her eyes fill with tears.

"Sorry isn't going to cut it," Byron said sadly, shaking his head. "Sorry doesn't matter to the judge."

Aria ducked her head as the officers pushed her into a waiting car, tumbling onto the smelly, faux-leather backseat. An officer checked her cuffs. A second officer strapped her in, then swung into the front seat, which was visible through a set of heavy bars. The reporters rushed the car, still screaming questions and snapping pictures. Aria could only imagine what sort of caption would accompany her pasty, bloated, tear-stained face on tomorrow's front page. She glanced out the window past the reporters, toward her grieving parents on the curb. There was a tug in her heart so painful she let out another sob. They looked destroyed.

She could just add them to the list of people whose lives she'd ruined.

"There's milk in the fridge," Ella said woodenly as Aria stumbled down to breakfast the next morning. Ella was sitting at the table in a dressing gown and a pair of embroidered silk slippers. Her gaze was on the *New York Times* Saturday crossword puzzle, though she hadn't filled in any of the squares. Several cereal boxes were also on the table, along with a bowl of fruit, a carton of orange juice, and a coffee carafe. Mike sat there as well, tapping incessantly on his phone.

"Okay," Aria mumbled, not sure if she should sit down with them or scuttle back up to her room with her breakfast. She wasn't in the mood to eat. Half the night she'd heard her mother sobbing. Byron had stayed, too, and

Aria had even heard *him* crying—and her dad hadn't cried even when an Icelandic pony trampled him in Reykjavík and broke three of his toes.

She poured a very small bowl of Weetabix and sat at the island on the very edge of the stool. Her new ankle bracelet clanked against the metal leg, and Mike winced, as though she'd just scraped her nails down a chalkboard.

"Sorry," Aria mumbled, hunching her shoulders. Needless to say, the cops had slapped the thing on her when they'd pulled into the Montgomerys' driveway last night—*and* they took her passport, fake passport, driver's license, Rosewood Day ID, cell phone, and anything else that could connect her to the outside world.

Ella scraped back her chair and looked at Mike. "So we have to pick up your tux in an hour, and then you're due at Chanticleer at noon. Dad's picking up Grandma at the airport, and I'm going to have to scramble around because Aunt Lucy is coming in from Chicago. So take the Subaru, okay?"

"Sure," Mike answered.

Ella nodded, then touched her face. "*And* I need to figure out how I'm going to fix my puffy eyes before tonight." She left the room quickly, her dressing gown trailing behind her.

Aria looked at her brother. "Your wedding's today. I forgot."

Mike sniffed. "Yeah, I guess *you've* been too wrapped up in yourself."

Aria hung her head. "I'm sorry." Fresh tears spilled down her cheeks.

The only sounds were Mike crunching his cereal and Aria's small, pathetic sniffs. Finally, Mike sighed. "So are you going to come?"

Aria flinched. A long beat passed. "You don't want me there," Aria answered.

Mike shrugged. "Get over yourself. You're still my sister. Hanna would probably like to see you, too."

Aria swallowed hard. Hanna probably hated her for disappearing and leaving her the burden of dealing with the trial on her own. Besides, things felt too tarnished after Emily, too damaged. Could they really be friends again, after all they'd been through?

She took a tiny bite of cereal. "I don't know."

"Come on. There will be Hooters girls."

Aria stared at him. "Hanna's letting you have Hooters girls at her *wedding*?"

"It's one of the reasons I'm marrying her."

Aria wanted to laugh, but she still felt too numb. "I'll think about it," she said.

Mike rolled his eyes. "You should be thrilled I'm inviting you. I'm pretty pissed, you know."

She peeked at him. "Because I got Noel in trouble?"

He stared at her crazily. "That's that dude's own fault. No, I'm mad because, one, no one has really *slept* since you took off. Pretty uncool, Aria. And two, because you went to Amsterdam without me—*again*! How many times have I told you that the next time you go, *you bring me with you?*"

He slammed his coffee cup into the sink, let out a groan, and stomped up the stairs. Aria watched him go, swirling her spoon in her cereal bowl again and again. *Huh.*

Then, she looked down at herself. Of course she should go to her brother's wedding—as long as she was with her parents, it was probably allowed. Suddenly, something struck her. Noel would probably be invited, too. Would the police let him attend? Maybe they'd get to talk. Maybe she could apologize. Beg for his forgiveness. Tell him that if she could serve his sentence for him, she would.

It was a tiny, shiny ray of hope. Aria might have to go off to prison for the rest of her life, but she would make things right with him before she did. Or else she would die trying.

23

I DO!

At T-minus thirty minutes until the big moment when Hanna walked down the aisle, Hanna, her mother, and Ramona stood in a dressing room at the Chanticleer mansion. Ramona held a tiny pair of nail scissors aloft. "Once you get this dress on, I don't want you sitting down," she instructed. "It'll wrinkle, and that's the biggest faux pas for any starlet on the red carpet—*and* any bride, for that matter. And since you're going to be both, you're just going to have to stand up for the rest of the day."

"Got it," Hanna answered obediently, pushing the Hollywood waves her stylist had created in her just-highlighted auburn hair over her shoulders. She looked at herself in the mirror and pursed her deep red lips and fluttered her eyelashes, which had just been fitted with extensions. She was probably the best-looking almost-criminal in the history of girls who were about to go to prison.

Not that she was dwelling much on that. Or the fact

that closing statements had been made and that the jury was now at the Rosewood Holiday Inn, deliberating her fate. Her wedding was today, and she was going to *enjoy* it, damn it. Even though she'd had only a week to plan, absolutely everything had come together. The weather was perfect for an outdoor ceremony, and the lines of chairs on either side of the aisle were decorated in fresh white roses. The rabbi her mother had found was young and tall and almost cute—well, for a rabbi, anyway—and the girls Hooters had sent to cater the wings and other Hooters stuff weren't the skankiest Hanna had ever seen. *Us Weekly* reps had already arrived to set up the red carpet in the grand hall. Hailey Blake had texted her several times asking if she could bring a few more famous actors and models as plus-ones. The cocktail-hour food looked delicious, and every waiter who would be passing out the canapés was more model-perfect than the last. The reception-room tables were exquisitely set with the most beautiful, silver-patterned china Hanna had ever seen. Ramona had booked the best fireworks company in Philadelphia to set off a serious display during the reception, and #HannaMarinWedding had been tweeted 981 times in the past three hours. Hanna was pumped and ready.

Ms. Marin, who looked stunning in an off-white Chanel shift, began to take Hanna's dress out of the plastic. Slowly and carefully, she slid it over Hanna's head and started to spread out the folds and fluff the train.

"Hanna," she breathed. "It's even more beautiful than I remembered."

Tingles traveled up Hanna's spine as she beheld her reflection in the mirror. The dress made her skin look rosy and her waist minuscule. The jeweled beading on the bodice sparkled in the light.

"It's fine," Ramona barked—which, Hanna realized, was as close to a compliment as she would get. Then she hurried out of the room, murmuring something about checking in on the flowers.

Hanna turned to her mother, who was dabbing her eyes in the back of the room. "So," she said, taking a deep breath. "Are you ready to walk me down the aisle?"

Ms. Marin nodded, her lips pressed tightly together. Maybe to keep from crying.

Hanna felt her eyes well up, too. "Thanks for being so cool through all this," she said. "I know it's sort of . . . unprecedented. And that I'm young. And that—"

"It's fine," Ms. Marin interrupted, rushing toward her and touching her bare shoulders. "It makes you happy. That's all I want to see. That's all I've *ever* wanted to see." She held Hanna's arms and looked her up and down. "Remember when we used to play wedding when you were little? I'd let you wear my slips?"

Hanna's lips parted. She'd forgotten that she and her mom had done that together—so many of her memories involved her dad and his special attention. But all of a sudden, she remembered her mom helping her pull the lacy slip over her head and putting ringlets in her hair. It made her feel sad that the memory had gone unacknowledged for so long. Or that Hanna had written off her mom for so long—maybe she shouldn't have.

Then a knock came at the door, and Hanna's head whipped up. Ms. Marin frowned. "Who could that be?"

"Maybe Ramona again?" Hanna murmured, leaping up to answer it. Hanna's vision adjusted as a tall figure walked into the small space. It was her dad.

"Oh," Ms. Marin said tightly.

Mr. Marin was dressed in a conservative black suit and a red tie. When he saw her, his face crumpled and his eyes went soft. "Oh, Hanna," he gushed. "My baby. You look beautiful."

Hanna turned away from him, instantly annoyed. "What part of *don't come* did you not understand?" she spat.

Mr. Marin crossed his arms over his chest. "Hanna. I know I've disappointed you in too many ways. And I know I've put myself first way too many times. I haven't been a father to you, and I'll never make that up to you, and you have a right to hate me forever. But please let me be here. Please let me see you get married. I want to walk you down the aisle."

"Uh, that job's already taken," Ms. Marin piped up. She placed a hand on Hanna's arm. "Do you want him to leave, honey?"

Hanna gritted her teeth. Her dad had done this *so many*

times. And so many times she'd forgiven him, only to be jilted again. But this time, she didn't feel the same pull to please him. All at once, she realized: Their relationship had changed. Her dad would never have the same place in Hanna's life as he had before. He'd lost that privilege for good.

At the same time, just seeing him standing there, that hangdog expression on his face, his hands pushed pathetically into his suit pants pockets, she felt something approaching pity. Maybe she should just give him this. Be the bigger person.

She let out a breath. "You can stay," she decided. "But Mom's right—*she's* walking me down the aisle. And that's final."

"Okay, okay. But thank you for letting me stay." Mr. Marin lurched forward to hug Hanna, and she obliged him, though she held him at arm's length so as not to wrinkle her dress. Out of the corner of her eye, she caught her mom rolling her eyes.

Then Ramona popped her head in again. "They're ready for you, Hanna."

Hanna felt a spike of nerves. She turned back to the mirror and smoothed down her hair, her heart suddenly going wild. She was doing this. Really marrying Mike. A huge smile stretched across her face. It was going to rock.

Her father had the good sense to slip out of the dressing room and into the crowd of guests. Hanna held tightly to

her mom's hand as Ramona led her there, her head spin-
ning. All sorts of scenarios suddenly plagued her. What if
she tripped on the grass? What if Mike wasn't under the
chuppah? Were they expected to say anything in Hebrew?
Of all the Jewish weddings she'd attended, she couldn't
remember for the life of her.

"Hanna? Oh my *God*!"

At first, Hanna thought that the two girls at the end of
the hallway were a mirage. Spencer, dressed in a goddess-
style beige dress, rushed forward, arms outstretched. Aria
followed behind her looking gorgeous in a long emerald-
green sheath. "Wow," Spencer gushed shyly. It looked
like she wanted to touch Hanna but wasn't sure that was
acceptable.

Hanna stared at her. "You came," she finally mustered.

Spencer squeezed her tight. "Of course I did, Hanna. I
wouldn't miss this."

"I'm so sorry," Hanna blurted.

"No, *I'm* sorry," Spencer said.

"And this is the *only* reason I'm glad the Feds caught
me," Aria added, worming her way into the circle.

Hanna turned to her. Aria looked tired, but otherwise
fine. "Are you okay?" she asked.

Aria shrugged. "You know. Not perfect, but whatever."

"Did Noel really go with you?" Hanna asked. "How
did *that* happen? And how did they catch you?"

Aria put a finger to her lips. "I'll explain it all later. This
is *your* time, Hanna."

Then Spencer cleared her throat. "It's been awful not talking to you, Han. I feel like such a jerk."

"It's okay," Hanna said, realizing that she should have said this days ago. "I've been a jerk, too. It's been so messed up, you know? The trial, Ali, Emily . . ."

Aria's face became pinched. "I miss her so much."

"I do, too," Spencer blubbered, erupting into fresh sobs.

"I keep *thinking* about her," Hanna exploded. "And Spence, it *wasn't* your fault. Of course it wasn't."

"Yes, it was!" Spencer pressed her hands over her eyes. "You were right, Han. I shouldn't have suggested we stay in Cape May. It's why I went into the water after her. I felt responsible."

"None of us is responsible," Aria urged. "We all loved her. We all wanted to protect her. And we thought *we* would keep her safe, all together in one hotel room. It just didn't work out that way."

Hanna pulled them in again. It felt so good to hug them. It was what they should have done at Emily's funeral. It wasn't anyone's fault. They'd all loved Emily. They'd all wanted the best for her.

Suddenly, Ramona appeared on the scene and let out a screech. "What the hell, girls?" she bellowed, inspecting Hanna's smeared makeup. She pressed the mouthpiece of her headset closer to her ear. "Is Janie still here? Get her over to the back vestibule so she can fix the bride."

The makeup artist arrived promptly and began dabbing

a foundation-filled sponge on Hanna's cheeks. Everyone moved down the corridor to where Ms. Marin was waiting to walk Hanna down the aisle. Hanna's flower girl, Morgan, waited there, too, looking like a little fairy in her white tulle dress. A cornflower-blue sash accentuated her eyes, and her long, light-brown hair had been pinned in a ballerina bun. When she saw Hanna, Morgan let out a squeal and gave her a hug. "You look so pretty!" she cried.

Hanna grinned happily at Morgan, and then turned to take her mom's arm. Spencer peeked out the door at the ceremony area on the lawn. The doors were open halfway, bringing in the bright, late-day sunshine, and Hanna could just make out the swells of the harpist Ramona had hired.

"There are tons of people here," Spencer whispered. "Including Hailey Blake and that cute guy from that new cop show."

"And Mike's already up there," Aria reported. "He looks *so* nervous. Although I don't know if it's because he's marrying you or because he's going to soon be surrounded by a ton of Hooters girls."

"You're having Hooters girls?" Spencer looked confused.

Hanna giggled. "Long story." Then she looked at her friends, suddenly realizing something. "Listen," she said. "I want you guys to be part of the wedding procession. As my bridesmaids."

Spencer and Aria exchanged an excited look. "Are you sure?" Aria asked.

"Of course I'm sure." Hanna thought about the headbands she'd bought for them, back at home. She wished she could retrieve them, but there wasn't enough time—and maybe that was okay. Instead, she grabbed two bouquets of flowers from the terra-cotta pots lining the mansion's doors, plucked a few stems from each, and wove them into the girls' hair. She placed the rest of the bouquets in their hands. "Here."

Aria looked like she was going to cry again. "This means so much, Hanna."

"I'm so glad you're doing this," Spencer whispered. "It's what Emily would have wanted."

"I think so, too," Hanna said.

The harpist broke into the opening strains of Pachelbel's Canon in D. Ramona frowned into her headset, then looked at the bridal party. "We're ready."

"Go," Hanna whispered, nudging Aria to start down the aisle. A few beats later, Ramona gestured for Spencer to go. And then it was Hanna's turn. Shaking, she grabbed her mother's elbow and took small, even steps, her head swimming. She wasn't sure she breathed until she was a few paces in, when she looked up and saw Mike in the most gorgeous tux ever, standing under the little tent, his eyes wide and his lips parted. His expression was a cross between loving adoration and the look of a horny, Hooters-loving adolescent who was dying to tear the dress off her.

Hanna breathed and laughed and maybe started crying again, overjoyed that he was there, and that he was hers. Her friends were back. Her mom was at her side. Hundreds of faces lit up as they turned and caught sight of her. Suddenly, Hanna felt a sense of overwhelming peace. Getting married before the trial verdict was delivered, no matter what the jury decided—it had been the best decision ever.

Everything, for once, was absolutely perfect.

24

DOES SHE STAY OR DOES SHE GO?

Even though Spencer wasn't normally the dance-at-weddings type, she'd spent the whole night grooving to "Shout," the "Cha Cha Slide," and the "Chicken Dance." She led a conga line around the tables, helped hoist Hanna's chair during the hora, and even sexy-danced with a Hooters girl in a cutoff tee and bright-orange boy shorts. It just felt so good to celebrate something. To forget, for a brief time, how scary her future was.

During a brief lull in the music, she sat down and took a sip from a champagne glass. The wedding had been truly spectacular—the music was amazing, the food was delicious, the Hooters girls were surprisingly well behaved, and the red-carpet photos of all the guests added a glittering touch. True, Hanna's grandmother Chelsea, who'd hastily flown in from Arizona, looked a little peeved and disapproving that Hanna was getting married so young, and Lanie Iler and Mason Byers, who'd long been a couple, had gotten into a colossal fight in the bathroom, and

Mr. and Ms. Marin had spent the whole evening more or less avoiding each other. But that was par for the course for every wedding, wasn't it? Spencer was just so happy that Hanna had a day she'd remember. And that *she* had gotten over her stupid pride and come to the wedding.

Aria sank into the seat next to her and grabbed a glass of wine from a passing tray. As she crossed her ankles, her tracking bracelet banged noisily against the chair rail. "You won't believe what I just saw in the bathroom," she said, eyes bright. "Kirsten Cullen's mom, making out with James Freed!"

"You're kidding!" Spencer made a wry face. "James always did have a MILF thing."

"Yeah, well, at least someone's getting some action tonight." Aria heaved a sigh.

Her gaze cut across the room, to where Noel Kahn, who also had a tracking bracelet on his ankle, was sitting with a bunch of guys from lacrosse. Noel looked up, perhaps sensing her, then quickly looked away again. Aria did, too.

"Do you want to talk about it?" Spencer asked quietly. Aria hadn't really gotten into what had happened in Amsterdam, though it was clear Noel was in big trouble for following her there and the two weren't exactly speaking.

Aria shook her head. "No."

It made Spencer feel melancholy that Wren wasn't there, too. Should she have invited him? She was dying to see him again. Then again, after last night—the way he'd just held her while she broke down, then drove her home sometime after midnight—she wasn't sure she could handle seeing him again. She worried that just the sight of him would make her lose all her resolve to leave.

And she had to leave—*soon*.

The big clock that hung over the second-floor balcony caught her eye. It was already 9. Her car was coming at 9:30.

"Have you seen Hanna?" she asked Aria. She gazed around the room for the only girl in a long, white gown.

Aria frowned and peered into the thick throng of guests. Almost everyone was on the dance floor, grooving to Katy Perry. "Not for a while."

There was no way Spencer was leaving without saying good-bye to Hanna. She rose and grabbed Aria's arm. "Come with me."

"Why?" Aria said, but her voice was swallowed up in the sound of the crowd. Spencer pulled her around the ballroom, her head swiveling this way and that as she searched for Hanna's lithe, elegant shape. Finally, she spotted her in the corner. Her heart broke a little as she took in Hanna's rosy cheeks, her huge smile, her expressive hands. How could she handle leaving her friends forever? What would they think of her when she didn't show up to the trial when it reconvened? Probably the way Spencer had felt when Aria hadn't shown up: kind of cheated, kind of jealous, and extremely hurt.

She hurried up to Hanna and flung her arms around her tightly. Hanna looked surprised. "Are you okay?"

"Of course I am," Spencer said in a choked voice. "I just . . . missed you guys while we weren't talking. And it just hit me all over again."

"Aw," Aria cooed in Spencer's ear, her skin smelling like the same patchouli perfume her mother wore. "I missed you guys, too."

Spencer pulled back and looked at them. "And no matter what happens, promise me you guys will be strong, okay?"

Aria's smile faded. Hanna's throat bobbed. "We'll always have each other."

"We'll be strong," Aria echoed.

Then Hanna's mom tapped Hanna's shoulder, thrusting an old relative toward her. Aria turned to Mike, distracted, too. Spencer took the opportunity to slip through a side exit, duck into the coatroom, and retrieve the bag she'd packed beforehand and brought with her so that she wouldn't have to go back into her house before Angela's car came. She rifled through it quickly, checking to make sure the jewels were all still there. Then she took one last look into the ballroom at all of the Rosewood people she'd known all her life. All the kids she'd sat next to at school. So many of the teachers she'd had, the neighbors she'd grown up around, the families she knew so well— even her own parents were here, her mom and dad being surprisingly civil.

A lump formed in her throat.

But then she turned and hurried down the stone steps toward the parking lot. There was the car service she'd arranged, chugging at the curb. She slipped inside.

As the car merged onto route 76, Spencer peered out the window wistfully, gazing at the twinkle lights on the row houses along the Schuylkill River. She'd always enjoyed that view driving out of the city. One more thing she'd never get to see again after tonight.

Her phone bleated, and she checked the caller ID. *Wren.* Spencer's finger paused over the IGNORE button, but then something made her answer.

"Spencer?" It sounded like Wren was smiling. "What are you up to?"

"Uh, nothing," Spencer said cagily, glancing out the window at the rushing traffic on 76. "Just, you know. Sitting in my bedroom."

"Would your ankle bracelet confirm that?" Wren asked. "It wouldn't say that, for example, you were at a fabulous wedding, getting your picture taken on the red carpet?"

Spencer shut her eyes. *Busted.* "I wanted to invite you," she blurted. "But it was so sudden. And I wanted tonight to be about my friends. We'd been fighting for so long, and we just made up, and–"

"It's okay," Wren cut her off. "I totally get it. You needed a night with them."

Tears suddenly filled her eyes. Wren understood her so well. He was so good at letting her be who she was. She hated that she would be leaving him.

"Now, look," Wren was saying. "Is there any way you can steal away from that fantastic wedding and hang out with me for a bit? I'll come to your house if you want. I just want to see you tonight."

Spencer checked the clock on the car's dashboard. 9:45. Only fifteen minutes until Angela. "I'm exhausted."

"I'm not taking no for an answer, okay? I'll be round in about a half hour. See you then."

"Wait!" Spencer cried, but Wren had already hung up. She pressed her hands over her face. Wren would come to the house and she wouldn't be there. What if he got suspicious? Called the police? He wouldn't do it to *tell* on her, of course . . . but out of concern. And that would risk everything. She needed this Angela thing to go off without a hitch.

But in the back of her mind, she fantasized about seeing Wren one more time. Somehow. Just once more before she went.

She'd give anything.

She only had five minutes to spare by the time she returned to her family's house. The night was warm and muggy, and her already-sweaty skin felt even stickier as she sat down on the curb to wait. Her house loomed behind her, so familiar. She'd lived here almost all her life. So many memories had been formed in the front yard, on the front porch, behind those walls. Because of all the A stuff, it felt like she'd been dwelling on the bad, but there were good memories, too. All those giggle-fest sleepovers with her friends. All the papers she'd written in her bedroom, all the plays she'd rehearsed for in the backyard, the times her dad had grilled burgers while she and Melissa wore tiaras and made crayon menus for their "restaurant." Soon, a new generation would be doing those same things here. She thought about Melissa's baby.

Spencer's thoughts returned to the little onesies Melissa had bought yesterday. After she vanished, Melissa certainly wouldn't want her to be the baby's godmother . . . Would Melissa even tell the baby about her? Or would everyone just pretend Spencer didn't exist?

Headlights appeared at the end of the road, and Spencer stood up. A black car rolled up, and the front window slowly descended. Angela's face peered out from the driver's seat. "Hand over the jewels. I'll look at them, and if they look good, you can get in."

But suddenly, Spencer found she couldn't move. All at once, there was no way she could just disappear without ever seeing Wren . . . or Hanna . . . or Aria . . . or even her family ever again.

She stepped away from the curb. "I'm sorry," she said in a small voice. "I . . . can't."

Angela stared at her. "Excuse me?"

"I . . . I changed my mind."

Angela chuckled lightly. "So you want to go to prison instead?" She rolled her eyes. "You're out of your mind."

Maybe Spencer *was* out of her mind. But there was something about reconciling with her friends today, something about all of them being *together*, that made her want to stay and face the consequences, whatever they were. It didn't seem fair that she would get to run away and start over while they had to remain here and serve out Ali's punishment. They were in this together, for better or worse. *We'll always have each other*, Hanna had said. And she was right.

And she'd have Melissa, too. And Melissa's baby.

"Suit yourself," Angela said. "So I guess I'll see you when I see you, huh?"

And then she peeled away. Spencer watched until her headlights disappeared around the corner, wondering if she'd made a huge mistake.

But she knew, deep down, that she hadn't. At least right now, she was still herself. Wren was on his way over, and she would take full advantage of every minute they had left together.

She would still get to be Spencer Hastings, the girl she'd always been, for a little while longer.

25

SO MUCH FOR A HONEYMOON

A little after 1 AM—after the fireworks display; the many toasts from Hailey Blake, Hanna's mother, Mike's lacrosse buddies, and even Hanna's father; after they'd taken a million red-carpet glamour shots and she'd kissed a zillion relatives and retweeted wedding pictures at least thirty times—Hanna's guests stood on the stone steps of the mansion, sending her and Mike off. People threw rice at their heads. Others blew bubbles. Hanna gazed through the crowd, searching for her friends but only seeing Aria. She wondered where Spencer had disappeared to. It was a shame she was missing this moment.

Then a glass of champagne appeared under her nose. She looked up and saw Mike smiling at her.

"One for the road?" He gestured to the circular drive ahead of them. A Rolls-Royce waited, its engine chugging.

Hanna raised an eyebrow. "Did *you* arrange for that?"

"Maybe," Mike said slyly. He smiled mysteriously and

took Hanna's arm. "Come on. Let's go."

Hanna glanced back at the straggling guests—her mom was tearing up as she waved at Hanna and Mike; her aunt Maude, who'd always been a lush, was still flirting with Mr. Montgomery; and most of the guests were holding up their phones, taking photos of the decor that would go straight to Instagram. She gave them a vague wave and took Mike's hand, then turned to him, excited about whatever this next surprise would be. They hadn't really talked about after the wedding . . . probably because Hanna and Ramona had been so wrapped up in the wedding itself. "Whatever you say, *husband*," she murmured.

"That's right, *wife*." Mike kissed her ear and opened the back door to the car. The scent of fresh leather wafted out. "So did you have a good time?"

"Incredible," Hanna breathed, sliding into the seat. Mike climbed in next to her, and the car zoomed away. Hanna laid her head on Mike's shoulder and closed her eyes, feeling a little bit dizzy and entirely content. Eventually the car pulled to a stop. When she looked up, Hanna wasn't in front of a luxe Philly hotel or even a quaint B and B, as she'd expected. They'd pulled up to her house.

"Oh," she said, a little disappointed. The only consolation, she supposed, was that her mother couldn't disapprove of them sharing her bed.

"You just wait," Mike said eagerly, easing her out of the car. A wide grin on his face, he led her around the back. When she saw her backyard, Hanna gasped.

Tiki torches were lit up in a row around the back patio, Hawaiian music swelled quietly out of the outdoor speakers, and the sound machine from Hanna's bedroom sat on the low wall, tuned to the Ocean Waves setting. Several kiddie pools had been filled with water, there were inflatable palm trees everywhere, and half the patio was covered with mounds of sandbox sand. Two slushy margaritas sat on the little table next to the chaises.

Hanna gave Mike a confused smile. "What is all this?"

"Well . . ." Mike twiddled his fingers bashfully. "I know you always wanted a tropical honeymoon, to Hawaii or the Caribbean or whatever. And I thought that since we couldn't take a honeymoon in the islands, I'd bring the islands to us. But if you don't like it, we can totally go back to the Ritz or whatever."

"I *love* it," Hanna said, touched more than she knew how to say. She pulled Mike close and squeezed him hard, tears burning at the corners of her eyes. With every passing moment of the night, from when she'd seen him at the altar to when they'd recited their vows to when he'd danced three dances in a row with her nebbishy relatives from Florida, she couldn't think she could love him more . . . but this might have topped it all. It astonished her over and over that Mike would do all this for her and still know, deep down, that he and Hanna would probably never be together. That their only time together would be in a prison visitation room, or in a courtroom, or during phone calls. And yet he still went through all of this.

Then again, who knew? There was always that hope, right?

"You really like it?" he asked, his chin tucked over her head.

"It's perfect. *You're* perfect," she said, running her hands up and down his back. "And you're going to make a great husband."

"Same goes for you," Mike said. Then he leaned back and looked at her, touching one of the delicate beads on the front of her dress. "And you know, this dress is beautiful and all, but maybe we should get you into something more comfortable."

"I second that," Hanna said flirtatiously, taking his hand and leading him inside.

Ding-dong.

Hanna groaned and rolled over, touching Mike's smooth, bare stomach. He sighed in his sleep.

Ding-dong.

She sat up and rubbed her eyes, looking around. Blankets and sheets were tangled around her and Mike, and Dot had wedged between them, his head on Mike's butt. Hanna stifled a giggle, then felt a swell of wistfulness.

If only she could have weeks, months, *years* of waking up together just like this.

There was a scuffle downstairs, and Hanna remembered the doorbell. Then there was a knock on her door. Hanna threw on a robe and opened the door just enough to see her mother's pale face and eyes. "The police are downstairs for you," her mother whispered. "The jury has made a decision."

"On a *Sunday*?" Hanna gasped. Instantly she was up and throwing on clothes.

Everyone was bleary-eyed when they pulled up to the courthouse. Hanna clasped Mike's hands tightly as they walked the distance from the parking lot to the steps. Flashbulbs popped in her face, and she couldn't help but think that her slapdash attempt at makeup and coarse comb-through of her hair, still gummy with hairspray from yesterday's updo, would probably get some jeers on Twitter. But those thoughts were quickly drowned out by the questions the reporters were yelling. "What do you think the jury will decide? How do you feel about going to prison? Do you think you'll go free?"

Once inside, Mike turned to Hanna and squeezed her arm tightly. "It's going to be okay."

Hanna nodded, too afraid to speak for fear she'd throw up. Somehow, her legs managed to get her to the courtroom. Spencer and Aria were already in their seats, their faces drained of blood. Wordlessly, Hanna slid in next to them and clasped their hands. Her pulse raced fast.

The jurors reassembled, the lawyers took their places, and the judge appeared at his bench. Her gaze wandered to the rest of the crowd—her parents, Aria's parents, a bunch of people from the press. Then she looked back at the jurors in their box. Suddenly, one of them met her gaze. A tiny smile appeared on the woman's face. Hanna felt her jaw drop. That had to be a good sign, right? Had the jury decided they weren't guilty?

The judge's booming voice rang out through the room, and all eyes turned to him. "Has the jury reached a verdict?" he asked.

A pasty-colored middle-aged guy who served as the jury's representative clutched a folded piece of paper tightly. "We have, your honor."

It seemed to take ages for the bailiff to walk the length from the jury box to the judge's bench. Hanna thought she might faint as the judge took the sheet of paper from him and studied it. Spencer's nails dug into Hanna's palm. Aria trembled next to her. For a few seconds, it didn't seem like a single person in the courtroom breathed.

The judge coughed, then lowered his glasses farther down his nose. He looked at the jury foreman and asked, "How do you find?"

The man replied, "We the jury find Hanna Marin, Spencer Hastings, and Aria Montgomery guilty of the murder of Alison DiLaurentis."

Hanna's mouth fell open. Someone near her screamed. Spencer's hand slipped from hers. Hanna glanced blindly around the courtroom, her gaze first landing on Mr. DiLaurentis, who was in his regular seat in the back. There was a small, tense smile on his face. Then Hanna found Mike in the crowd. His skin was ashen. He was blinking hard, maybe to hold back tears. Hanna held his gaze as long as she could, but she couldn't offer a brave smile, and neither could he. That was when she realized. Mike hadn't really thought this was ever going to happen.

Maybe she hadn't, either. But the reality sank in, and made her dizzy: She was never going to see him again, except in a prison visitor's room. She was never going to see *anyone* again.

The judge said more after that—something about the girls serving their life sentences immediately, as they were all flight risks, and for that sentence to be served at the Keystone State Correctional Facility, but Hanna barely registered it. Her vision began to dim. *Guilty. Guilty. Guilty.* It rang in her head like a gong. *Life in prison. Forever.*

And then everything went dark.

26

PRISON BLUES

Aria usually had a cast-iron stomach when it came to motion sickness, but something about the way the bald, burly, khaki-jacketed prison worker drove the van to the Keystone State Correctional Facility sent her stomach tumbling all the way until they rolled through the prison gates. Maybe it was his jerky driving, or maybe it was the way he *smelled* like jerky—beef jerky, the scent of it literally leaking from his pores.

The car came to a halt, throwing Aria, Spencer, and Hanna forward roughly against their seat belts. The worker glared at them, got out, and yanked open the sliding back door to the van. "End of the line," he ordered, then chuckled. "Welcome to your new home, bitches."

Aria shuffled out of the van as best she could with the shackles around her ankles. Hanna and Spencer followed, neither of them saying a word. They hadn't spoken since the verdict had been passed down, actually. Cried into one another's shoulders, yes. Stared at one another in horror, definitely. But what was there really to *say*?

Guilty. It was still too horrible to believe. Anything Rubens had said, any *logic* about what might have happened, any assurance that they'd appeal as soon as they could, went in one of Aria's ears and out the other. A panel of people had found them guilty. It made her feel lower than low. People actually thought she was a murderer. They'd listened to that ridiculous case and took Ali's side. She couldn't believe it.

The worker shoved them toward an open metal door. Another guard, a portly woman with short brown hair and a jowly face, waited for them, a metal basket in her outstretched hands. Aria glanced at the name on her badge. BURROUGHS. She'd read somewhere that people went only by last names in prison—first names were too personal. Or maybe they gave you too much of an identity. So in here, Aria would no longer be Aria, but simply Montgomery. No longer an individual, but a number. No longer an artist, but a killer.

"Turn over all your belongings," Burroughs ordered Spencer, who was first in line. "Any jewelry, anything you got in your pockets, give it here."

Spencer took off a pair of earrings and dropped them into the basket. Aria had nothing to fork over—she'd removed the Cartier bracelet Noel had given her earlier and handed it to Ella for safekeeping. She'd told her to give it back to the Kahn family, though even saying that had choked her up. She wished now that she hadn't chickened out of talking to him at Hanna and Mike's wedding. He'd just looked so . . . pissed. And he hadn't come to her trial. Then again, his own trial was probably soon. She wondered what he thought when he heard she'd been found guilty. Maybe he didn't care at all.

Suddenly Burroughs had pushed her up against the wall, Aria's chin banging against the cinder blocks. She felt Burroughs's hands move roughly up and down her body, prodding her armpits, cupping the space beneath her boobs, and doing a full sweep between her legs. Burroughs stood back and looked at the three of them with narrowed eyes. "Before we go inside, I don't want any funny business," she growled. "No talking. No looking at the other inmates. No complaining. You'll do what you're told, and you won't make waves."

Aria raised her hand. "When can I make a phone call?"

Burroughs snorted indignantly. "Honey, phone privileges are *earned*. And you certainly haven't done anything to deserve that yet." She glared at the others. "And so are bathroom privileges, sleeping privileges, even eating privileges."

"*Eating* privileges?" Spencer repeated, her voice cracking. "That doesn't seem humane."

Whap. The woman's hand flew out and struck Spencer's jaw so fast Aria almost didn't catch it. Spencer pitched to the right and made a tortured sound. Aria turned to her, wanting to comfort her, but feared the woman might hit her, too.

"I said *no complaining*," Burroughs hissed. Then she pushed them down a long, dirty corridor that smelled like feet, sweat, and the grimiest Porta-Potti ever, until they came to an entrance to what looked like a bathroom, though it didn't have a door. "Time to shower," she instructed, pushing them into the room.

Aria stared at the dingy tiles, the dripping faucets, the open toilet stalls. The place was teeming with other women—terrifying looking women with tattoos and vicious sneers and hunched, masculine postures, all strolling around totally naked and unashamed. A couple of them were shouting at each other as though on the verge of a brawl. A thin Asian girl was huddling in the corner, muttering something in a language Aria had never heard. One woman, who was plucking her eyebrows at the sink, had a scar running the length of her face. When she saw Aria staring, she broke into a wide, weird smile, tweezers held aloft. "*Hi*, there," she teased.

Aria shrank into herself. Her feet wouldn't move. She couldn't shower here. She couldn't even *stand* here. How was she going to do this? How was she going to stay strong? She thought of what Rubens had told them after the verdict had been passed down: "It's going to be okay. We'll appeal. We still might be able to beat this."

"And if we don't?" Hanna had sobbed.

Rubens had pulled his bottom lip into his mouth.

"Well, then, you might be looking at twenty-five years. Twenty maybe, if you have good behavior. I've even seen some prisoners get out in fifteen."

Fifteen years. Aria would be thirty-three by then. Half her life would be gone. Noel wouldn't have waited for her anyway, even if they had stayed together.

Somehow, she made it into the shower, which had no curtain. She tried her best to cover herself up and scrub down at the same time, though the soap was slippery, didn't really suds up, and smelled like vomit. Burroughs loomed close by in the corridor, arms crossed over her chest, watching each of them for reasons Aria didn't really understand—maybe just to get them used to the humiliation. Just outside the stall, the prisoners circled like sharks. "New girls?" Aria heard one of them ask the guard. "They're awfully pretty," said another. "They look like bitches," someone else said. Aria leaned her head against the filthy wall tile and let the tears fall.

After about three minutes, the guard ducked in and turned off the water, ordering Aria out. "Clothes back on," she barked. Aria, Spencer, and Hanna dried themselves off as best they could and quickly got into their orange jumpsuits. Aria's skin now smelled like the rank soap she'd used. Her wet hair dripped down her back, a feeling she'd always hated.

Then Burroughs motioned for them to follow her down yet another dark, windowless corridor—the whole place reminded Aria of one of those mazes scientists put rats in for psychological experiments—and past an open room of women's bunks. Prisoners prowled around the space aggressively. Hip-hop floated through the air. There was more yelling from a back corner, though a guard's voice rose up sharply, telling whoever it was to shut the hell up.

The guard took a turn down yet another hallway, but she took only Aria's hand, instructing another guard to lead Hanna and Spencer elsewhere. "Orientation for you, Montgomery. D'Angelo, send Hastings and Marin to their bunks."

Aria gasped. "We can't all go together?"

Burroughs snickered. "Sorry, sweetheart."

Aria met Spencer's eye. Spencer gave her a look that was so terrified, so trapped, Aria's own heart quickened. Hanna held up a hand in a wave. Something about it seemed finite, like they might never see one another again. The guards must have known how close they all were and that they'd allegedly committed the crime together. If their goal was to make everyone in here miserable, then of course they'd do everything they could to keep friends apart.

You can do this, Aria told herself. But really, she wasn't so sure.

Burroughs held tight to Aria's forearm and shoved her into a small conference room at the end of the hall. It was peppered with a few folding chairs and was so hot and stifling Aria immediately started to sweat. She shut her eyes, trying to pretend that she was in a hot yoga class—minus the yoga—but it really didn't do any good.

A skinny blond woman with a dramatic overbite stood at the front of the room. "Sit," she said to Aria, pointing at some empty chairs. A few seats were already occupied by other women in orange jumpsuits. Aria looked at each of them, wondering who on earth she could sit near without fearing for her life. There was an overweight Latina with a tattoo at her temple; a pale girl who was trembling a little, either in detox or on the verge of a psychotic break; a cluster of women all sitting together who, by their identical menacing expressions, looked like members of the same gang; and a tall black girl in glasses who was motionless at the back of the room, as watchful as a cat.

Aria looked at the black girl hopefully. She looked sane. Head down, Aria grabbed a chair next to her and folded her hands in her lap, wondering what would come next.

Olive, aka Overbite Lady, shut the door, which only increased the stuffy feeling inside the room. She walked over to the corner and clicked on a small desk fan, but then angled it only in her direction. "Welcome to the Keystone State Correctional Facility," she said in a bland voice. "I'm here to tell you everything you need to know, including rules, the schedule, your employment assignment, cafeteria hours, medical concerns, special privileges, and what to do if you start to feel suicidal."

Aria pressed her hands over her eyes. She *already* felt suicidal.

Olive went on for a while about various prison protocols, transforming the tiniest civil rights—having a few moments to see family every Saturday morning, being allowed to purchase things like hairbrushes or flip-flops from the commissary if adequate funds were provided, a regular half hour each day of outside time in the prison yard—seem like luxuries. Aria wished she could ask Olive if there was a library, or if she'd be able to purchase materials to paint, or if there was a psychologist on staff who might be able to walk her through how, exactly, she was going to get through this without losing her mind. But she'd already accepted the fact that she'd probably get none of those things.

She leaned back in her chair and stared up at the ceiling, a bead of sweat rolling slowly down her forehead. The black girl with the glasses shifted next to her, and as Aria turned, she caught her eye. Aria dared a shy smile. "Hey," she whispered. "Is this your first day, too?"

The girl nodded and smiled back. Aria's heart lifted—she seemed so normal. Maybe even a new friend. She'd need as many of them as she could get. Then the girl added, "But I've been here before, Aria."

Aria blinked hard, feeling as though the positive image had suddenly turned to a photo negative. "H-how do you know my name?"

The girl edged closer to Aria until their bodies almost

touched. "Because I've been waiting for you," she whispered. "You're the girl who killed Alison DiLaurentis, right?"

Aria's jaw hung open. It took too long for her to find the words to respond. "N-no," she said, her voice trembling. "I didn't kill her. The verdict was wrong."

The girl faced forward again, her smile now knowing and bitter. "Yeah, you did. And we all know it. She's a hero to some of us, you know. She's what keeps us going."

Every cell in Aria's body started to quiver. She wanted to leap up and tear away from this girl, but she was almost too stricken to move. *She's what keeps us going.* The girl's chin was held high, her expression certain and righteous. She believed what she was saying about Ali—believed in Ali herself. And then, when Aria looked down, she noticed a scabby, black tattoo on the inside of the girl's wrist. It was of a single letter: *A*.

Aria's blood ran cold. She instinctively patted her pockets for her cell phone, but of course there was nothing there. But if she'd had her phone on her, she would have texted her friends immediately. *SOS*. There was an Ali Cat—*in prison*.

All at once, Aria revised her prognosis in here. It would be a miracle if she survived the next fifteen years. She might not even survive until tomorrow.

27

THE BIGGEST SURPRISE
WITNESS OF ALL

Monday afternoon, Spencer hunched on her hands and knees on the floor of the women's bathroom, a sponge surely teeming with toxic mold in her hands and a bucket of filthy, rancid-smelling water next to her. Trying not to breathe, she plunged the sponge into the water and then slopped it onto the floor, making slow, even circles. She even threw in a few intense, centering, yoga fire-breaths that had always helped her before. But after breath number three, she heard someone snickering above her and looked up.

A scrawny-looking girl with olive skin and an eye patch leaned on the sink, smiling at Spencer with crooked, rotted teeth. "Little rich bitch can't handle bathroom duty, huh?"

"I'm fine," Spencer answered. She winced, wishing she hadn't said anything. She remembered from Angela's book that the key was *not* to engage with the other prisoners—it was a sign of weakness. And this girl, whose name was Meyers-Lopez, had been following Spencer around all morning, trying to get a rise out of her.

Meyers-Lopez hiked herself up onto the sink. "I bet you never thought you'd come here," she hissed. "I bet you thought you'd get away with it. She told me all about you, you know. She told me how much of a tight-ass you were. How much of a spoiled bitch."

Spencer winced and made bigger circles with her sponge. *Please let a guard walk in right now, please let a guard walk in right now,* she willed. This was the most terrifying part about prison so far. Not the fact that women argued violently well into the night, as Spencer had experienced yesterday evening, logging a total of forty-five minutes of sleep. Not the fact that the food was the lowest-grade possible and infested with all sorts of bacteria—she'd been terrified to choke down a waffle this morning for fear she'd go into botulism-related convulsions immediately. Not that she hadn't seen Aria or Hanna even *once*, or that she'd probably have to live the next thirty years sleeping next to someone whose nickname was Miss Vicious, as she had last night, the woman so haunted-looking that Spencer had been sure she'd wake this morning with bruises all over her body.

No. It was that several inmates had come up to Spencer in the past twenty-four hours and mentioned how they worshipped at the high church of Alison DiLaurentis.

How they'd claimed she'd *spoken* to them, *told* them about Spencer and the others—and who knew? Maybe Ali had. Whatever the case, these women were most definitely Ali's minions, and they'd threatened Spencer that soon, they would get their revenge.

Which meant . . . *what*? They were going to kick her ass? *Kill* her?

She scrubbed vigorously, ignoring Meyers-Lopez's hateful stare. It made perfect sense. Not only had Ali constructed a foolproof plan to get them convicted—Spencer was pretty sure Ali had paid off some of the jurors—but she'd also planted some Ali Cats inside the prison to make sure the next few decades of Spencer's life were miserable. And were the Ali Cats communicating with Ali, too, on the outside? Could that, in some way, prove Ali was alive? *Yeah, right*, she thought as the dirty water lapped against the bottom of the sink. She'd never be able to prove it. Ali and her minions were way smarter than that.

She took the sponge into one of the stalls. The door banged shortly after, and when Spencer emerged from the stall, the bathroom was empty. She smiled, feeling like she'd won a tiny victory. Meyers-Lopez must have gotten tired of Spencer and left.

She walked over to the bucket, but when she plunged the sponge into the water, her fingers hit something slimy and firm. She wheeled back. Something black floated on top of the water. Then she noticed a tiny paw, a whisker, a *snout*. Spencer screamed. It was a dead rat.

"Oh my God, oh my God," she said, staring at her outstretched hand. She'd just touched a dead rat. *She'd just touched a dead rat.* She was probably going to get the plague. From somewhere in the hall, she swore she could hear Meyers-Lopez laughing.

"Hastings?"

Spencer whipped around. Burroughs, the guard who'd showed them in yesterday, now stood in the doorway. For a moment, Spencer thought she was going to blame *her* for the dead rat. "I need you to come with me," the guard grumbled.

"F-for what?" Spencer dared to ask.

The lines in Burroughs's forehead furrowed even deeper. "Your lawyer's here, okay? And he wants to talk to you."

Spencer stared at her. *Her lawyer?* What could Rubens possibly have to say? Was he ready to appeal already?

"Well, come on!" Burroughs bellowed.

Head down, Spencer hurried out of the bathroom to Burroughs's side. They walked down a series of hallways until they got to the rooms where prisoners met with their attorneys. Burroughs unlocked the last door on the right and pushed it open. Rubens was standing, facing the barred window. Aria and Hanna were sitting at the table, looking just about as shell-shocked as Spencer was.

Spencer gazed between all of them. "What's going on?" she asked, feeling circumspect.

Rubens's expression was hard to read. He clasped his hands together. "You girls are coming with me."

Spencer frowned. "Where?"

"To the courthouse."

Hanna looked worried. "*Why?*"

Rubens glanced back and forth worriedly. A couple of inmates loitered outside, trying to look busy. "I can't get into it here," he said cagily. "You just need to come, okay? *Now.*"

A series of guards shoved them down the hallway past the cafeteria and to the double doors that led to the outside. Spencer huddled close to her friends, thrilled to see them again, even if it was for something so mysterious. "What do you think is happening?" she whispered.

"Maybe we're being moved," Aria said. Her expression darkened. "God, I bet that's it. We're being moved to somewhere even *worse.*"

Hanna swallowed hard. "There can't be anywhere worse than this. They have me working in the cafeteria with this woman who has already decided she hates me. She trapped me in the walk-in refrigerator twice." She looked around, as though the woman was listening. "And then, when I came out? She made fun of my cold, pointy nipples. She made *everyone* in the kitchen look at them."

Aria squeezed Hanna's hand. "I'm in laundry, and I think one of the other girls replaced the water in my bottle with bleach yesterday. Thank God I didn't drink it."

Spencer swallowed hard, thinking about her experience with the rat. "Did those women mention Ali?"

Aria's eyes widened. "The girl I met in orientation did."

"The kitchen bitch didn't, but I think my cellmate knows about Ali," Hanna whispered. She glanced back at the prison doors. "She *looks* totally normal, and she's new like us, but she has an *A* tattoo on the inside of her wrist and she already knew my name."

Aria's eyes widened. "I might have met the same girl. She's definitely an Ali Cat."

Hanna shut her eyes and moaned. "Did you know she's a knitter? She can legally have knitting needles in her bunk. I was so afraid last night that I was going to . . ." She made a stabbing motion with her arm.

Burroughs wheeled around and glared at them. "No talking!"

They were outdoors by then. The sun on Spencer's face felt delicious, but she couldn't relish it for very long because the guards were shoving them into a waiting van. Hanna and Aria tumbled in after her, and the same guy who'd escorted them to the prison manned the front seat. Rubens climbed into the passenger side. Spencer stared at the back of his head, trying to figure out what the hell was going on. What was so important that they were being led back to the courthouse? Was the jury going to sentence them to immediate *death*?

After a long, almost intolerable silence, the courthouse appeared on the hill. The van rattled into the parking lot and pulled up to the curb. Spencer peered out the window. "Why are there press people here?" she asked.

The lawyer jumped out of his seat and slid open the doors. "Let's go," he said roughly.

Hanna climbed out, almost tripping over her ankle chains. "Are we going to be ambushed with something? You have an obligation to tell us, you know."

"Y-yeah," Aria said shakily. "If this is bad, you have to let us know now."

But the reporters had already descended upon Rubens and were bombarding him with questions. "What's going on in there?" they shouted. "Why was everyone called back to court?" "What's happened?"

"No comment, no comment," Rubens said, gripping Spencer's hand hard and pulling her up the steps. The other girls followed. Spencer was acutely aware of all the flashes going off, getting pictures of her in her orange jumpsuit and messy hair and, most likely, filthy-sweaty-grimy face. But she was far too curious about what was happening inside to worry. Guards whisked her through the metal detector, and soon enough she was standing just outside the courtroom.

Rubens stood in front of them, his hand on the door-knob. There was a jittery expression on his face, but Spencer couldn't tell if it was good or bad. "Okay, ladies," he said breathlessly. "Brace yourselves."

"For *what*?" Hanna squeaked.

The door swung open, and several people who were

already in the courtroom, including the judge, swiveled around and clapped eyes on them. Then Hanna gasped. Aria made a small breathy sound that was a cross between a hiccup and a sob. A tall, familiar girl stood at the front of the courtroom. It was a girl Spencer had thought she'd never see again. A girl she'd thought about far too many times, who'd appeared in far too many dreams, who'd haunted her endlessly since she vanished.

"E-Emily?" Spencer managed to say, shakily pointing at the girl at the front of the courtroom. She looked at Rubens.

He smiled. "I just got the call an hour ago. She was escorted here this morning."

Spencer looked again. Tears filled Emily's eyes. She broke into a wide, careful smile. "H-hey," she said. And it was, indeed, Emily's voice. Emily's *everything*.

She was alive.

28

BACK ON DUNE STREET

One week, two days earlier
Cape May, NJ

"Do you smell that?" Emily said excitedly, gesturing into the garage of the closed-up beach house that belonged to Betty Maxwell, Nick's grandmother.

She watched as her friends stuck their heads into the garage and sniffed. "Is that . . . vanilla?" Aria finally said.

Emily nodded, feeling like she was going to burst. "We should call the police. This is proof she's still alive!"

But her friends just shifted, looking uncomfortable. Spencer peered back into the empty house. "Em, that's not enough to get the police here." She sighed. "Besides, she's not here *now*."

Emily couldn't believe it. Okay, okay, Ali wasn't here now—but it was still an amazing lead, right?

They all just shrugged and looked at her like she was nuts. And maybe she *was* nuts—the Ali voice in her head was cackling so loudly Emily could barely think straight. She couldn't believe that, once again, Ali had gotten the best of them. It was yet another slap in the face.

Emily tried to tell herself this was the end. But she couldn't just let it go so easily.

Emily heard her friends say they should stay here for the day, catch some rays, have a nice dinner. She felt herself nod along only because fighting would worry them more. But as they walked away, she felt detached from her body—from the whole scene, really. Her entire mind, her whole being was back in that house. There had to be a bigger clue there, something they'd missed.

She had to find it.

As they headed to the beach, Emily mentally reviewed the places in the house they'd searched. There was nothing in the kitchen, nothing in the bedrooms, nothing in the closets. But what about that vanilla-stinky garage? They'd only poked their heads in. Sure, the place had *looked* empty . . . but maybe it wasn't.

It haunted her as they played in the waves and listened to music through Spencer's iPod speakers. It plagued her as they changed for dinner. It needled her as they ate fresh seafood and ordered margaritas and tried to act upbeat. Her friends kept trying to pull her into the conversation, but she could only reply with stiff, one-word answers. *We have to go back*, she wanted to tell them. *Something is there. I just know it.*

But she knew her friends wouldn't go back to that

house. They'd already taken a huge risk breaking in this afternoon. They were taking a huge risk even *being* there. No. If she wanted to satisfy her hunch, she would have to do it alone.

They tumbled into their shared hotel room that night and turned on the TV to Comedy Central. Emily bided her time, watching as each of her friends had settled into bed, Spencer turning on the AC, Hanna pulling her eye mask over her face. After a while, the room grew silent, and someone turned down the TV volume. Emily waited an extra half hour to make sure they were all asleep, then crept out of the hotel room, key in hand.

The walk to Betty Maxwell's house took fifteen minutes, her flip-flops smacking loudly on the sidewalk in the quiet night. It had to be about two in the morning, and Emily worried a cop car might stop her, wondering what she was doing out so late. But luck was on her side. She didn't see any cars at all.

The beach house was eerier after dark, the walls creaking, strange shadows skittering in the corners, an odd clanking sound coming from somewhere in the back. Armed with a flashlight, Emily headed straight to the garage. It still smelled strongly of vanilla—of *Ali*. She stepped into the dark, small space, leftover sand gritting under her flip-flops. Hands shaking, she felt around the metal shelves along the garage walls, desperate to find something other than dust bunnies. Her fingers grazed spider webs. She pressed against the cinder-block walls, hoping for a loose brick that was concealing something secret. In the corner of the garage was an industrial-looking tool chest; she opened it and felt to the very back, but there was nothing inside.

Then she saw the trash can.

It was just a normal blue trash can with Cape May's city logo on the front, but Emily heard warning bells go off in her mind. She scampered over to it, lifted the plastic lid, and shone the flashlight inside. There were no bags in there, and the bottom was dark. But then the light caught the edge of something crusted along the bottom. Emily reached as far down as she could, unpeeling the piece of paper from the plastic. She pulled it out, barely able to breathe. It was an envelope smeared with dried oil. It should have smelled like trash, but it, too, smelled like vanilla.

She ran back inside, placed it on the kitchen island, and shone her flashlight over it. There was no addressee, just Betty Maxwell's house number and the Cape May ZIP code. In the corner, though, was a return address. Someone had written, *Day, 8901 Hyacinth Drive, Cocoa Beach, FL.*

Emily turned the envelope over. It had already been opened; whatever was inside had been removed. The vanilla smell was so strong it made her dizzy. Had *Ali* received this? Who was *Day*? The name seemed significant, for some reason, but Emily couldn't recall why.

She was so wrapped up in thought that she barely

remembered the walk back to the hotel. This was definitely, *definitely* a clue. Should she tell the others? Or would they reprimand her for going back, then shoot her down? They wouldn't actually believe it was anything, would they?

Certainly not that the envelope was worth traveling to Cocoa Beach, Florida to follow up on. But Emily just . . . *felt* something, a premonition stronger than any she'd ever had. She *needed* to see what this was. She had to go there. It would mean abandoning her friends—and the trial. But as much as she hated to do that, she knew this was probably their last shot. She would just have to go without them.

She didn't want anyone knowing about it, though—not her friends, not her family, not the cops. She couldn't afford to be looking over her shoulder the whole time. And she didn't want Ali to see her coming. How could she manage that?

She slipped back into the hotel room and took her place next to Hanna on the bed, her mind churning. And then, all at once, it came to her. It was so easy: Ali had already done it, after all. She'd faked her murder, and everyone believed it. If Emily faked her suicide, everyone would believe it, too.

She lay awake the rest of the night, planning the logistics. She would use the hurricane—everyone would think that it had killed her, but she knew she was a good enough swimmer to get through. At 5 AM, when she scrawled a note to Spencer, Aria, and Hanna, she knew what they'd believe. After all, she'd been legitimately distraught for weeks. She might as well capitalize on that now.

She pinned a Ziploc bag full of cash to her swim bottoms, walked down to the beach, and stepped into the waves. As she got deeper, the current was trickier to navigate than she'd originally thought, but she tried to stay calm and trust her swimming skills. She saw her friends rush to the shore, their faces masks of horror. Emily pretended to struggle, simultaneously feeling guilty for what she was putting them through but also confident in her decision that this was the only way no one would come looking for her.

What she didn't bank on was Spencer walking into the waves after her. "No!" Emily screamed, thrusting her arms over her head. She watched as the ocean pulled Spencer under again and again. "Stop struggling!" By the time the rescue teams arrived, Emily feared the worst. Several EMTs dragged Spencer's limp body onto the beach. Emily watched as the rescuers crowded around her and her friends stood in shock. But then, Spencer's body bucked, and she coughed and rolled to her side. Everyone seemed to relax a little. The rescuers loaded her onto a stretcher and carried her up the beach.

The coast guard helicopters swooped overhead, still searching. Emily ducked under, choking up salt, feeling the jellyfish stings, thrashing her legs through the waves. She let the current carry her farther out, terrified the whole time. A jetty was to her left; all she had to do was get out of the riptide and then swim underwater toward it.

But the waves crashed at her right and left. Several times she was pushed under for so long she was sure her lungs would give out. She surfaced, gasping, again and again, only to be pulled under once more. Her back hit the bottom roughly. Her elbow smashed against an outcropping of rocks. She caught sight of blood on her skin, terrified it might draw sharks. The waves rolled in again and again, showing no sign of slowing. A single image of Ali's hideous, angry, menacing face blazed in her mind, pushing her forward. She was doing this to find her. She was doing this to end the nightmare.

There was a break in the tumult, and Emily bobbed to the surface, breathing hard. The helicopters were farther down the beach, searching a different spot. She breathed and paddled hard toward the jetty, which wasn't far at all. She almost cried when she reached it, clinging to it and letting her legs bang against the posts. After a lot of breaths, she hefted herself up onto the wooden deck. Mercifully, there was no one on shore to see her, and the cuts on her legs from the jetty weren't that bad. After a while, shivering and weak, she staggered onto the cold, wind-swept beach and took refuge under a lifeguard stand. Her fingers touched something soft, and she unearthed a red Under Armour sweatshirt someone had left behind. She squealed with delight, pulling it on quickly and immediately feeling comforted by the warm, soft cotton. Then she patted her swim bottoms—the Ziploc was still pinned securely. Both things together felt like a wonderful boon. Maybe this really was going to work.

Once Emily regained her strength, she started up the walkway and headed into town. Thank goodness this was a beach town and walking into places in only a sweatshirt and a bathing suit was commonplace—when she walked into Wawa, no one paid any notice to her strange attire. Katy Perry's "Roar" was playing loudly over the speakers, which nicely drowned out Emily's pounding heart. She kept her head down and her eyes averted as she canvassed the aisles, selecting a giant-size iced tea, several soft pretzels, flip-flops, and a pair of gym shorts with a Cape May logo from among the small clothing section.

She pretended she had a hangover as she handed the bills to the man at the counter so she wouldn't have to make eye contact. Once outside, she pulled on the shorts quickly and stuffed the pretzels into her mouth, desperately ravenous. It was still so early in the morning, the sky a dull gray. There weren't many cars in the parking lot. Across the street, the town's famous pancake house was closed, maybe because of the storm. One helicopter circled the sky, perhaps still looking for her . . . and here she was, eating a pretzel, drinking iced tea, fine.

It was kind of crazy, and certainly drastic. What if it didn't work? What if she'd just made a horrible mistake?

She waited, listening for the Ali voice to chime in, but she was silent. Then Emily felt inside the Ziploc that was now tucked into her new shorts, pulling out a folded piece of hotel stationary. *8901 Hyacinth Drive, Cocoa Beach, FL*, she'd written. The ink hadn't smeared one bit—and that felt like a good omen, too. She held it between her hands, her heartbeat speeding up. She'd have to figure out the best way to get to Florida.

She only hoped she'd find what she was looking for once she got there.

29

One week and one day after Emily's dive into the ocean, she had made her way down to Florida. The oppressive humidity hit her the moment she stepped off the Greyhound bus, but it was a welcome change compared to the rank, bologna-smelling, bone-rattling contraptions she'd been a prisoner of for the past week. She shaded her eyes and looked around. Palm trees swayed majestically down the boulevard. Fluffy, midday clouds drifted overhead. A big electronic sign loomed large on the side of the building. *Today is Sunday*, scrolled red digital letters. *Welcome to Cocoa Beach.*

Emily was finally here. She cocked her head, still expecting an Ali-voice comment, but Ali had been silent ever since Emily's plunge into the sea. And so Emily relied on the old superstitious trick she'd used so many times since she was a kid, gazing out at the rushing traffic on the highway. *If a semi truck passes in the next ten seconds, you'll find her. If it doesn't, you won't.*

She started to count. At seven, a semi rushed past. Her fingertips tingled with possibility.

She followed the crowd of people into the depot, cagily looking back and forth for fear that someone might recognize her. But no one was even glancing in her direction. Then again, she didn't exactly *look* like the Emily Fields from the news, but instead like a skinny, bedraggled ragamuffin who hadn't showered or eaten a proper meal in days. She'd had to transfer seven different times to ensure the cheapest bus to southern Florida. She'd read the same discarded copy of *Golf Digest* for four days in a row just to keep from going insane. She'd slept with her head against a bus window or curled up on a depot bench. She'd almost gotten pickpocketed twice, countless skeevy travelers had hit on her, and an old lady had screamed at her in Portuguese—Emily suspected she'd put a hex on her. She'd suffered a lot on this trip. Risked a lot, too.

But it was worth it. She was on a mission.

The depot was frigid and smelled like cleaning products, and an announcement blared over the loudspeaker in Spanish. Emily pushed into the women's bathroom—the toilet on the bus had become entirely too gross to use by the end of the trip, and she'd been holding in pee since the Georgia/Florida line. Inside the stall, she reached into the plastic bag she'd been carrying, pulled out the burner cell she'd bought at a stopover in North Carolina, and went through the steps to activate it. She hadn't wanted to use a cell phone before this, but now that she was here, she wasn't sure what sort of situation she might run into. After the screen announced that the phone was active, she slipped it into her pocket, feeling every ounce of its weight.

Outside the bathroom was a big map of the Cocoa Beach area. It took some searching, but Emily located Hyacinth Street in a development several miles away. She pulled out the pen she'd swiped from a rest stop in South Carolina and wrote the directions on her hand. Then, something on the TV hanging over the ticket window caught her eye, and she looked up. Hanna's and Spencer's solemn, sober faces flashed on the screen, filling Emily with even more guilt. They looked so *tortured*. She'd caught snippets of the trial during the journey, and with each new story, she'd felt even worse for leaving them to deal with it all on their own, especially since Aria had taken off for Europe. She also hated that her suicide wasn't a vote of confidence to the jury that they were innocent.

Then she noticed the headline. *Pretty Little Liars Found Guilty*, read big red letters. Emily's jaw dropped. The trial was over. The jury didn't believe them. They were going to *jail*.

She had to get to that house, *now*.

She found the bus line to Hyacinth Street and jogged to the stop just as a bus was pulling up. After paying the fare, she collapsed into a seat, AC blaring on the back of her neck. Art deco buildings swept past out the windows. Palm trees swayed. A woman near the front was listening to loud, lively music over headphones. Emily knew Ali had a grandma in Florida; was she hiding her now? But who had helped her *get* here? Who had paid her way the whole distance down the coast?

How had Ali passed unnoticed by everyone yet *again*?

The bus reached her stop, and Emily hurried off and onto a desolate stretch of sidewalk. Small stucco houses lined the streets. Two yards down, an older woman in curlers tended a flower bed. Across the street, an elderly man was walking a Lakeland terrier. A pack of senior citizens in matching tracksuits disappeared around the corner, their arms pumping, power-walker style. All the cars parked on the street looked like something her grandparents would drive: either big, boatlike cruisers or efficient little Toyota Corollas.

Emily's throat felt dry as she walked up the block and took a right at Hyacinth. More pretty stucco houses lined the block, all painted in cheerful pastels. Emily gazed at the sprayed-on numbers on the curb—8879 . . . 8881 . . . 8893 . . . and suddenly, there was 8901, just ahead. It was a cheerful pink house with white shutters and a white fence. A sprinkler sprayed the green grass in the yard, and tropical plants grew in a few flower beds near the windows. On the porch was the same statue of a droopy-eyed dog that the old lady who lived three doors down from Emily back in Rosewood had on *her* porch. The driveway was empty of cars.

Emily crouched behind a giant palm. Was this right? The place seemed like a retirement community. What if Ali had planted that envelope in the trash can for Emily to find? What if she was watching from somewhere, laughing her head off?

Emily thought about her friends' faces on the news again. *Prison.* It was unthinkable. They were going through hell, and she wasn't by their side. What if this was a trap and she was caught? She'd go to jail and probably get double the sentence for faking her death. Her friends would hate her. Her family would hate her. *Everyone* would hate her. They'd think she was even more nuts than before. Maybe she would end up at The Preserve.

But then the front door opened.

Emily crouched down. A figure stepped down the front path and crossed the lawn toward the driveway. It was a woman, her hips swinging and her hair bouncing, and she didn't look nearly as old as the other residents in the neighborhood. Her hair was still a fresh, buttery blond. Her body was trim and young, as if she did lots of yoga. She was wearing a sundress, blue espadrilles, and a sparkling diamond pendant at her throat.

Emily frowned. That diamond pendant looked familiar—*really* familiar. Just then, she got the strangest memory: It was seventh grade, and she and the other girls were dressing up Ali to go to the high school's Valentine's Dance—she'd been asked by a cute freshman boy named Tegan. Emily had thrown herself into helping Ali get ready, fussing over her hair and makeup, *ooh*ing and *ahh*ing over the teardrop-shaped diamond necklace Ali got to wear that night, on loan from her mother.

Day. All of a sudden, Emily knew why that name was significant. Before the DiLaurentises moved to Rosewood, they'd been known as the *Day*-DiLaurentises. But when they'd moved away because of their daughter's violent outbursts, wanting to change over and start fresh, they'd dropped the first half of their name.

Could it *be*?

The woman strode toward the back of the house, that familiar diamond pendant thumping at her throat. As she opened the gate, the sun struck her face, illuminating her fine-boned features, from her slanted nose to her big blue eyes to her bow-shaped lips. Emily's mouth dropped open. A scream froze in her throat.

It was Ali's mother.

Emily was so stunned that her knees gave way. But suddenly, it made so much sense. This was why Mrs. D hadn't attended the trial. This was why she hadn't commented to the press. Maybe the press didn't know where she *was*. And Ali might have been insane, and Mrs. D might have fully understood that, but Ali was still her daughter. And as her mother, Mrs. D probably felt an obligation to protect her. It was something Emily could easily empathize with: *She* had a daughter, too, little Violet. It hadn't been that long ago that A had hinted that Violet might be in danger. Emily had gone crazy with worry, desperate to keep Violet safe.

Maybe that's what Mrs. D was doing, too. Not quite thinking things through, Emily shot across the street and onto the property. She unlatched the white metal gate at the front and crept through the side yard, her heart pounding. It was cooler in the backyard, the area shady with palm trees, and a water feature bubbled noisily near the sliding door.

Mrs. D stood with her back to Emily. A white curl of cigarette smoke snaked above her head, and a glowing red cigarette tip extended from between her fingers. She looked so vulnerable, standing there, having no clue Emily was behind her. Emily felt vulnerable, too. She still had no idea what she was going to say or do.

Taking a deep breath, she covertly pressed the CALL screen of the burner cell. Fingers trembling, she dialed 911. Someone answered immediately. "What's your emergency?" a woman's voice blared.

Mrs. D's head shot up, and she turned at the noise. When she spied Emily, her eyes narrowed, then widened.

"H-hi," Emily heard herself say, her voice so small.

"What's your emergency?" the voice said again. Emily just hoped the dispatcher wouldn't hang up before certain things were said. Didn't they record 911 calls?

The color drained from Mrs. D's face. Up close, she

looked older than Emily remembered. There were dark circles under her eyes, and her skin seemed drawn against her face, her body too gaunt.

"What are *you* doing here?" Mrs. D finally hissed, backing up. "Didn't you . . . *drown*?"

She sounded scared, Emily realized. Maybe trapped. "I'm looking for Alison," Emily said in the steadiest voice she could manage, her gaze on Ali's mom. "I think you've seen her."

Mrs. D looked at Emily crazily. Her mouth opened, but no words came out.

"I think you know where she is," Emily went on. "I understand what you're doing, Mrs. DiLaurentis. I have a daughter, too. If I thought she was in danger, I'd do anything to help her. But you need to do what's right. Your daughter has hurt a lot of people and ruined a lot of lives."

Mrs. D dropped the cigarette to the pavers. "I don't know what you're talking about," she spat. "My daughter is dead. *You* killed her."

There was a slight hiccup in her voice, and she averted her eyes. Emily's heart jumped. "You know that's not true," she said loudly. "You've been in touch with her. In fact, I think she's *here*."

Mrs. D shook her head. "I've heard things about you. They said you'd gone crazy. I figured you were the one that killed Alison. I bet it was you alone, wasn't it?"

"I *didn't kill her*," Emily roared. "She almost killed *me*."

"I read the things she wrote about you in her journal. You girls are monsters."

"Hello?" the dispatcher said. "Is someone on the line?"

Mrs. D glanced at Emily's pocket. "Who are you talking to?"

Emily touched the phone through the fabric. "I've called the police. They're on their way. So you'd better start telling me the truth."

Mrs. D's bottom lip started to tremble. Something about her tough expression collapsed. "The *police*?" she squeaked. "W-why would you do that? They'll come after *you*, you know. Haven't you heard? Your friends were found guilty."

"They won't come after me. You know that. Just tell me where she is. I'm not going to hurt her. I promise."

Though it was difficult, Emily didn't break her poker face. Mrs. D's eyes darted back and forth. She looked like she was going to crack.

"Hello?" the dispatcher said again. "Ma'am, we're . . ."

But Emily didn't hear the rest. She felt someone yank her from behind, pinning her arms behind her back. She let out a scream. Mrs. D's eyes widened. And then Emily felt something cold and hard press at her temple. Her whole body went slack. It was a gun.

"Don't move, bitch," a voice growled.

A figure stepped in front of her, swimming into view. Emily saw a heavyset girl with sallow skin and dull, brown hair. It was the eyes, though, that Emily recognized right away—crystal-blue eyes that sparkled when they smiled. And the mouth, too. That beautiful, kissable bow-shaped mouth.

Ali.

30

NOT GOING DOWN WITHOUT A FIGHT

"What are you *doing*?" Mrs. DiLaurentis screamed at her daughter. "Go back inside!"

"Oh, because you have this covered?" Ali howled, tightening her grip on Emily's arms. And now her voice sounded utterly familiar, that beautiful and horrible voice Emily would never forget. "You told me you had this under control. But I *saw* you. You were about to tell her everything!"

Mrs. D rushed over and tried to pry Ali off Emily, but Ali shoved her away, sending her careening into the wrought-iron table. Mrs. D recovered quickly and gave Ali a plaintive, desperate look. "Just go inside, okay? *Please*. She said she called the police. Just go to that place we talked about. It's safe."

But Ali didn't seem to hear her mom. She yanked Emily closer until her mouth was against Emily's ear. "You made a big, big mistake looking for me, bitch. And now you're going to pay."

Mrs. D trembled on the other side of the patio. "Alison, *stop*," she said sternly. "*Go inside.*"

Ali pointed at her mother. "This is your fault, you know. You should have prevented this. I *trusted* you."

Mrs. D slapped her arms to her sides. "If you just go to that place we talked about, this will be fine!" She pointed at Emily. "I've got her covered. She's a *murderer*. Everyone is looking for her. The police will take her away."

"Or we could just get rid of her now," Ali said, turning on Emily. At the same time, Emily yanked away from Ali with a quick spin, shot out her hand, and knocked the gun away. It clattered along the patio, coming to a stop by a large stone birdbath.

"You bitch!" Ali lurched for the weapon, but Emily tackled her and pushed her to the ground. She climbed on top of her, wrapping her legs around Ali's thickened torso. Her breath heaved. Ali wriggled under Emily's weight, her chubby face wincing, her teeth gnashing.

Ali spit in Emily's face. "What are you going to do to me?"

"I could kill you," Emily whispered.

Ali snickered. "Yeah, *right*. You don't have it in you."

"I don't?" Emily bellowed in a voice entirely not her own. She reached out and clenched her hands around Ali's neck. Ali's eyes bulged. Emily could feel the muscles and tendons at Ali's throat, and she willed herself to squeeze and squeeze and squeeze. "I *don't?*" she repeated. Dimly, she realized that Mrs. D was screaming.

The furious smirk on Ali's face turned to something more fearful. Emily relished the terror in Ali's eyes—for once, she understood what they'd been through all these years. All she wanted was to get rid of this girl once and for all. All she wanted was for Ali to *pay*.

But then she realized: It wouldn't solve anything. And she really *would* be Ali's murderer. No better than Ali was.

She pulled her hands away. Ali turned her head and coughed violently. Emily leaned down, close to her ear. "No. You don't deserve to die. I'm going to make you rot in jail for the rest of your life."

"Not if I have anything to do with it."

There was the sound of a short, sharp *click*. Emily whirled around. Mrs. D stood behind them, holding the gun. "Put your hands up," she whispered.

Emily leapt off Ali. Ali rolled onto her side, still groaning and coughing and clutching her throat.

Mrs. D's hands might have been unsteady, but she was composed enough to release the gun's safety. Her jaw was tight. Cords stood out from her neck. "Don't touch my daughter," she whispered.

Emily nodded weakly. She glanced back and forth for something to battle Mrs. D with, but there was nothing nearby. She was trapped. Mrs. D had her.

"I'm sorry," she heard herself say. So this was it. She really *was* going to die. No one would ever know she'd searched valiantly for Ali. And Ali would get away . . . *again*.

A sound rose up from down the street. Emily perked up her ears. It was a siren—so the 911 dispatcher *had* heard her. "Back here!" Emily dared to scream. "Help!"

After that, everything happened so quickly: She heard the sounds of footsteps and the *clang* of the gate. The officers exploded onto the patio, and Mrs. D dropped the gun. The cops ran and picked it up, and then there was more shouting and confusion. "What's going on here?" the cops bellowed. "Everyone, hands where we can see them!"

"This girl was trying to break into my home!" Mrs. D pointed at Emily. "She's Emily Fields, the girl who's supposed to be dead! She's a murderer!"

The cops turned and stared at Emily. The tall one grabbed her wrist. The dark-haired one reached for his walkie-talkie. "Wait!" Emily cried. "The girl I supposedly murdered? She's here!"

She gestured to where Ali had fallen—and gasped. Ali was gone.

There was a tinny, clanking sound at the edge of the property. Emily turned and caught sight of a shadowy figure scaling the chain-link fence. Ali was halfway up by now. "It's Alison DiLaurentis!" Emily screamed to the cops, who were next to her. "You know who she is, right?"

The tall cop, who was still holding Emily's wrist, glared at her. "Isn't she dead?"

The other cop shouted up the fence. "Hey, you! Come

back down. *Now*." But Ali kept climbing. The short cop climbed up the fence after her. Ali let out a wail and scurried as quickly as she could, but her excess weight slowed her down. The cop caught her by the ankle and dragged her back. Ali's legs kicked, and her fists flew. "Don't touch me!" she screeched. "You're hurting me! You can't do this!"

"Stop struggling," the cop said, shoving Ali to the dirt. Her hair fell in her face. Her too-small T-shirt pulled unattractively across her stomach. But as she twisted around to spit in the cop's face, he looked at his partner, recognition dawning. The second cop leaned down and stared into Ali's face, which was pushed against the grass. Now it was his turn to look baffled . . . and maybe a little bit frightened. He pulled out his walkie-talkie. "I'm going to need backup. Will you send two more black-and-whites to 8901 Hyacinth Drive?"

Mrs. D touched the cops' arms. "Don't believe a word that girl says," she warned, her eyes on Emily. "She's insane. My daughter's name is Tiffany Day, not Alison DiLaurentis."

"Yeah?" Emily felt heat in her face. "Do you have ID?"

Ali twisted around and looked at her mother. "Get my ID, Mom."

Mrs. D stood very still. The corners of her mouth turned down. "S-she doesn't have ID."

Ali's eyebrows shot up. "Of course I do."

Mrs. D averted her eyes. "I didn't get it yet," she whispered to her daughter. "There wasn't enough time."

Ali just stared. There was a look of horror on her face.

The dark-haired cop reached for a pair of handcuffs and clapped them around Ali's wrists. "Let's all go down to the station so we can talk. You, too, Mrs. . . ." He looked searchingly at Ali's mom, then shrugged and clapped cuffs around her wrists, too.

Mrs. D looked stunned. "*We're* not the ones you want." She nodded her head toward Emily. "It's *her*."

"Oh, we're bringing her, too," the dark-haired cop murmured. "We'll get all this sorted out."

It took all of the first cop's strength to restrain Ali enough to get her into the squad car, and Mrs. D howled the whole way to the curb. Emily, however, walked calmly and patiently. She could feel a big smile spreading across her face. Sure, the cops would bring her in and ask her questions. But she knew she wouldn't be in trouble. Once they realized who Ali was—once they realized everything—she wouldn't be in trouble at all.

A second police cruiser had pulled up, and two officers loaded Mrs. D and Ali into the backseat. Just as Ali was about to climb inside, she twisted around and gave Emily a damning look. Her features were small and tight. She was so angry that her jaw was shaking.

"This isn't over," she hissed at Emily, little droplets of spit flying from her mouth. "We're not even *close* to being done."

But Emily knew they were. She knew, finally, she'd won.

31

THE GANG'S ALL HERE

Present, Monday,
Rosewood, Pennsylvania

"Emily?" Hanna gaped at the girl at the front of the courtroom. It was the most incredible thing she'd ever seen. There was Emily, whole, undamaged, bright-eyed, almost *excited* looking at the front of the courtroom. Not pulled out of the water, dead. Not huddled in a corner, crazy. *Alive.* Smiling.

Hanna tore down the aisle to her friend. Emily stretched her arms out and gave her a huge hug. It felt so good to breathe in Emily's lemony smell and look into her eyes. Hanna didn't even realize she was crying until she tried to speak and her words came out all blubbery. "I can't believe it," she said. "You're . . . *here.* Really here!"

"I'm here," Emily answered, tearing up, too. "I'm just sorry I'm late. You had to go to prison. I didn't mean for that to happen."

Hanna waved her hand. "You're alive," she whispered. "That's all that matters."

The others had approached and flocked around Emily, too. "How is this possible?" Spencer asked.

"How did you survive that storm?" Aria cried.

"Where have you *been*?" Hanna asked. She wondered, too, why Emily was back here. Had she survived only to turn herself in?

But Emily was looking back at the doors through which they'd all just come. Hanna swiveled around, too, and so did everyone else in the courtroom—which was mostly empty except for the judge, the lawyers, and some official-looking note-taking people. The double doors had opened, and someone new had just been escorted through. Hanna's jaw dropped.

"*Ali?*" she whispered.

At least she *thought* it was Ali. The girl's hair was stringy and brown. Layers of fat concealed her fine-boned face and made her blue eyes look all squishy and piggish. The black T-shirt she was wearing didn't remotely fit across her stomach or her boobs. A single thought bubbled to the surface of Hanna's mind: If this girl had been at Rosewood Day, and if the old Ali were still around, she would have ruthlessly made fun of her. Ali had become her own worst nightmare.

The rest of the courtroom exploded into whispers as a guard led Ali to the front of the court. Ali shuffled despondently. Hanna's heart was pounding so hard. Their almost-killer, the mastermind who'd gotten them sentenced to life in prison, was standing just feet away. Part of her wanted to break free from the others and pummel Ali to the ground. Another part wanted to run far away as fast as she could.

She wheeled around and stared at Emily. All at once, she understood why Emily was here. It wasn't a coincidence that both Emily and Ali were in the courthouse at the same time. Somehow, Emily had survived her death and . . . *found* Ali, wherever she'd been hiding.

She gawked at her friend. "I don't believe it."

"Where *was* she?" Aria asked at the same time, her eyes wide.

Emily gave them a patient smile. "I'll tell you the whole story soon," she whispered.

They all turned back to Ali, who was standing at the judge's bench, her head down. The judge looked from Ali to the girls. "It seems we have another surprise witness," he said wryly. "The murdered girl, arisen from the dead."

Ali's head snapped up. "They *did* try to kill me," she suddenly blurted. "You don't understand. They did everything I said in my journal. They tied me up. They hurt me. Everything I told you is true."

"Yeah, right," Spencer shouted.

Ali sneered at them, her face twisted and terrible. "They're horrible bitches," she told the judge. "They deserve to go to jail."

The judge stared at her evenly. "Watch what you say, Miss DiLaurentis. Everything that comes out of your mouth can and will be used against you—in your trial."

Ali's eyes widened. She opened her mouth to speak, but a man in a pin-striped suit who'd joined her at the bench, presumably her lawyer, placed a hand on her arm to silence her. Ali wilted, letting out a small, weak whimper.

Hanna felt a triumphant flurry in her chest. In every situation, Ali had gotten the better of them. Until now. It was the best feeling in the world. The judge then turned to them and gave the news that Hanna thought she'd never hear: All four of them were cleared of their murder charges, since the victim was *still alive*. "Not just *alive*, either, but she faked her own death and has been on the lam, evaded the law, tried to escape, and threatened Miss Fields here with a gun," the judge added, glancing in Emily's direction.

Hanna gawked at Emily. "She tried to shoot you?"

Emily shrugged. "Her mom did, too."

Spencer's mouth dropped open. So did Hanna's. She was too dumbstruck to ask questions.

The judge cleared his throat. "Now, there are some charges we will need to clear up with you girls. Miss Fields, you put a lot of people through a lot of strife, thinking you were dead. Not to mention you deliberately broke your court-ordered mandate to stay in the state of Pennsylvania and took off for Florida. But I suppose we'll let those charges rest, considering the ordeal you've been through."

Emily let out a huge sigh. "*Thank* you," she gushed. Hanna squeezed her hand.

"And Miss Montgomery." The judge flipped a page on his desk. "You fled the country, which is a bigger offense. But I think we can negotiate community service in lieu of prison time."

Aria's eyes brightened and she clapped a gleeful hand over her mouth.

The judge flipped more pages. "As for everything else with you girls, you've been cleared. You're free to go."

Spencer looked down at her prison uniform. "We can take this off?"

The judge nodded. He motioned toward a guard in the corner. The man strode over to the girls and began removing their ankle shackles one by one. The weights fell to the ground with a satisfying clunk.

Hanna took a moment to relish what was happening. She wasn't going back to prison! She wouldn't have to shower in plain sight or starve for fear of the disgusting food or sleep next to a murderer. She'd get to be with Mike again. She'd get to do *everything* again!

Hanna stared at Emily. "You actually did it. You found her. You got us all free!"

Emily grinned, still seeming a bit stunned herself. "It's crazy, isn't it? The whole time I wasn't sure if I could actually do it. But you guys were what kept me going. I thought of you the whole time—and that's why I did what I did."

They moved together into another group hug, everyone crying a little. Then Aria pulled back, sniffing, crying tears of joy. "You know, Em, we thought you were suicidal. We were so worried."

Emily nodded. "I *was* struggling a lot, ever since what Ali did to Jordan. And I know I took a huge risk going after her—it probably *was* crazy. I had no idea if I would actually find her." She slung one arm around Hanna's shoulders and another around Spencer's. "I'm just sorry that I had to leave you guys the way that I did. I felt terrible that I wasn't there during the trial. It looked awful."

"It was," Spencer said. But then she shrugged. "I get it. What you were doing was far more important. We'll never be able to repay you."

"You never have to," Emily said quickly. "You would have done the same for me."

Hanna turned to the judge. He was flipping another page, his gaze on Alison. "As for you," he said, the courtroom falling silent again. "You're a flight risk, you're a menace to society, you faked your own death, and you're unsafe on your own, so you will await your trial in prison." He banged his gavel. "Take her away."

Two guards appeared at Ali's sides and grabbed her arms. Ali let out a little grunt but let her limbs go limp. As they dragged her down the aisle, she glared at Hanna and the others. A shiver ran up Hanna's spine as their eyes met.

Neither of them blinked. Ali stared at Hanna and the others with disdain and a seething fury. It was a look Hanna had never quite seen from her before, probably because Ali had always been the one in control. This look said, *I can't believe this is happening to me.* Ali wasn't used to being on the losing end. The last time she'd lost, *really* lost, was after Courtney switched places with her, sending her to The Preserve.

And just like that, everyone in the courtroom was rising and filing out. No guards rushed up to Hanna and the others to escort them away. Slowly, the girls turned and walked out on their own. Through the doorway, Hanna caught sight of her mom and Mike waiting in the lobby. She squealed.

"Is this a dream?" she asked her friends, her grin stretched wide.

"Maybe," Spencer said, looking just as dazed. Then she reached out and took Hanna's hand, breaking out into a smile. Hanna reached for Emily on her other side, and Em reached for Aria.

Hand-in-hand, the four girls walked into the lobby together. Reporters pounced on them immediately with questions, microphones thrust in their faces. "What did you think when you saw Alison today?" one yelled. "Do you think she'll get the death penalty?" "Emily, how did you find her?" "What are your thoughts on this whole ordeal?"

For some reason, Hanna felt compelled to answer that last one. She leaned toward the reporter and took a deep breath. "What are my thoughts on this whole ordeal?" she repeated, pausing to contemplate. And then she thought of the perfect answer. "Ali didn't manage to kill us," she said. "She only made us stronger."

32

A CLEAN SLATE

The smell of something salty and delicious woke Aria from a deep dream. She opened her eyes, expecting to feel the immediate aches and pains of sleeping on a hard prison mattress, but instead she was lying in her old, familiar bed, surrounded by a million pillows. Her art posters hung on the walls, and her pig puppet, Pigtunia, peered out from the foot of the bed. Her recently returned cell phone blinked cheerfully on her desk.

She shot up like a start, everything rushing back. A miracle had happened. She was *home*. And Ali was in jail.

Aria leapt out of bed and grabbed her phone. There were a ton of Google Alerts for Ali, all of them mentioning her capture. Aria scrolled down to the bottom, searching. There was no mention of Ali escaping from jail this morning, though. No prison attacks, no strange disappearances. Ali was behind bars, for real.

But Aria still felt uneasy. Last night before bed, she'd checked every window and door to make sure it was locked. When she'd called her friends, they'd seemed just as paranoid. It would take a little time for them to shake the Ali fear. Aria just hoped it would go away eventually.

She pulled on her favorite robe, slipped the phone in her pocket, and strode downstairs.

Her mom stood at the stove, scrambling eggs. She looked up at Aria and smiled. "Morning," she said, pushing the hair out of Aria's eyes. "How did you sleep?"

"Really well," Aria said in a froggy voice, still feeling a little bewildered. "I guess a sleepless night in prison will do that."

Ella paused from making eggs to wrap her arms around Aria. "I'm so sorry you had to go through that," she said gently.

Aria shrugged. "I'm sorry I took off for Europe without telling you." She peeked at Ella. "Are you really mad?" she asked in a small voice.

Ella sighed. "Just don't do it again, okay?" She shook a spatula at her. "I mean it. You have nothing to hide now. Everyone believes you about Alison."

Her gaze drifted toward the TV in the corner. Not surprisingly, Ali's face flashed on the screen. The report was a rehash of yesterday's events—Ali coming into the courthouse, the ruling overturned, the girls going free, and Ali being locked up. The latest news, though, was that Ali had been put into the prison's psych ward, and she'd suddenly changed her story, confessing to framing the girls, faking the journal, and constructing an elaborate murder scene.

The prison psychiatrist appeared on TV. "Miss DiLaurentis keeps calling herself *A*," he told the reporter. "She has said, repeatedly, *I'm A. I did it. It was me all along.*"

"Whoa," Aria whispered. Ali, confessing to being A? *That* was a new one.

Ella let out a *tsk*. "I guess she's trying to plead insanity. Otherwise, why would she admit to all that?"

Aria winced. "Does that mean she might get out sooner?"

Ella shook her head. "Doubtful. In prison, you serve your sentence, and then you can go. At the psych ward, they can extend your stay indefinitely."

Aria rolled her jaw. Maybe that was so, but Ali was smart. She wouldn't have gotten herself thrown into the psych ward if she didn't think there was something in it for her. Probably she thought she could figure out how to escape from it.

Then Emily appeared on the screen, giving a brief recap of how she'd tracked down Ali in Florida. Aria beamed with pride. Emily had told them the whole crazy story yesterday, including the part about Mrs. DiLaurentis hiding Ali, and Emily confronting her, and Ali popping out with the gun. She'd also explained how she'd called 911 but left the phone in her pocket, banking on the call being recorded and the police realizing something terrible was happening. It had been a risk, Emily said, but it had paid off, as the cops arrived just in time to save Emily from Ali's wrath. Aria couldn't believe the good luck of it all. It felt like fate had intervened, like the universe had realized that Ali couldn't get away with it *again*.

Then the news showed a shot of Mrs. DiLaurentis. Ali's mom's head was down, her hands were cuffed, and two police officers were leading her into what looked like a jail. "Jessica DiLaurentis is being charged with harboring a known criminal," blared a reporter. "Her trial is set to begin next week."

Then Ali's father, looking bewildered and exhausted, popped on camera. "I had no idea my wife was hiding our daughter," he said, the corners of his mouth turning down. "I have nothing else to say on the matter." For whatever reason, Aria believed him.

"So that's that," Ella said softly as she scraped the eggs from the pan and onto a plate. She handed Aria one serving and kept another for herself, and the two of them sat down to eat. After picking at moldy prison food, the eggs were the most delicious thing Aria had ever tasted.

"So that's that," Aria repeated, looking down.

Ella cocked her head. "You don't seem so thrilled."

"I am . . ." Aria trailed off. "It's just . . . *weird*, you know? We were so used to no one believing us. I even got a call from Jasmine Fuji yesterday, apologizing." *That* had been a huge surprise. It certainly felt good to hear Fuji say she was sorry. "But it's hard to actually let go," Aria added. "I keep thinking Ali's still out there, plotting her next move against us."

Ella chewed thoughtfully. "Are you worried about the Ali Cats?"

Aria fiddled with the napkin on her lap. "Maybe," she admitted. "What if she gets in touch with them in prison? What if she asks them to hurt us, somehow?"

Ella shook her head. "They won't let her have visitors, and they won't let her use the internet." She patted Aria's hand. "You can't keep being afraid of her. You have to live your life. Otherwise, she really has won." Then Ella brightened and pushed her cell phone across the table. "And actually, I have some news for you. In the past weekend, demand for your artwork has gone up tremendously. *Everyone* wants an Aria Montgomery piece now. Which means *you*, my dear, have to get painting."

Aria looked at the email on Ella's screen. It was from Patricia, her agent in New York, stating that six people had put bids on yet-to-be-painted Aria works. "Wow," she breathed.

"Right?" Ella's eyes shone. "You're going to get to live the life you want after all, honey. And you shouldn't let anyone keep you from being happy."

Aria tried to smile, but suddenly she felt another twinge. She *did* feel happy. But one thing was missing: Noel. Another Google Alert had said that Noel might receive two years in prison because he'd followed Aria to Amsterdam, but in the Ali scuffle, Aria hadn't heard anything more. She'd called him the moment her phone had been returned to her, but his phone went to voicemail every time. Was he already in jail? What did he think about all this?

She looked up at her mom, suddenly determined. "I have to go do something," she blurted, and rose from the table. Ella looked at Aria curiously, but she didn't ask any questions as Aria, still wearing her pajamas and a robe, grabbed the car keys and headed out the door.

The gate to Noel's family's house was open, but Aria still parked on the street, feeling apprehensive about dropping in unannounced. As she walked up the path, she relived all the times she and Noel had lay in the front yard, gazing at the stars, or having a picnic, or making a snowman. It was strange to return here with the situation so changed. The grass looked the same, there were the same flowers in the beds, but she was so different . . . and Noel was, too. Maybe *too* different.

Swallowing hard, she rang the bell, praying Noel's mother didn't answer the door—Aria hadn't seen much of Mrs. Kahn after they'd reconnected, but Noel's mom hadn't been a fan of her after Noel was attacked at prom, and she probably blamed Aria for dragging Noel to Europe. Three chimes rang out, and Aria tapped her toe nervously. After a moment, she heard footsteps. Then the door flung open. Noel was on the other side.

He wore a hoodie over a faded T-shirt, and his sneakers

were untied. The first thing Aria did was search for an ankle tracking bracelet peeking out from under his jeans. She didn't see one.

"Hey," she said bashfully, suddenly not sure what to say.

"Hey," Noel said back.

There was a long, strange pause. "Are you okay? Are you going to prison?" she blurted out, before he could slam the door in her face.

Noel shook his head. "They dropped my charges. My dad hired a good lawyer, and after all the Ali stuff . . ." He waved his hands. "I got a slap on the wrist, had to pay some fines, that sort of thing—and, I mean, my family is really pissed." He made a face. "But I'm free. And it looks like you are, too." His mouth twisted into an almost-smile.

"Yeah," Aria said, her eyes filling with tears. Suddenly, she felt overcome with . . . well, she wasn't sure what. Shame, maybe. And also gratitude. And simple exhaustion. "I'm so sorry, Noel," she said.

He held up his hand. "*I'm* the one who's sorry. You guys were going through so much, and you were so paranoid, and you were *right* to feel that way. Have you read any of Ali's confessions? She's crazy. She doesn't just talk about that journal, she talks about assembling an Ali Cat army and then *killing* some of them when she had no use for them anymore. Everything you guys worried about, everything you were running from, all those crazy fears no one believed? It was all true."

Aria nodded shakily. She knew it was true. She'd lived it.

Noel took her hands and squeezed. "And as for what you said in Holland—look, you have to know that I don't care about Ali anymore. I don't love her, I don't think of her, I don't *anything.* All I think of is you."

Aria's heart did a little flip. "Okay," she said, head down.

"We've been through too many cycles of getting mad at each other over Ali and reconciling. Our argument in Holland proved it. I don't want to go through that again."

"I don't, either," Aria said quickly.

"So I guess I need to know." Noel took a deep breath. "*Do* you forgive me for Ali? In your heart, for real?" He stared up at the clouds. "Because I'm *sorry,* Aria. I'm sorry I lied to you. I'm sorry I didn't tell you everything I should have. I'm sorry I was involved with her at all. If you don't forgive me, that's okay. But I don't know if we can be together, you know? It wouldn't feel . . . right. You'd always be mad at me, deep down. I'm just wondering if we can just . . . start over. Like it never even happened."

Aria sank down onto the stone bench next to the fish-pond. The fight they'd had just before they were arrested swirled in her mind. It was a hard thing for Aria to let go of—the fact that he'd sympathized with Ali for so long, kept it from Aria.

But that was exactly what Ali wanted: to remain in their consciousness, to be an obstacle between her and

Noel even from behind bars. It was the perfect A strategy, actually: manipulation and mind games from afar, with Aria's own self-sabotage leading to her downfall.

Aria squared her shoulders. "Yes," she said. "Let's start over. I'm done letting Ali take away the things—and the people—I care about the most."

Noel grinned. "I love you, Aria Montgomery," he said, and kissed her softly.

Eventually they just leaned their foreheads together, staring into each other's eyes. Aria glanced at the T-shirt he was wearing. All at once, she realized it was his lucky Nike University of Pennsylvania tee he'd had for years. It was the same shirt he'd had on the day she'd re-met him in Rosewood when her family had returned from Iceland.

She paused to reflect on that day. Noel had tried to strike up a conversation with Aria, but she'd blown him off, thinking there was no way he could have had a crush on her. She'd felt so . . . *above* him, she supposed, assuming he was just some Typical Rosewood who lacked culture and style. Totally not her type.

Boy, was she wrong. Who knew they'd be *here* in a few short years?

Then Aria remembered the internet search she'd done in the car, just before coming over. "I have something for you."

"For me?" Noel looked confused.

Aria pulled up the email on her phone and showed him the screen, which had a logo for Japan Airlines. *Your upcoming itinerary*, it read. Noel's brow furrowed, but he scrolled down. The email was a confirmation for two seats on a flight to Tokyo, leaving next week.

He looked up at her. "Really?"

Aria nodded excitedly. "My accounts were unfrozen, and I've sold a few more paintings. I thought you and I could take that trip to Tokyo we were talking about." She peeked at him shyly. "If you still want to . . ."

"Of course I'll go!" Noel said, throwing his arms around her once more. "We'll do everything we talked about, right? Touring the pagodas, eating sushi, the skiing . . ."

"Except no international incidents," Aria advised. "No hiding in hotels."

"No sneaking off trains," Noel agreed.

"No strange men arresting us in dark alleys."

Aria giggled. Looking at Noel again, she felt a rush of love. All at once, things really *were* right. "It's a date," she said, and kissed him again.

33

SPENCER EMBRACES IT ALL

The following evening, Spencer and Wren sat next to each other at a long dining table in the Rosewood Country Club's formal dining room. The sun was setting, the outside lights cast a pretty pink glow against the ninth green, and Spencer's skin tingled every time her knees bumped Wren's. Melissa, Darren, Spencer's mother, Mr. Pennythistle, and Amelia were there, too—and, interestingly, so was Spencer's father. Both of her parents were on their best behavior—for good reason. It was a celebration of all kinds of things: Melissa's pregnancy, her engagement, and, most of all, Spencer's exoneration. They had a million things to be thankful for, and what better way for the Hastings family to celebrate than with dinner at the club?

Spencer gazed around the dining room with a smirk. The Rosewood Country Club would never change: It had the same heavy mahogany furniture, the same sea-life mural on the wall, even the crotchety jazz band in the corner playing the same rendition of "All of Me." The same preppy boys in their blazers and girls in their pleated skirts snuck sips of their tight-lipped parents' gin and tonics. As Spencer gazed around her own table, she half expected her family to launch into a rousing game of Star Power, comparing their accomplishments and desperately trying to one-up each other. It used to be a Country Club Dinner staple.

When *was* the last time they'd played that game, though? It seemed like a lifetime ago, and things were so different now. There was Melissa on Spencer's other side, shooting Spencer a sweet smile, all animosity between them gone. Melissa held Darren's hand—a guy who'd almost *ruined* Spencer, thinking she'd killed Courtney, and a guy *she'd* suspected, too—and Darren raised his glass to Spencer's for a toast. Mr. Pennythistle, who Spencer thought she'd never grow to like, pushed a plate of the club's famous mussels toward Spencer, urging her to have a bite. Even prissy little Amelia had poked Spencer's arm a few moments earlier to show her a funny dog video on YouTube, almost like they were friends.

Then there was her dad, at the end of the table. Spencer watched as he straightened his tie and signaled his favorite bartender for another glass of Scotch. Mr. Hastings was clearly on the fringes of the group, but she appreciated that he was part of this tonight. Still, Spencer had to wonder: Did he grieve for the monster he'd created in Ali? Was he sad that she was so crazy, and that she would probably spend her whole life in jail? Spencer didn't dare ask him—they didn't exactly talk about the fact that he was the DiLaurentis twins' secret father. But she had a feeling the grief weighed on him. Bertie, the waiter who'd been at the club ever since Spencer could remember, appeared at Mr. Hastings's elbow. "Big group tonight," he announced, looking down the table, his brow crinkling at the obvious incongruity of Mr. Hastings, Mrs. Hastings, *and* Mr. Pennythistle. On one hand, it *was* kind of weird—definitely unprecedented for a Hastings family dinner. But as Spencer leaned back and looked at the pink cloud mural above her head, she realized that maybe the Hastings were more unprecedented than she thought.

After Bertie took their dinner orders, Spencer looked over at her sister, who was gently touching her as-yet-nonexistent belly. "Do you feel any kicks yet?" she asked hopefully.

Melissa giggled. "Not *yet*, silly—it's way too early. But don't worry. You'll be the first to know."

"You'd better tell me, too," Mrs. Hastings said mock-sternly from across the table.

"I'll tell you both at the same time," Melissa said, smiling. "How about that?"

"I suppose that's fair," Mrs. Hastings demurred. Then she rolled her eyes and touched Spencer's hand. "After all, you *are* going to be the godmother. And you'll make a good one, I'm sure of it."

Spencer looked over at her mom, feeling a tiny twinge. Ever since she'd been released, her mom had tried really hard to apologize for the way she'd treated Spencer during the trial. What would she think, though, if she knew Spencer had almost sold off her jewels? Spencer had put them back as soon as Angela drove away, but she still felt bad for doing it in the first place. And why hadn't Amelia told on her? She'd seen the ring on Spencer's finger and the guilty look on her face. It would have been such an easy way to get Spencer in trouble. And yet, for whatever reason, she hadn't.

Spencer glanced at her stepsister across the table, then experimentally stuck out her tongue. Amelia looked up, eyes wide, and then stuck out her tongue back. Her smile was genuine. Maybe Amelia wasn't so bad after all. Spencer promised to give her more of a chance, now that she was free.

Then Mr. Pennythistle turned to Spencer. "So. What are your plans? Off to Princeton after all?"

Spencer ran her tongue over her teeth. Once again, Princeton had reinstated her place at school that fall. Alyssa Bloom from HarperCollins had called, too, re-extending her book deal. She'd received a ton of emails in the past day to start up the bullying site once more.

Which she would . . . but maybe not this week. Maybe not next week. "You know, I've been thinking about taking a gap year," she said, glancing nervously at her mother—this was the first Mrs. Hastings was hearing about it—and then at Wren, with whom she'd discussed the plan at length. "I talked to Princeton, and they said it would be okay to defer until next year."

Mrs. Hastings took a sip of her cocktail. "What would you do instead? I'd rather you didn't just lie around the house."

Spencer took a deep breath and looked at her father down the table. "Well, Dad got me an internship at a Legal Aid office in Philly. I'd help represent people who don't have money to pay for lawyers." She shifted in the plushy seat. "I guess the trial got me interested in the legal system. And I'd work on the bullying book, too."

Mrs. Hastings crossed her arms over her chest, considering this. "Would you live here?"

Spencer couldn't tell if that was a plea for her to stay in the house or for her to get the hell out. "Maybe in the city. With roommates? I don't know." Spencer looked at Melissa. "I want to be close to the baby when he or she is born."

It wasn't that she didn't want to go to Princeton someday . . . just not in a few months. It was funny: Only when she'd really considered disappearing for good did Spencer truly appreciate what she had here.

"I think it sounds like a great idea," Melissa said softly.

"Yeah, it sounds cool," Amelia chimed in.

Wren squeezed her knee. "You'd make a great lawyer, Spence."

"That's what I've always told her, since she loves to argue," Mr. Hastings said, rolling his eyes.

Mrs. Hastings let out a breath. "Well, I suppose it's your decision. As long as Princeton has given their blessing about deferring."

"Really?" Spencer cried, her whole face erupting into a smile. "Thank you, Mom!"

She circled the table to give her mother a hug, but Mrs. Hastings swished her away. "I'll wrinkle," she said, gesturing to her linen dress. But then after a moment she smiled, and hugged Spencer anyway.

Wren touched Spencer's arm and asked if she wanted to get some air on the patio. They walked outside together, taking in the pretty vantage. The golf course was so green, the trees behind it so lush. Spencer could just make out the Hollis Spire through some of the branches.

"That went well, don't you think?" Wren murmured.

Spencer nodded. "Better than I thought."

Wren touched the tip of her nose. "I'm so glad you're going to be in Philly. Because you know what *else* is in Philly, besides the Legal Aid office?"

Spencer put a hand to her chin, pretending to think. "Um, the Liberty Bell?"

"Not that," Wren said playfully.

"Independence Hall?"

Wren chuckled. "How about *me*?"

Spencer's heart did a flip. "Oh, right!" she exclaimed, in mock surprise. Then she sighed. "I can't wait to spend more time with you," she said softly. She was really excited at the prospect of getting to know Wren better.

Wren leaned in, and their lips met in a passionate kiss. Spencer shut her eyes, sinking into the sensation. Her world felt utterly right. She was so glad she hadn't disappeared. She'd remained Spencer Hastings, and she didn't have to give that up for freedom.

But then her gaze drifted back into the dining room, landing on a certain table near the window. She'd probably sat at every table in this place at one point or another, but that particular table carried a particular memory. It was shortly after Courtney had tapped them for her new clique, right after they'd all become friends, and Spencer had brought the girls to the formal dining room to show off her parents' expensive country club. They'd all dressed up, and everyone had tried to act extra-genteel, ordering complicated items off the menu and behaving with impeccable manners. Aria had even spoken with an accent.

Halfway through, however, Hanna had knocked over an enormous carafe of iced tea, which had doused their sweet potato fries, the candle in the middle of the table, and somehow even sprayed the grumpy old couple sitting to their left. For a moment, the room had been absolutely silent. The old woman stared at Hanna with disdain, her ugly white suit ruined. Spencer had glanced at Their Ali—Courtney—certain she'd blacklist all of them for Hanna's clumsiness. But to her surprise, Courtney had thrown back her head and laughed. And then the *rest* of them had laughed, hooting so loudly and uncontrollably the waiter had asked them to leave. They'd tumbled onto the golf green, holding one another, not even sure what was funny anymore. Spencer had never loved Courtney as much as she had that day. And she'd loved the others, too—just as much as she loved them now.

Spencer's attention drifted to the TV above the bar, in the casual lounge side of the restaurant. Not very coincidentally—for Ali was *everywhere* right now—the Ali story was on the news. There was a picture of an overweight brunette being led into prison in handcuffs. *Psychopath Awaits Trial in Psych Ward*, read the banner underneath.

Suddenly, the girl turned and stared straight into the camera. Her mouth was small. Her expression didn't change. Her eyes didn't look scared or sad, but angry. A shiver traveled up Spencer's spine. It felt like Ali was looking straight at *her*. And her eyes were saying, *We're not over. There's still a lot of fight left in me. You just wait.*

One of the guards yanked Ali hard to turn her around, and they shoved her into prison, slamming the doors shut behind her. Heavy iron doors, Spencer was happy to note, with industrial-size locks, guarded by vicious dogs and men with high-powered rifles. Ali wouldn't be escaping any time soon.

And Spencer would never have to worry about her again.

34

THE JOYS OF MARRIAGE

On Thursday morning, Hanna and Mike sat at Hanna's kitchen table for breakfast. They were dressed in monogrammed, terry-cloth bathrobes they'd received as wedding gifts, plaid pajama pants, and interesting footwear. Hanna's high-heeled slippers with a pouf on the toe were a wedding gift from Hailey Blake. Mike was wearing the ugliest Icelandic-wool socks Hanna had ever laid eyes on. When she asked him to take them off, he'd just looked at her and said, "These are my favorites. They keep my feet warm."

Those were the intimate details you were forced to deal with when you married someone. You learned to take their ugly socks. You witnessed their drool on the pillow while they slept. You kicked them gently when they snored. She'd gotten all of that and more the past few nights.

And it had been *wonderful.*

Now they were plowing through the enormous pile of wrapped gifts on the floor. Even though Hanna had explicitly said *No Gifts* on the invitation, people had bought them all kinds of crap anyway. And not just their wedding guests, but people from all over the country who'd felt for Hanna after Ali reappeared and their verdict was reversed.

"Oh look, another SodaStream!" Hanna exclaimed, removing the drink-carbonating machine from its wrapping paper. She peered at the accompanying card. "It's from a Mrs. Mary Hammond in Akron, Ohio." She glanced at Mike. "Anyone you know?"

"Nope, sounds like a Hanna fan." Mike made a face. "I don't even *like* sparkling water."

Hanna added it to the duplicates pile, which also included three Keurig coffeemakers, two waffle irons, four eggbeaters, and two complete sets of kitchen knives. She let out a sigh as she took in all the loot. "Let's just hope Macy's lets us exchange this for cash."

"Not this one!" Mike said, slicing open a small envelope. It was a twenty-five-dollar gift card to Hooters from someone in New Mexico. He tucked it into his pocket. "I'm totally treating Noel to some wings and boobs."

"You're gross," Hanna told him, wrinkling her nose in mock horror.

"Just kidding." Mike grinned. "I won't even *look* at the girls."

"Damn right," Hanna said as she opened yet another salad spinner.

Mike peeked at the card, which was again from someone neither of them knew. "But you know that means you can't work out with any of the hot male trainers at the gym anymore."

"What?" Hanna pouted. "That's not fair!"

Mike grinned. "You have to give up some stuff for marriage, remember?"

"Fine, I guess it's worth it." Hanna sighed dramatically.

"It's *totally* worth it," Mike said, and leaned in to kiss her. When he leaned back, tucking a stray hair behind her ear, Hanna looked into his bright blue eyes. "Promise me we won't turn into a boring married couple?" she blurted out. "I don't want to be those people who sit around and watch TV and don't talk to each other."

Mike picked up a big gift with pink-and-white striped wrapping paper. "Obviously not. We're going to be the cool married people. We'll go to parties, have tons of friends . . ."

"And we'll live in New York," Hanna said, smiling at the thought of the Fashion Institute of Technology. She'd gotten a call yesterday saying she was still welcome there if she wanted to attend. The idea of getting out of Rosewood to somewhere exciting like New York City was pretty thrilling. She was sick of this place.

"Yeah, my parents are thrilled I got into Stuyvesant," Mike said, referring to the prestigious public school in Manhattan. You had to take an exam to be admitted, and Mike had surprised everyone by passing easily—except for

Hanna, of course, who always knew he was smart. She felt guilty that he would spend his senior year of high school somewhere new, but he'd assured her that he was ready to leave Rosewood, too. And that he wanted to be wherever Hanna was. "Plus, Aria will be there. Hey," Mike said, his eyes lighting up as he got an idea. "Maybe we should get a big apartment with her and Noel. How awesome would that be? You guys could, like, girl-talk every night, Noel and I could watch football, we'd always have drinking buddies . . ."

Hanna shoved him playfully. "We are not having *roommates*, Mike. We're married."

She was about to say something else, but she trailed off, her attention turned to the object Mike had pulled from the pink-and-white wrapping. It was a robin's-egg-blue Tiffany box.

"Ooh!" she squealed, yanking it from Mike and opening the lid. Inside, instead of a pair of crystal champagne glasses or one of those gorgeous silver picture frames like she'd expected, was a silver bracelet with a Tiffany heart charm. She blinked. It was exactly like the one she'd shoplifted from the King James Mall years before. That bracelet had landed her in the police station and had triggered the first message from A, about looking fat in prison garb. Except there was one difference: This charm had an initial engraved on it. The letter *A*.

There was a note with the bracelet, too. Hanna opened it up.

I'll always be watching. —A

Hanna felt the blood drain from her face. Was this from the *real* A? Maybe before Emily apprehended Ali in Florida? She wished she knew when UPS had delivered the box.

Mike grabbed the note and stuffed it in his pocket. "We'll turn it over to Fuji. But you shouldn't worry about it."

"Uh huh," Hanna said quickly.

But that didn't stop her heart from pounding. It was going to take some time to really understand that Ali was truly gone. Nick wouldn't be getting out of prison, either, and even Mrs. DiLaurentis had been arrested for hiding Ali and pulling a gun on Emily. And even if, by a horrible twist of fate, Ali *did* escape from prison, at least Fuji believed them this time. Hanna and the others were no longer the Pretty Little Liars but the Pretty Little Truthtellers. Not that that had a particularly good ring to it on the cover of *People*.

Her phone chirped, and she put the strange box aside and looked at the number on the caller ID, afraid for a split second that A might be calling. It was a number from Los Angeles. Puzzled, Hanna answered and heard a gruff voice. "Hanna? This is Hank Ross."

"Oh!" Hanna shot up from her chair. Hank was the director of *Burn It Down*. "H-how are you?"

"I'm all right, Hanna, though probably not as well as

you are." Hanna could tell by the tone of Hank's voice that he was smiling. "Congratulations on everything. I also heard you got married?"

"Uh, yeah," Hanna said. She looked over and Mike squeezed her arm. *Who is it?* he mouthed, but she held up a finger, indicating she'd tell him in a moment.

"So listen, Hanna." Hank cleared his throat. "You might not know this, but our production has been put on hold for a little bit. The story kind of got . . . *bigger* than what we'd written. Alison faking her death, Emily also faking her death and finding Alison in Florida—we wanted to use all of it."

"Yeah," Hanna said faintly. "Emily is a hero."

"Indeed," Hank agreed. "So we've gone back to the drawing board and rewritten quite a few of the scenes. Compressed some stuff, added a bunch of new drama as well. But our backers and the studio are very, very impressed with our new script, and we've gotten the green light to continue. It's going to be an even more incredible movie than before."

"That's great," Hanna said. It made sense to tell the story all the way to the end.

"I think you should come back and play yourself," Hank said. "If you're still interested, that is."

Hanna held the phone outstretched. "Really?"

"Absolutely. Everyone loves you. And now that you've gotten the trial out of the way, there's only one catch: The movie is filming in L.A. now, not Rosewood. A few of our stars had dual commitments out West, and because we didn't want to lose them we were forced to relocate. We'll shoot it at the Warner studio in Burbank this summer. It'll have the same feel and look as Rosewood though, don't worry. So what do you say?"

Hanna peeked at Mike. He stared back excitedly, probably sensing what the call was about. "I'm supposed to go to college in the fall . . . ," she said, trailing off.

"Not a problem. We plan on wrapping in mid-August, so that will give you plenty of time. We do start shooting next week though," Hank said, sounding nervous.

"I'll have to check with my husband," Hanna told him. "I'm assuming the salary package is competitive?"

"Naturally," Hank answered quickly. "We'll give you a raise from your last offer."

"Good to hear," Hanna said in a clipped voice. "Well, my agent will get back to you shortly."

Then she hung up, placed her phone on the table, and selected another gift from the floor. Mike blinked at her hard. "Um, hello? I'm dying over here!"

Hanna looked up at him, ready to explode from excitement. "How would you feel about going to L.A. for the summer?"

Mike's eyes gleamed. "Is my wife going to be a star?"

"I think so," Hanna said giddily. "So what do you say? Will you come with me?"

Mike opened his arms. And Hanna knew, just from the way he hugged her, that he was going to say yes.

Six months later

35

REAL LIFE

Emily sat on her bed, looking around her old bedroom. She hadn't been in here in months, and it felt both the same and different. The same old Michael Phelps posters were on the walls, and some of her old clothes still hung in the closet. But Carolyn's side was now overrun by a big Singer sewing machine and a bunch of plastic bins full of thread and fabric. The carpets had also been changed to pale white instead of their old candy pink. The room felt emptier, no longer as full of life.

And as Emily sprang out of bed and looked at herself in the mirror, *she* was different, too. Her face was no longer drawn and freaked-out looking. Her hair still had highlights from the summer she'd spent working at the surf shop in Monterey, California. She felt utterly . . . well, *herself.* To be honest, it actually felt stifling being back in the house—she'd left soon after she came back from Florida, and she hadn't had a ton of contact with her parents since. But she was only here for a night to celebrate the big premiere of *Burn It Down.*

She was dressed in her new uniform as of late: Toms shoes, oversize snowboarding-style pants, and a fitted Hurley shirt—a perk of being one of the new faces of the brand, thanks to her newfound fame. With one more glance at her reflection, she rolled back her shoulders and padded downstairs. The Christmas tree was up in the family room, and lights were strung on the staircase. Her mother was in the kitchen, stuffing some things in a large, holiday-themed basket. When she turned and saw Emily, she broke into a twitchy smile. "Want breakfast?"

Emily didn't answer, her eyes on the basket. It was yet another one of her mother's Welcome Wagon efforts for someone who'd just moved to the community. It gave her a spiky twinge. More than two years before, her mom had prepared a basket just like this one—albeit autumn-themed—for Maya St. Germain's family, who'd moved into Ali's house. As it turned out, though, she'd been totally *un*welcoming to them, after she found out Emily was in love with Maya.

Her mom noticed Emily's gaze on the basket and flinched. Emily could tell her mom was groping for a way to break the ice. Last night, when Emily had gotten in, Mrs. Fields had looked at her in the same longing way, full of questions she didn't feel like she could ask anymore. Emily knew her well enough to know what they might be: *Are you going to go to college? Why are you still living at the beach? Why won't you* talk *to me?*

But Emily wasn't going to take her family back that easily, not after what her friends had told her about the funeral. Emily had confronted her mom about not letting Hanna, Spencer, or Aria speak, and Mrs. Fields had just given her a crazy jumble of excuses. "We were so confused about what had happened," she'd said in a scattered voice. "We didn't know if your friends were the problem or the solution."

"Yeah, but they knew me best," Emily had snapped. "And if it was really *my* funeral, with my wishes, you would have let them speak no matter what they had to say."

Her mother had shrugged and said that was out of the question. And all at once, it had hit Emily. *She* was out of the question, too—at least in her parents' eyes. Her parents were so worried about how she appeared to other people—first when Emily wanted to quit swimming, then when she came out to them, and then the domino effect of Ali and A and everything else. They couldn't even eulogize her properly. They'd been forced to turn her into the perfect little Emily they'd always *wanted*.

But she wasn't that Emily, and she never would be. What she had to understand, though, was that her parents weren't going to change, either. And so she'd let her family go for a while. She would always love them, but it was easier to do so from afar, at least until they came to terms with who she really was. And for now, that was okay.

Because she had another family, a *real* family, people who accepted her no matter what.

Her friends.

Her phone buzzed, and she looked at the screen. *I'm out front*, Hanna texted. "See you," Emily said to her mother, grabbing a bagel from the platter and heading out the door.

The December air was crisp, and huge piles of leaves overran the lawn. Emily skipped across the grass to Hanna's parked Prius. She whooped when she saw Spencer, Aria, and Hanna inside. "Oh my *God*!" she squealed, yanking open the door.

All three girls inside yelped, too. "You look awesome!" Hanna, who was wearing a short, studded dress she'd designed herself during her first semester at FIT, cried.

"Are you, like, a pro surfer by now, Em?" Aria asked. "When are you going to teach me?"

"Whenever!" Emily lilted, sliding in next to her. "But you have to come visit. It's been too long."

It *had* been too long. In late June, Emily had visited Hanna in L.A., where she was filming *Burn It Down*, but they hadn't seen each other since. The northern and southern parts of the state weren't exactly close. And then the film had wrapped and Hanna and Mike had returned to New York, where Hanna was going to FIT and Mike was finishing up high school, and they were living together in what Hanna claimed was "the cutest West Village one-bedroom you've ever seen." Aria was living in Brooklyn, painting and schmoozing the art gallery circuit and going to Parsons—and Noel was in New York, too, but uptown at Columbia, where he'd walked on to the lacrosse team. Aria and Hanna said that they saw each other, but not as much as they wanted given their grueling school schedules. And Spencer had taken a job at Legal Aid in Philly and was still dating Wren.

Emily had meant to visit all of them in the past six months, but she'd been busy, too. Sure, by most standards she'd been a beach bum, learning how to surf, logging long hours at the shop, doing a few Hurley ads, and giving a few lucrative interviews about her harrowing debacle with Ali. She'd also met a pretty new surfer girl named Laura and . . . and started *something*, though it was too early yet to tell what. Mostly, Emily had been finding herself. Being truly *her*, which was something Rosewood had always prevented. Not that she knew that until she left.

"It is so weird to be back in my house," Hanna moaned as she pulled away from the curb. "My dad keeps calling, like, every hour, wanting to see me. And my mom keeps giving me marriage tips." She made a face. "Stuff like, 'Don't go to bed mad.'"

"It's weird for me, too!" Aria sighed. "Especially because Mike and I are both gone. Ella is mooning around, moaning that her kids grew up too fast."

"And doesn't everything seem so . . . I don't know, *small* here?" Emily looked at the houses swishing past.

"I don't remember the Wawa being so teeny-tiny. Even Rosewood Day doesn't seem as impressive."

"That's what happens when you leave somewhere," Spencer teased, cuffing her playfully on the shoulder.

Hanna drummed on the steering wheel. "Listen, I have everyone booked for hair at eleven and makeup at noon, and then we'll try on a bunch of dresses my stylist brought in so we look totally and completely fabulous for the event. Okay?"

"You don't have to do all that, Han," Aria complained, crossing her slender, leather-clad legs. She was wearing the most fabulous black studded booties Emily had ever seen, and with her new, choppier haircut, she looked like a true New York City artist.

Hanna snickered. "Of course I do. *Rosewood's* footing the bill—when they found out we were holding the premiere here, they said they'd pay for everything, including a spa day for all of us."

"Well, they owe us," Spencer sing-songed, stifling a giggle.

"Agreed," Emily said.

Spencer frowned into the rearview mirror. "Shit, guys. I just realized I left my camera at home—I really want to document all of this. Mind if we swing by and grab it?"

"Sure," everyone said in unison, and Hanna turned into Spencer's neighborhood.

"So," Hanna said. "From now on, we are hanging out at least once a month, okay? I'm going to fly all of us out to L.A. in February. Which will be perfect, since it's freezing in New York around then. What do you say?"

"Totally," Aria answered, and Emily let out a cheer.

"As long as Melissa doesn't have the baby early," Spencer reminded them. "She's due right around then, and she wants me to be her labor coach." She made a freaked-out face, then glanced at Emily, who smiled sadly. "I can only imagine, Em," she said softly. "I wish I'd been there to help you through it." It hadn't been so long ago that they'd all been there in Emily's hospital room for her C-section.

"How is Violet, anyway?" Hanna asked, seeming to read their minds.

Emily grinned. "She's great. She's even starting to say some words!" That was something else that had changed: After the Ali stuff, Emily had decided that she wanted some contact with Violet, after all. She'd reached out to Violet's family, saying that things were absolutely safe—no A was going to swoop down and try and steal Violet away—and they'd given her regular updates on the little girl, who was now a year and a half old. The family was planning to take Violet to Disneyland in California once she turned two, and they'd invited Emily along. She couldn't wait.

They pulled up to Spencer's house, and Spencer entered the key code into her gate. "Be right back," she said, dashing inside.

Emily sat back and gazed at Spencer's lawn, which was covered in a fine layer of frost. Even though she'd been there a thousand times since, all she could think of, suddenly, was the seventh-grade sleepover, when she and her friends and Courtney had convened on this very street. She could almost hear their words verbatim: *I'm so glad this day is over. I'm so glad seventh grade is over.* And then, from Mona Vanderwaal: *Hey, Alison! Hey, Spencer!* It was hard to imagine that a second DiLaurentis twin had been watching from the window the whole time. Waiting. Scheming. And that, hours later, Courtney would be dead.

Three months before, Real Ali had been officially sentenced to life in prison. Emily had considered going to the arraignment, but she decided she didn't need to see Ali again. Still, she sometimes woke up in the middle of the night, certain that Ali was out there. Something about all of this felt unfinished. Emily wished she could have made Ali understand exactly what she'd done to them. But maybe she needed to let that go. Ali was crazy. She didn't listen to reason.

"What the hell is *that*?"

Hanna pointed at something on the DiLaurentis's curb. There was a jumble of candles, several stuffed animals, and a few bouquets of flowers wrapped in cellophane. A vanity license plate propped among them read *Alison* in glittery pink letters.

Emily's insides seized. Another Ali shrine? *Really?*

Aria made a disgusted face. "Wonder how long *that's* been up."

Spencer swung back into the car with her camera, then

glanced where the girls were looking. "Oh, yeah." She made a face. "*That*. Amelia says it went up right after Ali was sentenced to life in prison."

Emily squinted. "Three *months* ago?"

"Uh huh," Spencer said.

Aria clucked her tongue. "I can't believe there are still Ali Cats."

"There probably always will be," Emily said softly. She perused Ali Cat boards every so often, astonished at how many people still sympathized with Ali's plight. "But we also know that the FBI has it under control. No one's talking to her in prison. And no one is going to hurt us."

"Damn right," Hanna said. She glanced at Emily in the rearview mirror. "*We* won this time."

Emily's phone beeped. She looked down at the screen, feeling suddenly worried. Maybe it was being back in Rosewood, maybe it was being *here*, in front of Ali's house, but she couldn't help but think she'd just received a new text from A.

But it was from Laura. *Miss you, chica*, it said. *Hope you're having fun!*

Emily looked up and smiled. She typed back that she missed Laura, too. Laura would never be Jordan, she knew. *No one* would be Jordan. But maybe that was okay. Emily was just happy going with the flow, seeing where things with Laura went.

Spencer cast one more glance at the Ali shrine, then shrugged. "You know what? Who cares if the Ali shrine is there. People can love Ali all they want. *We* have better things to do."

"Hells yeah!" Hanna whooped, shifting into drive. "We have a premiere to get to!"

And just like that, the four of them took off, leaving the Ali shrine—and maybe Ali herself—far behind. To Emily, it felt like a huge moment. They were going off into their new lives. Into a world where they were understood and safe. Into a world where they could be anything they wanted.

And into a world where they'd always have each other.

36

BEHIND CLOSED DOORS

The four blank cinder-block walls gave Alison a lot of time to think. Hours upon hours—she had no sense of time—days upon days, months upon months. Who knew how long she'd been in here? Her psychiatrist wouldn't tell her, almost like it was above her level of privileges to know. Her psychiatrist barely told her anything, actually, except to push a Dixie cup full of pills to her and watch as she swallowed them down. The pills did little to help her sleep or even buoy her mood. But they didn't cut through her scheming mind, either, so Ali dutifully took them. She wanted to be the perfect patient. She wanted them to fall in love with her like everyone else.

The psych ward in the prison sucked, but another year of this, maybe two, and she'd be moved to a different psych ward outside a prison. She'd done her research. She knew what the protocol was. And in a basic mental hospital—well, she would practically have free rein. She'd lived long enough inside The Preserve to know how to work the system. All she had to do was hold on for a little bit longer. Endure the pills, deal with the leather straps that sometimes tied her down, get over the freaky moaning in the middle of the night. Get lost in her head, thinking of the way she was going to change things next time.

She thought about everything that had gone wrong. Enlisting Nick. Choosing the wrong Ali Cats. Relying on her mother. Not checking and double-checking every detail. Next time, she would be smarter. *Flawless*, in fact. She'd find different Ali Cats. Snag a better Nick. Become a perfect Ali. She had already lost all the weight she'd put on to conceal her identity. Here in prison, she had better doctors, and they'd treated her burns more properly than Nick's nurse had, and her skin was looking better, too. She'd gotten a fake tooth to replace the one she'd pulled out. She was on her way to being Ali D again—the brilliant, beautiful, *perfect* Ali D. The girl who could make anyone do anything. Including scheme for her. Kill for her.

Carry out her every wish.

She measured her days by mealtimes and pill times and lights-out, but she knew this wouldn't be forever. *Soon enough*, said a voice in her head as she envisioned Spencer, Aria, Emily, and Hanna. *Soon enough, I'm coming to get you all.*

ACKNOWLEDGMENTS

So this really and truly is the end of the PLL saga, and I'm beyond grateful that I have been able to live and move within Rosewood for nine lovely years. I owe this to the brilliance of the people at Alloy Entertainment, including Les Morgenstein, Josh Bank, Sara Shandler, Lanie Davis, Katie McGee, Kristin Marang, Heather David, Romy Golan, and Stephanie Abrams. You guys have been invaluable to work with all these years, and I hope the fun doesn't end!

Thank you to everyone at HarperCollins, past and present, who championed Pretty Little Liars and made it a success. Much gratitude to Jen Klonsky, Kari Sutherland, and Alice Jerman for your keen insights. Thanks also to all of the dedicated PLL readers, tweeters, blog writers, and fans—I love you all. Love to my parents and Michael for your constant support. Kisses to Ali, the original A, and Caron—I had so much fun at the PLL season finale event in March. Thanks to Gennaro Monaco for the great new website and Theo Guliadis at Alloy for diligently and enthusiastically tweeting the PLL episodes (and posting awesome content!). Huge hugs to Kristian, naturally, and love to little Henry—when this series began, I couldn't imagine you, but now that you're here I can't imagine life without you.

YOU DON'T HAVE TO BE *GOOD* TO BE PERFECT.

Read on for a sneak peek at Sara Shephard's next series

The Perfectionists

IN MANY WAYS, BEACON HEIGHTS, Washington, looks like any affluent suburb: Porch swings creak gently in the evening breeze, the lawns are green and well kept, and all the neighbors know one another. But this satellite of Seattle is anything but average. In Beacon, it's not enough to be good; you have to be the *best*.

With perfection comes pressure. Students here are some of the best in the country, and sometimes, they have to let off a little steam. What five girls don't know, though, is that steam can scald just as badly as an open flame.

And someone's about to get burned.

On Friday night, just as the sun was setting, cars began to pull up to Nolan Hotchkiss's huge, faux-Italian villa on a peninsula overlooking Lake Washington. The house had wrought iron gates, a circular driveway with a marble fountain, multiple balconies, and a three-tiered, crystal chandelier visible through the front two-story window. All the lights were on, loud bass thumped from inside, a cheer rose up from the backyard. Kids with liquor spirited from their parents' cabinets or bottles of wine shoved into their purses sauntered up to the front steps and walked right inside. No need to ring the bell—Mr. and Mrs. Hotchkiss weren't home.

Too bad. They were missing the biggest party of the year.

Caitlin Martell-Lewis, dressed in her best pair of straight-leg jeans, a green polo that brought out the amber flecks in her eyes, and TOMS houndstooth sneakers, climbed out of an Escalade with her boyfriend, Josh Friday, and his soccer friends Asher Collins and Timothy Burgess. Josh, whose breath already smelled yeasty from the beer he'd drunk at the pregame party, shaded his brown eyes and gaped at the mansion. "This place is freaking sick."

Ursula Winters, who desperately wanted to be Timothy's girlfriend—she was also Caitlin's biggest soccer rival—stepped out of the backseat and adjusted her oversize, dolman-sleeve shirt. "The kid has it all."

"Except a soul," Caitlin muttered, limping up the lawn on her still-sore-from-a-soccer-injury ankle. Silence fell over the group as they stepped inside the grand foyer, with its checkerboard floor and a sweeping double staircase. Josh cast her a sideways glance. "What? I was kidding," Caitlin said with a laugh.

Because if you spoke out against Nolan—if you so much as boycotted his party—you'd be off the Beacon Heights High A-list. But Nolan had as many enemies as friends, and Caitlin hated him most of all. Her heart pounded, thinking about the secret thing she was about to do. She wondered whether the others were there yet.

The den was filled with candles and fat red cushions. Julie Redding held court in the middle of the room. Her auburn hair hung straight and shiny down her back. She wore a strapless Kate Spade dress and bone-colored high heels that showed off her long, lithe legs. One after another, classmates walked up to her and complimented her outfit, her white teeth, her amazing jewelry, that funny thing she'd said in English class the other day. It was par for the course, naturally—everyone *always* loved Julie. She was the most popular girl in school.

Then Ashley Ferguson, a junior who'd just dyed her hair the same auburn shade as Julie's, stopped and gave a reverent smile. "You look amazing," she gushed, same as the others.

"Thank you," Julie said modestly.

"Where'd you get the dress?" Ashley asked.

Julie's friend Nyssa Frankel inserted herself between the two. "Why, Ashley?" she snapped. "Are you going to buy the exact same one?"

Julie laughed as Nyssa and Natalie Houma, another of Julie's friends, high-fived. Ashley set her jaw and stomped away. Julie bit her lip, wondering if she'd been too mean. There was only one person she wanted to be mean to deliberately tonight.

And that was Nolan.

Meanwhile, Ava Jalali stood with her boyfriend, Alex Cohen, in the Hotchkisses' reclaimed oak and marble kitchen, nibbling on a carrot stick. She eyed a tower of cupcakes next to the veggie tray longingly. "Remind me why I decided to do a cleanse again?"

"Because you're insane?" Alex raised his eyebrows mischievously.

Ava gave him an *uh-duh* look and pushed her smooth, straight, perfect dark hair out of her eyes. She was the type of girl who hated even looking at cross sections of the human body in biology class; she couldn't stand the idea that *she* was that ugly and messy inside.

Alex swiped his thumb on the icing and brought his hand toward Ava's face. "Yummy . . ."

Ava drew back. "Get that away!" But then she giggled.

Alex had moved here in ninth grade. He wasn't as popular or as rich as some of the other guys, but he always made her laugh. But then the sight of someone in the doorway wiped the smile off her face. Nolan Hotchkiss, the party's host, stared at her with an almost territorial grin.

He deserves what he's going to get, she thought darkly.

In the backyard—which had high, swooping arcades that connected one patio to another; huge potted plants; and a long slate walkway that practically ended in the water—Mackenzie Wright rolled up her jeans, removed her toe rings, and plunked her feet into the infinity-edge pool. A lot of people were swimming, including her best friend, Claire Coldwell, and Claire's boyfriend, Blake Strustek.

Blake spun Claire around and laced his fingers through hers. "Hey, watch the digits," Claire warned. "They're my ticket to Juilliard."

Blake glanced at Mac and rolled his eyes. Mac looked away, almost as if she didn't like Blake at all.

Or perhaps because she liked him *too* much.

Then the patio door opened, and Nolan Hotchkiss, the man of the hour, sauntered onto the lawn with a smug, *I'm-the-lord-of-this-party* look on his face. He strolled to two boys and bumped fists. After a beat, they glanced Mac's way and started whispering.

Mac sucked in her stomach, feeling their gazes canvass

her snub nose, her glasses with their dark hipster frames, and her large, chunky knit scarf. She knew what they were talking about. Her hatred for Nolan flared up all over again.

Beep.

Her phone, which sat next to her on the tiled ground, lit up. Mac glanced at the text from her new friend Caitlin Martell-Lewis.

It's time.

Julie and Ava received the same missives. Like robots, they all stood, excused themselves, and walked to the rendezvous point. Empty cups lay on the ground in the hall. There was a cupcake smashed on the kitchen wall, and the den smelled distinctly of pot. The girls convened by the stairs and exchanged long, nervous glances.

Caitlin cleared her throat. "So."

Ava pursed her full lips and glanced at her reflection in the enormous mirror. Caitlin rolled back her shoulders and felt for something in her purse. It rattled slightly. Mac checked her own bag to make sure the camera she'd swiped from her mom's desk was still inside.

Then Julie's gaze fixed on a figure hovering in the doorway. It was Parker Duvall, her best friend in the world. She'd *come*, just as Julie hoped she would. As usual, Parker wore a short denim skirt, black lace tights, and an oversize black sweatshirt. When she saw Julie, she poked her face out from the hood, a wide grin spreading across her cheeks and illuminating her scars. Julie tried not to gasp, but it was so rare that Parker allowed anyone to see her face. Parker rushed up to the girls, pulling the hoodie around her face once more.

All five of them glanced around to see if anyone was watching. "I can't believe we're doing this," Mackenzie admitted.

Caitlin's eyebrows made a V. "You're not backing out, are you?"

Mac shook her head quickly. "Of course not."

"Good." Caitlin glanced at the others. "Are we all still in?"

Parker nodded. After a moment, Julie said yes, too. And Ava, who was touching up her lip gloss, gave a single, decisive nod.

Their gazes turned to Nolan as he wove through the living room. He greeted kids heartily. Slapped friends on the back. Shot a winning smile to a girl who looked like a freshman, and the girl's eyes widened with shock. Whispered something to a different girl, and her face fell just as quickly.

That was the kind of power Nolan Hotchkiss had over people. He was *the* most popular guy at school—handsome, athletic, charming, the head of every committee and club he joined. His family was the wealthiest, too—you couldn't go a mile without seeing the name *Hotchkiss* on one of the new developments popping up or turn a page in the newspaper without seeing Nolan's state senator mother cutting a ribbon at a new bakery, day care facility, community park, or library. More than that, there was something about him that basically . . . *hypnotized* you. One look, one suggestion, one command, one snarky remark, one blow-off, one public embarrassment, and you were under his thumb for life. Nolan controlled Beacon, whether you liked it or not. But what's that saying? "Absolute power corrupts absolutely." And for all the people who worshipped Nolan, there were those who couldn't stand him, too. Who wanted him . . . *gone*, in fact.

The girls looked at one another and smiled. "All right, then," Ava said, stepping out into the crowd, toward Nolan. "Let's do this."

Like any good party, the bash at the Hotchkiss house lingered into the wee hours of the morning. Leave it to Nolan to have an in with the cops, because no one raided the place for booze or even told them to cut the noise. Shortly after midnight, some party pics were posted online: two girls kissing in the powder room; the school's biggest prude doing a body shot off the star running back's chest; one of the stoners grinning sloppily, holding several cupcakes aloft; and the party's host passed out on a Lovesac beanbag upstairs with something Sharpied on his face. Partying hard was Nolan's specialty, after all.

Revelers passed out on the outdoor couch, on the

hammock that hung between two big birch trees at the back of the property, and in zigzag shapes on the floor. For several hours, the house was still, the cupcake icing slowly hardening, a tipped-over bottle of wine pooling in the sink, a raccoon digging through some of the trash bags that had been left out in the backyard. Not everyone awoke when the boy screamed. Not even when that same someone—a junior named Miro—ran down the stairs and screamed what had happened to the 911 dispatcher did all the kids stir.

It was only when the ambulances screeched into the driveway, sirens blaring, lights flashing, walkie-talkies crackling, that all eyes opened. The first thing everyone saw were EMT workers in their reflective jackets busting inside. Miro pointed them to the upper floor. There were boots on the stairs, and then . . . those same EMT people carrying someone back down. Someone who had Sharpie marker on his face. Someone who was limp and gray.

The EMT worker spoke into his radio. "We have an eighteen-year-old male DOA."

Was that Nolan? everyone would whisper in horror as they staggered out of the house, horrifically hungover. *And . . . DOA? Dead on arrival?*

By Saturday afternoon, the news was everywhere. The Hotchkiss parents returned from their business meeting in Los Angeles that evening to do damage control, but it was too late—the whole town knew that Nolan Hotchkiss had dropped dead at his party, probably from too much fun. Darker rumors posited that perhaps he'd *meant* to do it. Beacon was notoriously hard on its offspring, after all, and maybe even golden boy Nolan Hotchkiss had felt the heat.

When Julie woke up Saturday morning and heard the news, her throat closed. Ava picked up the phone three times before talking herself down. Mac stared into space for a long, long time, then burst into hot, quiet tears. And Caitlin, who'd wanted Nolan dead for so long, couldn't help but feel sorry for his family, even though he had destroyed hers. And Parker? She went to the dock and stared at the water, her face hidden under her hoodie. Her head pounded with an oncoming migraine.

They called one another and spoke in heated whispers. They felt terrible, but they were smart girls. Logical girls. Nolan Hotchkiss was gone; the dictator of Beacon Heights High was no more. That meant no more tears. No more bullying. No more living in fear that he'd expose everyone's awful secrets—somehow, he'd known so many. And anyway, not a single person had seen them go upstairs with Nolan that night—they'd made sure of it. No one would ever connect them to him.

The problem, though, was that someone had seen. Someone knew what they'd done that night, and so much more.

And someone was going to make them pay.

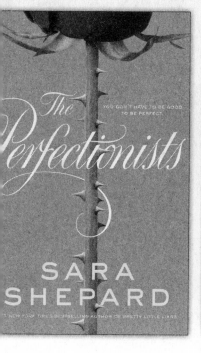

Don't miss a single scandal!

EVERYONE IN ULTRA-EXCLUSIVE ROSEWOOD,
PENNSYLVANIA, HAS SOMETHING TO HIDE . . .

DISCUSS THE BOOKS AND THE HIT TV SHOW AT
WWW.PRETTYLITTLELIARS.COM.

ALSO BY SARA SHEPARD

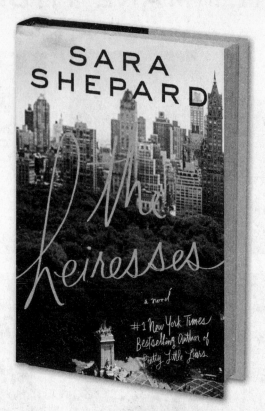

THE HEIRESSES
A Novel

"A wonderfully escapist thrill ride, *The Heiresses* is an all-access pass to a glamorous world of privilege and prestige that will keep you guessing to the very last page."
—Kimberly McCreight, *New York Times* bestselling
author of *Reconstructing Amelia*

From Sara Shepard, the #1 *New York Times* bestselling author of *Pretty Little Liars*, comes *The Heiresses*—a novel about the Saybrooks, a diamond family blessed with beauty and fortune. Beauties, entrepreneurs, debutantes, and mavens, the Saybrooks are the epitome of high society. Anyone would kill to be one of them. Then tragedy strikes the prominent family on a beautiful morning in May when Poppy, the most remarkable Saybrook of them all, flings herself from the window of her office. Everyone is shocked that someone so perfect would end her own life—until her cousins receive an ominous warning: One heiress down, four to go.

Pretty Little Liars
5 YEARS
FORWARD

TUESDAYS 8/7c

abc family
is becoming
#FREEFORM